SWEET MASQUERADE

It *was* her.

Jack could scarcely believe it, but there could never be two such ladies in all the world. Yet, what was she, a lady, a fair flower, doing in a dirty alleyway, dressed like a housemaid and, apparently, all alone? His mind reeled with the possibilities and came up empty. What was she up to? He glanced around to see if she was truly alone, or if her guards were with her. There was no one. He really ought to keep an eye on her—heaven only knew what could happen to a lady alone.

He just opened his mouth to ask her what in Hades she was up to, but she stopped him by reaching for his hand and cradling it tenderly in her two small, soft palms. She stood so close that he could smell the lilac scent of her hair.

She was every bit as lovely as she had been at the reception, but without the trappings of her formal gown and rich jewels, she was no longer as remote as the moon. Her eyes, her skin, her very demeanor were transformed—they glowed and sparkled with life, with energy. She was so close to him he could lean his head the merest inch and take a surreptitious breath of her scented hair, brush his hand on her arm.

Delicious.

LADY IN DISGUISE

AMANDA McCABE

A SIGNET BOOK

SIGNET
Published by New American Library, a division of
Penguin Group (USA) Inc., 375 Hudson Street,
New York, New York 10014, U.S.A.
Penguin Books Ltd, 80 Strand,
London WC2R 0RL, England
Penguin Books Australia Ltd, 250 Camberwell Road,
Camberwell, Victoria 3124, Australia
Penguin Books Canada Ltd, 10 Alcorn Avenue,
Toronto, Ontario, Canada M4V 3B2
Penguin Books (N.Z.) Ltd, Cnr Rosedale and Airborne Roads,
Albany, Auckland 1310, New Zealand

Penguin Books Ltd, Registered Offices:
80 Strand, London WC2R 0RL, England

First published by Signet, an imprint of New American Library,
a division of Penguin Group (USA) Inc.

First Printing, September 2003
10 9 8 7 6 5 4 3 2 1

*To my grandmother, Laura Ruby Smith,
who introduced me to the "romance novel habit"
in the first place!*

Chapter One

June 1814

"*E*mma, dear! Close that window and sit down. You must cease behaving like a gawking peasant this instant."

Lady Emma Weston sighed at her aunt's words and at the bang of her walking stick against the carriage floor. That admonishing sound was as familiar to her as her own voice, and she knew it meant she had best obey with alacrity. She took a deep breath of cool, blessed fresh air, then ducked back into her seat and let her maid, Natasha, close the window. They had traveled for so long, for what seemed like eternity, and the carriage had become stuffy and dull, with only the occasional glimpse of passing scenery on the Dover Road to relieve the monotony.

Just like my life, Emma thought wryly. She had hoped the journey to England as part of Tsar Alexander's retinue to attend the peace celebrations would bring some excitement, some magic into her existence. She had been born in England but had not seen it since she was six years old—since her parents died so tragically young and she went to live with her aunt and uncle in Russia.

Yet, now she realized this voyage was just more of the same, more of the rules and protocols she had lived under in her aunt and uncle's home. More of maintaining perfect outward decorum, while screaming inside for something, *anything*, different.

Her aunt—the sister of her late mother and long married to a Russian nobleman—loved her. Emma knew that. Yet Aunt Lydia and Uncle Nicholas had a position to maintain, and it was Emma's duty to help them do that. She did not mind, truly—they had given her a home when she was young and frightened, had looked after her, cared for her when she was scared and bewildered by her sudden change of homes. But, oh! How she had dreamed of what things would be like once the hated Napoleon was driven from Russia and she could leave her family's country estate and be presented at the court in St. Petersburg! Books, her only real companions, had fueled fantastical dreams of handsome dance partners, beautiful gowns, dashing sleigh rides and skating parties.

Emma sighed, and shifted restlessly on the carriage seat.

She had the gowns now, to be sure, but not much else. Every handsome young man who dared to approach her was frightened away by her aunt's stern glances or her uncle's lofty position as one of the Tsar's chief advisors.

Now she was on her way to London, one of the greatest cities in all the world! Not only that, but her nineteenth birthday was fast approaching, and she would at last be considered grown up, a lady. The world should be a glorious place for her. But all she saw stretching ahead of her was more rules, more restrictions, more protocol.

She almost sighed again and slumped back against the cushions, but she managed to stop herself in time. A *lady* maintained proper posture at all times. She always appeared serene and cheerful. She never laughed too loud or danced too long with any one partner.

Natasha reached up to fuss with Emma's bow-trimmed bonnet and the collar of her blue velvet spencer, while her aunt peered at her closely.

Aunt Lydia, the Countess Suvarova, looked far younger than her fifty-something years, and her green eyes were sharper than those of many a young miss. Or of any sharpshooter in the army, which was a more apt description, since Emma always felt she was caught in the fireline when her aunt looked at her in that way. Aunt Lydia folded her gray-gloved hands atop the ivory head of her stick and continued to watch Emma. Her expression was fond but exasperated, like a mother's looking at a toddler who had spilled its milk for the fourth time.

"Were you looking at those soldiers, Emma?" she asked.

"Indeed, no, Aunt Lydia!" Emma protested. She hadn't been watching the Tsar's outriders in their handsome green uniforms—she knew that was a waste of time. Aunt Lydia would surely never approve of any of them, even if Emma did see one she liked. "I was looking at the scenery."

Aunt Lydia glanced briefly out the window, at the passing hedgerows and meadows. "It does not look like something that would engage your interest."

"I have not seen England in a very long time. And anything is better than being on that ship, with only water to look at."

Lydia's expression softened. "Poor Emma. We *have* been traveling a very long while. And we have not seen your uncle since he came to England with the Grand Duchess of Oldenburg in March. But we will soon be in London, and things will be more interesting for you there."

Interesting if one enjoyed state dinners and balls where one could only dance with elderly relatives, Emma thought. She just smiled at her aunt, though, and said, "Of course. It will be wonderful to see Uncle Nicholas again."

Lydia gave her a sly little glance. "A young man called Sir Jeremy Ashbey will be there, as well. Your uncle has written to me about how much he likes him. Perhaps we will meet him at the military review tomorrow."

Emma looked at her, puzzled. Whoever was Sir Jer-

emy Ashbey? An Englishman her uncle knew? She could
not recall her uncle or her aunt ever mentioning him.
"Sir Jeremy Ashbey?"

"Perhaps you heard of him when you were a child.
His family's estate marches with the one your parents
left you, Weston Manor."

Since Emma's parents had died when she was six and
she had been in Russia ever since, it was hardly surprising that she did not remember him being mentioned. She
shook her head.

"He was attached to the British embassy in St. Petersburg but returned to England with the Grand Duchess's
party. Your uncle writes that he is very impressed with
his manners."

Emma felt a faint stirring of interest and trepidation,
perhaps even dread. This was the first time her aunt had
ever spoken of *any* young man, except to warn Emma
to stay away from them all. Who was this Sir Jeremy
Ashbey, and what did her praise of him mean? Surely if
her aunt and uncle liked him, he lived a life just like
theirs—bound by duty.

Her questions would have to wait, however, for they
had at long last reached the edge of London itself.

Emma leaned over as far as she dared to watch the
city move past the window. London was very different
from St. Petersburg with its gold and cream and pale
blue colors and canal-laced streets. The colors here were
darker, the houses narrower, the streets crowded with
excited merrymakers. The carriage jostled as it struck the
uneven cobbles of the city streets.

She was rather disappointed by the lack of bright colors, but she was enthralled by the shop window displays.
They passed drapers, stationers, confectioners, booksell-
ers, all with windows full of shimmering, enticing goods
and draped with flags and bunting. She wondered if she
could persuade her aunt to agree to a shopping expedi-
tion later.

Yet, even more enthralling than the shops were the
people. People in simple attire stood on the walkways

alongside well-dressed individuals, jostling to watch the carriages pass, hoping for a glimpse of the Tsar himself. One little girl, an adorable cherub in a pink muslin dress and tiny straw bonnet, looked so amazed and wide-eyed that Emma could not help but wave at her.

The delighted child waved back.

"Emma!" Aunt Lydia cried disapprovingly. "Do not *wave*."

"I'm sorry, Aunt Lydia." Emma folded her hands demurely in her lap, but she could not quell her growing excitement.

London was truly splendid, so full of glorious life and energy. If only she could walk about and explore it all, really take it all in! She wanted to smell all the strange scents, talk to people, *hear* them. Not just peer at them from inside the carriage.

All too soon they reached their destination, the Pultency Hotel, where the Tsar's beloved sister, the Grand Duchess Catherine of Oldenburg, waited to greet him and where the entire Russian delegation would stay.

Emma accepted the footman's arm as she stepped down from the carriage after her aunt. Her gaze swept over the magnificent building, whose sparkling windows overlooked what her aunt said was called Green Park. Crowds gathered at the edge of the park cheered and shouted.

Something wonderful *was* going to happen here, Emma thought, as she took in the whole colorful scene. No place so splendid as this could ever be ordinary. "It must," she whispered wistfully. "Or I will surely shrivel up and die."

"Emma," Aunt Lydia said, as she straightened her muff on her arm and planted her walking stick firmly on the marble steps. "Do cease talking to yourself and come along, dear. Your uncle will be waiting."

Emma tore her gaze away from the crowd and followed her aunt into the hotel. "Yes, Aunt Lydia," she said obediently. But her mind was already busy with plans.

*   *   *

". . . wouldn't you say so, Jonathan? Jonathan!"

Jack Howard, Viscount St. Albans, looked up from his dinner plate, startled by his father's suddenly loud words. In truth, he had not been paying heed to his parents' conversation at all. He had been thinking of the appointment he must keep, the very important appointment, after he was released from this family supper.

He took a quick swallow of wine and said, "I beg your pardon, Father?"

The Earl of Osborn's lips compressed into a tight, disapproving line. "I would appreciate it if you would pay more attention when I am speaking to you, Jonathan. I do not talk just to listen to myself."

Jack thought that might be a debatable statement. He remembered childhood scolds where his father would go on for hours, not even noticing his son's glazed, far away expression. Things had not changed much over the years, either. Jack was now nearly thirty years old, a veteran of the Peninsular campaign and still bored by his father's pontifications.

He almost laughed aloud at the absurdity of it all but then thought better of it and just said, "No, sir. Of course I was listening. I merely lost myself for a moment in the glories of Cook's mint sauce." He prodded with his fork at the congealed greenish mass on his lamb cutlet. The Howards' cook had been with them for many years and did a divine trifle, but sauces were not her forte.

His father peered at him suspiciously. "Are you trying to be funny, m'boy?"

"Certainly not," Jack muttered. Trying to be funny here would have been a complete waste of time.

"Good. Because I do not approve of levity during supper. Your mother works very hard to select these menus for us, and we should take the time to properly appreciate them."

"Oh, I do not mind . . ." Jane, Lady Osborn, said, her delicate voice floating down the table for the first time since the soup had been served. She was still a lovely woman, with silvery curls and bright blue eyes, but she always seemed to melt into the wallpaper of whatever room she happened to be in.

"Nonsense, Jane!" her husband boomed, and she subsided back into her chair. "Now, Jack. Tell me what thoughts you were so engrossed in that you could not pay attention to our conversation. Some mischief, no doubt. As usual, since you returned home from Spain."

Jack could hardly tell his father the truth. He had to maintain the facade of careless licentiousness, that he had so carefully built up since returning to England— even if it pained him deeply to be thought of as nothing but a useless fribble. He shrugged and gave his father a reckless grin that hinted of plans he could not speak of in front of his mother.

Lord Osborn frowned. "Ah, well," he said. " 'Tis of no matter what you do tonight, I suppose. For you will join your mother and me at Lady Bransley's house tomorrow evening."

This was certainly the first Jack had heard of it. "Lady Bransley's?"

"Yes. Surely even *you* have heard of the occasion, even though I doubt you ever read any serious newspapers. Lady Bransley is hosting a reception in honor of the visiting monarchs."

"It is an honor to your father's diplomatic work that we are invited," Jack's mother said.

Lord Osborn puffed up like a proud pigeon, the pearl buttons on his waistcoat swelling. In his youth, before he ascended to the earldom, he had worked for the diplomatic corps in France and Prussia. He was immensely proud of those days and would speak of them endlessly to anyone who would listen. It was a great bone of contention between himself and his son, for he had always exhorted Jack to follow in his footsteps, to no apparent avail.

If only he knew.

"Indeed it is," Lord Osborn said. "King Frederick William of Prussia himself requested that I receive an invitation. The Tsar and his sister will be there, and Count and Countess Lieven, as well as Count and Countess Suvarov. It is very important that you attend with us, Jonathan."

It fell in with Jack's own purposes perfectly. But he could scarcely show that to his parents. A useless dandy would hardly be looking forward to such a stuffy and proper event. He shrugged again and swallowed the last of the wine in his glass. "If you wish, I will attend with you," he said in a bored tone.

Before his father could answer, the dining room door opened quietly, and Spencer, the butler, slid inside.

"Yes, Spencer, what is it?" Lord Osborn said impatiently. He had obviously been working up to a good lecture on Jack's expected behavior at the reception and was not happy to be cut off.

"I do apologize for interrupting, my lord," Spencer answered smoothly. "But Mr. Stonewich has called for Lord St. Albans."

"Oh, yes. We have very important things to do this evening—the theater and such." Jack rose from his chair with alacrity, grateful for the interruption. He kissed his mother's cheek and said, "Wonderful to see you, Mother, as always. I will meet you both here before the reception tomorrow evening. Just send word of the time to my lodgings."

Before his father could swallow his bite of lamb and begin bellowing, Jack hurried out of the dining room into the foyer, where Bertie Stonewich waited.

"There you are, Jack," Bertie said, examining his reflection in a tall, gilt-framed mirror. He straightened his pale blue cravat and smoothed his neatly pomaded light gold hair, the very image of a Society dandy. "We're supposed to meet everyone in an hour. I hear it's devilish impossible to get into this new gaming hell!"

"So sorry for the delay, Bertie old boy. I was just finishing supper with the parents." Jack grabbed up his hat and walking stick and almost pushed his friend out the front door to the waiting carriage. He couldn't take the chance, no matter how remote, that his father would follow him into the foyer and continue the lecture.

Once the vehicle moved out into the flow of Mayfair traffic, Bertie's vacuous facade fell away and his previously empty gaze hardened. "They do not suspect, do they?"

"Of course not," Jack answered. "I never realized before that I possessed such acting skills. I ought to be treading the boards, truly. They think I care for nothing but the cut of my coat and winning my next wager. In fact, they had to practically beg me to attend Lady Bransley's reception with them tomorrow night."

Bertie arched one brow. "The Bransley reception? That *was* a bit of luck."

"Yes," Jack murmured. "A bit of luck indeed."

The town house foyer Jack and Bertie were ushered into was dark and dusty, with a shabby carpet and no paintings on the brown-papered walls. It was quite a contrast to the rich environs of Jack's parents' house, and any stranger happening to glance into it would not be at all impressed. But for those in the know—as Jack and Bertie were—this bland foyer concealed some of the inner workings of England's great military machine.

They did not have a long wait before a footman, dressed in inconspicuous dark livery, showed them into a library. This room was also plain, but a cheerful fire burned in the grate, and comfortable leather-upholstered chairs were drawn up about a round table. Already seated at that table were two men, the colonel of Jack's regiment, for whom he had performed many surreptitious "errands" while they were in Spain, and a tall, slim older gentleman, plainly dressed and somber faced. Jack had met this man once or twice before soon after he arrived home in London, but he knew him only as Mr. Thompson. Not, in all likelihood, his true name. Yet he seemed, for all his quietness, to be in the know about everything of importance in the kingdom.

"Ah, St. Albans, Stonewich," Colonel Smith-Aubrey said. "Right on time, as usual. Brandy?"

"Yes, thank you, sir," Jack answered. As he and Bertie took their seats, the footman poured the snifters of brandy and departed, closing the door silently behind him. The four men were left alone in the cocoon of the book-lined room.

"Very sorry to take you away from all the celebrations, but no rest for the wicked, eh?" the colonel said, with a little chuckle.

"No, indeed, sir," Bertie said, reaching for his drink.

Mr. Thompson studied them with his calm, still, gray gaze, his long fingers steepled before him. "Most people would think this would be a quiet time for us, that our work would be finished. But, of course, it is not. It is only just beginning, in many ways. This time is crucial for the future of Europe, for the whole world. Nothing must be allowed to mar it."

Jack remained silent, toying with his glass. He waited to hear what might be coming next, what might be threatening this new, tenuous peace, what his task might be.

Mr. Thompson did not disappoint. He withdrew a small packet of papers from inside his coat and pushed them across the table to Jack. They were of a plain off-white vellum, heavily sealed.

"These must be delivered to Count Suvarov at the Pulteney Hotel, day after tomorrow," Mr. Thompson said. "You may wish to dress inconspicuously, Lord St. Albans. Many people are watching the hotel. Many we know of—some we do not."

Jack tucked the letters neatly into his own coat. As far as errands went, this was among the simplest he had ever been asked to perform. "Of course."

Mr. Thompson nodded and sipped impassively at his brandy. "Colonel Smith-Aubrey was just telling me how invaluable your—help was in Spain and here at home, as well. I hope both you and Mr. Stonewich will be ready to continue to lend assistance when needed."

"Of course," Jack said again.

Mr. Thompson nodded, as if satisfied. "The visiting monarchs should enjoy their time here, unmarred by any trouble. Perhaps you could help them to achieve that enjoyment by keeping an eye on them? Only informally, of course. Especially the Tsar and his party. The Russians can be so—unpredictable. Don't you agree?"

Jack thought once more of the reception he was to attend with his parents tomorrow evening—the reception in honor of the visiting monarchs. This new task seemed fated.

"Yes," he answered. "Russians are most unpredictable."

Why did she always seem to end up staring out of windows? Emma thought, as she looked through the glass at the crowds on the street below. She rubbed one finger absently along the rich brocade of the drapery and swayed slightly to the faint strains of some lively, distant music.

Behind her, in one of the sumptuous drawing rooms of the Pulteney Hotel, the Russian delegation gathered before supper. The Tsar and his sister held court, surrounded by the glitter of the men's medals and the women's silken gowns and jewels while Emma, having made her curtsy to them and then been forgotten, drifted over to the window.

The conversation in this lavishly decorated room was low and muted, respectful, punctuated only occasionally by low laughter. Beyond this glass, though, the night seemed full of life. Full of celebrating people, who waited outside to cheer the Tsar.

How Emma longed to breathe the fresh evening air! To wander free and laugh as loud and as long as she liked.

She closed her eyes and leaned her forehead against the cool glass.

"Emma, dear?" She heard her aunt's voice behind her and felt a light touch on her arm. Her eyes flew open, and she straightened her posture immediately.

"Yes, Aunt Lydia?" she said, turning to face the room, and her aunt, again.

"Are you quite all right?" Aunt Lydia asked. She looked all that was proper, as always, in her dark blue satin gown and with every hair in place beneath a peacock feather–trimmed turban. But her brow was creased in concern, and she drew off her glove to gently touch Emma's cheek. "You feel a bit warm."

Emma took her aunt's hand in her own and said, "I am just a bit tired, Aunt Lydia."

"Of course you are. It has been a very long day. But we must do our duty." Her tone changed subtly but unmistakably from one of concern to one of stoic resolve.

Duty. Always duty. "Of course," Emma murmured.

"It should not be a terribly long supper, though, and then you must go straight to bed." Lydia reached out to adjust the puff of Emma's white muslin sleeve. "Now, dear, come with me. Your uncle has someone he would like you to meet."

Emma sighed inwardly. It was probably some elderly general or prince, with cold, bony hands and sour breath, whom she would have to sit beside at supper. "Of course," she said again.

As if divining Emma's reluctant thoughts, Lydia smiled indulgently. "Now, my dear, it is nothing like that. This is young Sir Jeremy Ashbey, who I spoke to you about earlier."

The name sounded rather familiar to Emma, but she could not exactly recall why. She had met so many new people today, with more to come at tomorrow's military review. "Did you, Aunt Lydia?"

"Of course I did, miss! I told you that he has been attached to the embassy in Russia, but his family's estate here in England is very near to the one your parents left you." Lydia laughed, in patient indulgence of her forgetful niece.

Oh, yes. Now Emma remembered—Aunt Lydia had spoken of him in the carriage today. Emma had thought it rather odd. Her aunt never spoke of eligible young men. "So, he is here this evening?"

"Yes, and quite eager to make your acquaintance." Lydia made one more adjustment to Emma's attire, twitching her pearl necklace into place, then took her arm to lead her back into the midst of the drawing room.

Her Uncle Nicholas stood near the fireplace, tall and handsome in his white uniform, his hair still dark and thick, his bearing military-straight. He was talking with the gentleman who stood beside him, whom Emma now studied surreptitiously. This must be the famous Sir Jeremy Ashbey. He *was* good-looking, she had to admit, almost as tall as her uncle, with pale golden hair brushed into neat waves and a carefully trimmed mustache. His figure was lean in his immaculately stylish evening clothes of dark blue velvet.

Yes, handsome, like a prince in a storybook. But Emma felt oddly detached as she approached him, as if she were watching herself from a distance, acting out some oh-so-socially correct scene. Surely she should be more excited when faced with a good looking gentleman who was obviously approved of by her aunt and uncle?

She pasted a smile on her lips and hoped it looked less strained than it felt. It was probably as her aunt had said—she was just tired, and all this would look very different in the morning.

Her uncle saw them and reached for her aunt's hand, raising it to his lips for a quick kiss. His smile for her was warm and personal; it was so obvious that they were delighted to be back together after their long separation. Emma couldn't help but smile at their happiness, a smile that was genuine now.

"Lydia, Emma, my dears," Nicholas said. "I would like you to meet Sir Jeremy Ashbey, who has been here with us in the Grand Duchess's party for the last few months. He is a most promising young man, and I have enjoyed his company. Sir Jeremy, may I present my wife, the Countess Suvarova, and my niece, Lady Emma Weston."

Sir Jeremy gave them both an elegant bow, his eyes a very pale green and slightly flirtatious as they turned to Emma. "It is my very great honor, Countess Suvarova, Lady Emma. Count Suvarov has been all that is kind since I was appointed here and has spoken of both of you so highly that I have been very eager to make your acquaintance. Though, of course, Lady Emma and I have met before, many years ago."

Lydia laughed. "And we have been eager to meet you, Sir Jeremy! I enjoy getting to know any friend of my husband. But I fear he is *so* fond of us that he tends to exaggerate our charms. I fear you will be disappointed."

"Not at all," Sir Jeremy answered gallantly. "You are both every bit as lovely as he said, and Lady Emma as lovely as I remember."

"How very charming," Lydia said, shifting a bit so that Emma was directly facing Sir Jeremy. "The count also tells me that your family lives very near my niece's own country estate."

"Weston Manor. Yes, I know it well." Sir Jeremy said. He looked once more to Emma, who still had a very odd sense of detachment from the scene. She remembered Sir Jeremy not at all, even though it seemed *he* remembered *her*.

But her social training was, as always, at the fore. She forced a polite smile to her face and said, "Yes, indeed. My father's estate, Holmsby Hall, the seat of the earldom, is now my cousin's, but Weston Manor was my parents' favorite place. More like a true home, my mother always said. I fear I have not seen it since I was six years old." Emma thought she was babbling, yet she could not seem to help it. She always became terribly sentimental when she thought of her parents and their home—even when she was in front of complete strangers.

Sir Jeremy's expression only radiated sympathy, though. "It is a very lovely place. I am not at all surprised that your mother was so fond of it. Perhaps we could go for a drive in the park soon and speak more of the country we both have ties to? I have many tales I could tell you of the neighborhood. We could speak of it further at the military review tomorrow morning."

Emma was greatly tempted, despite the fact that she was so strangely unmoved by Sir Jeremy Ashbey himself. She longed to hear more about the home she had only vague memories of.

She glanced at her aunt, who gave her a tiny nod of approval. "Yes, thank you, Sir Jeremy. I would enjoy that."

Chapter Two

"Which gown will you wear tonight, my lady?" The brisk question echoed through the ornate bedchamber as Natasha, Emma's lady's maid, and really her friend since they were both little girls, sorted through the array of gowns hung neatly in the wardrobe.

Emma shifted her feet in the basin of warm water, sighing at the comforting feel of the liquid lapping against her skin. How could she think about gowns now when she was still tired from standing all day, watching the endless military review under the hot sun? All those different regiments, with all the names she would never be able to remember. It had gone on for hours, along with the English Prince Regent's terrible jokes.

She lifted a throbbing foot out of the water and examined it. If her feet became too horribly swollen, they would never fit into her satin slippers.

Now, *there* was an idea! If she could not put her shoes on, she could not possibly attend the reception at this Lady Bransley's house. It would never do to appear in her stockinged feet.

Yet, even as the fanciful thought flitted through her mind, she dismissed it. Her aunt and uncle would surely insist she attend, even if she had to do it in her bedroom shoes.

"My lady?" Natasha prompted.

Emma looked up at her. "Hm?"

"Which gown would you like to wear? This one . . ."

Natasha held up a pale pink silk creation, lavishly embroidered with silver thread and pearls. "Or perhaps this one?" Out came a heavy cream-colored satin.

Emma glanced at them both without really seeing them. "You choose, Natasha. You always have such perfect taste."

"This one, then." Natasha laid down the satin on the bed and put the pink silk back into the wardrobe. "You can wear the pink one at Lady Hertford's ball."

As Natasha fussed with the gown and matched slippers and jewels to the rich fabric, Emma continued to swirl her feet about in the cooling water, even when Madame Anastatia Oblonovskaya, Aunt Lydia's secretary, hurried into the room. As usual, Madame Ana, as she was always called, was impeccably neat in her black silk gown, her dark brown hair pulled back in a sleek knot, her gold-framed spectacles balanced carefully on her nose. She was actually not a great deal older than Emma herself, but her air of brisk efficiency made her seem a veritable matron.

"Good evening, Lady Emma," she said crisply, flipping through the pages of her ever-present notebook.

"Good evening, Madame Ana," Emma answered in a small voice. She knew very well what was coming.

"Your aunt has asked that I review with you what will occur this evening."

Emma nodded politely, but inwardly she thought there was no need for any sort of "review"—she knew exactly what would happen. She would stand in a receiving line for hours, her feet aching even more as she smiled at countless people, inclining her head to some, curtsying to a few. She would make conversation with elderly countesses and statesmen with ear trumpets and a faint smell of mildew about them, would not pay too much attention to any one young man, and would always, always stand up straight and smile.

Oh, wonderful, she thought wryly. *Delightful. I am almost leaping with joy.*

"There will be no dancing tonight," Madame Ana was

saying, writing in her notebook with her little gold pencil.
"So we need not worry about suitable dancing partners.
Lists of those, of course, will be drawn up before the
Marchioness of Hertford's ball."

"Of course," Emma murmured.

"Tonight, you will be introduced to the guests by
Count and Countess Lieven, the Russian ambassador and
his wife, whom you met today at the review. The
Prince Regent . . ."

"Who, we hope, will *not* be an hour late, as he was
today!" Emma said with a laugh. She remembered the
disgruntled impatience, as everyone had been kept waiting by "Prinny" at the military review.

Madame Ana gave her a sharp look, then went on as
if there had been no interruption. "The Prince Regent
will attend, as will Princess Charlotte. The Duke of . . ."

She went on with a long list of dukes, marquesses,
earls and viscounts, and instructions on how she was to
greet each one, but Emma only half-listened. She swirled
her toes in the now cold water and listened instead to
the sounds outside her window. Laughing, cheering
crowds had been passing the hotel all day in the obvious
hopes of catching a glimpse of the Tsar and his sister.
Emma stopped to peer at them from between her curtains whenever she could.

They all appeared to be having such a grand time.
They did not have to remember who to curtsy to and
who was simply to receive a nod and a small smile.

Emma wished that she could join them, could laugh
and dance and be free for just a moment . . .

The sharp snap of Madame's notebook closing brought
her back to reality.

"That should be the entire guest list for the reception,"
Madame said. "The supper before will be a small one,
and you will be seated next to Lord Eversworth."

Emma remembered Lord Eversworth from the military review. He was seventy if he was a day and had hair
growing out of his ears. She had stared at that hair in
fascination, unable to hear anything of what he said.

She shuddered.

"Thank you, Madame," she said.

Madame Ana nodded, then bustled out of the room as quickly and efficiently as she had entered.

Natasha came and lifted Emma's feet out of the basin, wrapping them up in warmed towels. "*Nye haroshya!*" she said. "Your feet are wrinkled like an old crone's. But at least some of the swelling has gone down."

Emma looked down at the top of Natasha's head, at the neat white cap that concealed most of her pale curls. "Natasha?"

"Yes, my lady?" Natasha did not look up from her task.

"What are you going to do tonight, after we have left for the reception?"

Natasha *did* look up at that question, to shoot Emma a curious glance before turning her gaze back to the white silk stockings she was smoothing over Emma's feet. "Tonight, my lady? I will press your gown for tomorrow's luncheon party."

"Surely that will not take all evening!" Emma said in a soft, cajoling tone. "You can tell me."

Natasha sat back on her heels, her eyes suddenly sparkling with shy fun. "Well, they say there are illuminations to be seen all over the city, after it grows dark. Some of the other servants are going, and they have invited me. If I have your permission, my lady?"

"Don't be silly, of course you may go! It sounds lovely. And the reception is sure to be very late." Emma sighed wistfully before she could stop herself. "I only wish I could go with you."

Natasha looked at her disbelievingly. "You, my lady? But you will be having a glorious time with all the grand lords and ladies and the Tsar himself." She crossed herself at the mention of the Little Father of Russia.

Having a deadly dull time, Emma thought. But she just nodded, and said, "Of course."

"We should be getting you dressed now, my lady, or you will be late!"

And what a tragedy *that* would be. Emma stood up and shrugged off her velvet dressing gown so Natasha could help her into her light stays and the stiff brocade.

"There must have been some handsome officers at the military review today," Natasha chatted on, as she fastened the myriad of small pearl buttons that marched up the back of Emma's gown.

"Hm, yes, a few," Emma said. She thought of Sir Jeremy Ashbey and his smooth, polite, blond handsomeness—and her aunt's agreement that she be seated next to him at the review. He really seemed to be everything a sensible girl could dream of, being good-looking and well connected. Yet, somehow Emma, no matter how hard she tried, could still feel nothing when he bowed over her hand or smiled down at her.

Nothing but a strange, vague restlessness.

Natasha laughed. "Only a few, my lady?"

"I did not have many opportunities to inspect them closely," Emma said, with a laugh of her own. "Not with my aunt right beside me the entire afternoon."

"Perhaps you will meet someone tonight. Someone wildly romantic."

Emma giggled. "Yes. A tall, dark Englishman!"

Now Jack remembered why he so seldom attended *ton* functions with his parents. It was not because he had to maintain his careful facade of careless rakishness—it was because they were so very dull.

Oh, it was certainly a great crush, to Lady Bransley's credit. Everyone who was anyone in Society was packed in to the very walls. People were wedged between the potted palms and the banks of heavily scented hothouse roses, dressed in their finest garments and most valuable jewels. Yet, despite the crowd, it was oddly quiet. Everyone spoke in hushed voices, as if in a great, solemn cathedral, craning for a glimpse of, hoping for a word from the visiting royalty.

The royalty themselves stood in the receiving line with Lord and Lady Bransley, greeting the guests who moved in a slow parade up the rose-twined staircase into the white and gold ballroom.

Jack had been standing with his parents for what seemed like a decade, choked by the stuffy, perfume-filled air. They were no closer to the receiving line of the greats than they had been ten minutes ago, but if he leaned slightly to the left he could just get a glimpse of them. Tsar Alexander of Russia, tall and splendid as a storybook king in his white uniform, stood beside his short, pale, strong-featured sister, the Grand Duchess of Oldenburg. Her black satin gown and the black lace veil attached to her tiara stood out starkly against the pastels of the other ladies. The florid-faced, portly Prince Regent stood on her other side, and when he attempted to speak to her, the glance she gave him was positively glacial.

Interesting, to be sure, but hardly useful. Everyone knew that the Grand Duchess loathed Prinny. Nothing appeared to be out of order here.

Jack's father swept the assembly an approving gaze. "An impressive group, are they not, Jonathan?" he said, his own medals and ribbons flashing in the candlelight.

"Indeed they are," Jack answered, only half-sarcastically. All those diamonds and yards of gold braid were enough to impress anyone. "We are fortunate to see so many heads of state gathered in one place." Even if they could all be such blasted nuisances.

His father gave him a startled look, as if he was surprised that Jack could devise any polite conversation. "Quite right, m'boy. Quite right. We shall never see the likes of this time again." The line moved forward then, preventing him from pontificating any further. He took his wife's arm and helped her up the last step into the ballroom.

Lady Osborn gathered up the train of her silver satin and lace gown and beamed at her husband and son. She had been the peacemaker, the one who smoothed things over, for so long that she was obviously delighted by the evening's amity.

"I see that the Count and Countess Suvarov are here,"

Lord Osborn said. "She is English, you know, the eldest daughter of the Duke of Barclay. And they say the Tsar trusts the Count's opinion more than any other. If I were just a young man again, with a diplomatic career ahead of me, I would certainly wish to make *their* acquaintance." He gave his son a significant look. "In this new order of ours, Russia is certain to be of great importance. Great importance indeed."

Before Jack could reply to this, or even puzzle out what his father was trying to say, they reached the guests of honor. He gave his most elegant bow to the Tsar and the Grand Duchess, and to the Prince Regent. After Prinny stood a very handsome couple, both of them tall and dark and even more regal than the Tsar and his sister. This was undoubtedly the Count Suvarov, the man who was to receive the papers Mr. Thompson had given Jack, and his wife.

Jack, who was very seldom fazed by anything life chose to hurl at him, *almost* began to feel intimidated by their cool stares. But their hostess intervened before he could do anything ridiculously gauche and schoolboyish. "Count and Countess Suvarov, may I present the Earl and Countess of Osborn and their son, Viscount St. Albans?" Lady Bransley said, in her perfect-hostess voice. "This is the Count and Countess Suvarov and their niece, Lady Emma Weston. Lady Emma is the daughter of the late Earl of Lindsey."

Then he saw her. He drew in a sharp breath, suddenly speechless. She was as still and perfect as a marble figurine, her expression exquisitely polite but distant. Yet she was far more lovely than any figurine, or indeed any woman, he had ever seen. She was small and slender, with milk-white skin dramatically set off by deep brown eyes and shining black hair. Her nose was perhaps a shade too long, but her cheekbones were sharp and soaring. The pearl and diamond tiara in her glossy, upswept hair sparkled as she turned toward them, her heavy, ivory-colored brocade gown rustling. The scarlet watered-silk sash of some order that looped over her shoulder shifted, emphasizing the small high line of her perfect bosom.

Jack looked quickly away. He was certain it was not the thing to be caught staring at such a lady's breasts!

She held her gloved hand out to him and said in a soft, lightly accented voice, "How do you do?"

Her demeanor was all that was perfectly proper. But he had the distinct impression that she did not really *see* him. Her dark eyes looked slightly past him, as if she was lost in her own world. A world far away from the crowded ballroom and the people gathered around her.

Jack wondered how he could join her there, this perfect ice princess in her own dream. He was not particularly vain, but he *did* enjoy a certain degree of success with women. To be so completely overlooked by one pricked just a bit—but also intrigued him.

All too soon, she withdrew her hand from his and turned to the next person in line, and Jack was forced to move away.

He could not help but glance back at her just once more. The man at her side, who had been introduced as Sir Jeremy something-or-other, attached to the English embassy to Russia, said some quiet words to her. His pale golden hair and mustache and deep green velvet coat made a picture-perfect contrast to her night-and-snow beauty.

She nodded and gave him a small smile.

Well, Jack though with a rueful laugh. Obviously diplomatic work *did* have its advantages, just as his father said. Perhaps he should rethink his choice of career.

"Would you care for a glass of champagne, Lady Emma?" Sir Jeremy asked solicitously, taking Emma's arm to lead her across the ballroom after they were freed from the receiving line.

Emma would indeed care for some champagne. She gave a longing glance to crystal flutes full of the golden liquid as a footman passed by with a laden tray. But she regretfully shook her head. Champagne made her feel all fuzzy headed and giggly, made her feel like kicking off her slippers and twirling about, and she knew *that* would be unacceptable at a time like this. Or anytime in her life.

"No, thank you, Sir Jeremy. Perhaps some punch?" Her throat was dry, and her lips felt cracked from so much smiling. The tepid-looking pink punch would be better than nothing.

"Of course. It would be my honor to fetch it for you." Sir Jeremy left her at her aunt's side and disappeared into the swirling crowd. His dark green coat was lost in the flash of jewels and bright silks.

Emma watched him go. He *was* handsome and eminently suitable, and he was quite charming and attentive. Also, her aunt and uncle seemed to like him, even allowing him to escort her into the ballroom tonight.

She should be laughing with joy, her heart pattering happily. This was what she had dreamed of, wasn't it? On all those lonely days in the country, reading all those books, she had imagined what it would be like to meet a handsome suitor.

But it was not exactly as she had imagined. In fact, it was awfully—flat. Much to her disappointment, Emma felt no different than she had two days ago. The same restlessness still tugged at her heart. She had even been daydreaming about the crowds outside when Sir Jeremy was standing right beside her in the receiving line! Daydreaming so deeply she scarcely saw the people in front of her.

But her Aunt Lydia seemed happy with her husband beside her, which was good because it kept her from turning her too perceptive gaze onto Emma quite so often.

Lydia smiled at her now and drew her close to her side. "Emma, dear, you know Countess Lieven."

"Of course." Emma inclined her head to the lady her aunt was speaking with. The elegant countess seemed quite friendly, but Emma felt small and awkward around her. Her gown felt pale and childish beside Countess

Lieven's vivid rose-colored creation and her sparkling parure of amethysts and diamonds. Emma had to resist the urge to reach up and make sure her hair was still tidy, coiled beneath the headache-inducing tiara.

"Sadly, we have not had much opportunity for conversation," Countess Lieven said. "I hope you will come to tea at the embassy while you are here, Lady Emma. And you, too, of course, Countess Suvarova. Perhaps the day after tomorrow?"

"We would be delighted." Aunt Lydia looked past the countess's shoulder, a smile of greeting softening her formal expression. "As, I am sure, my husband will be."

Nicholas came up to his wife and smiled down at her before bowing politely over Countess Lieven's silk-gloved hand. "Now, what is it I would be delighted to do?" he said, his voice lightly teasing. "What have you embroiled me in now, my dear?"

Lydia laughed, and tapped at his sleeve with her folded fan. "Only tea at the embassy with the Countess. Nothing *too* onerous."

Emma smiled at the gentle banter, relaxing a bit for the first time all evening. They were obviously in good humor tonight.

When she was a little girl, Emma would sometimes imagine that one day her husband would be a bit like her uncle Nicholas–tall, dark, with a ready smile to go along with his devotion to duty and family. She had hoped her marriage would be like that of her aunt and uncle, a union of true partners whose love would never waver, even in the face of frequent separations.

Now, of course, she knew the truth of how difficult those separations, this etiquette-bound life, could be. She knew she did not want it for herself, but she did not know how to escape it, either.

She bit back a sigh and turned her attention to the conversation around her. Perhaps she was not giving Sir Jeremy a chance, she told herself. They had not even had their promised drive yet.

"There is someone I would like you to meet," Countess Lieven was saying. "In his younger days he was quite invaluable in England's diplomatic service, or so my husband tells me. Now, alas, he is retired, but my husband and I have enjoyed his company and that of his sweet wife since we have been in London."

She lifted her elegant hand and summoned a gentleman to her side. He had obviously been quite handsome in his youth and was still distinguished despite an expanded girth and receded hairline. Emma vaguely recalled him from the receiving line, but she had been lost in her daydream then and could not quite remember his name. Her aunt would surely scold her soundly for that lapse, though, so she smiled and prayed that someone would mention his name before she had to address him.

"Lord Osborn, of course you have met the Count and Countess Suvarov and their niece, Lady Emma Weston," Countess Lieven said, rescuing Emma from her dilemma. "They are relations of our Tsar, and quite indispensable to our country."

"A great honor to meet you," Lord Osborn said. He bowed first over Aunt Lydia's hand, then Emma's. "We are indeed privileged to have such lovely ladies grace our city with their presence."

"You are too kind, Lord Osborn," Lydia said.

"No, indeed, Countess Suvarova. No, indeed. Merely honest." Lord Osborn gave Emma an oddly speculative glance. "I should so much like you to meet my son. He is conversing with our hostess at the moment, but perhaps later?"

"We should like that, Lord Osborn," Emma answered, since the man was still looking at her. "Countess Lieven tells us that your wife is also very charming."

She watched him as he made some reply and wondered if his son was as carefully polished, as artificial, as the father was. If so, she wasn't sure she could face him just now. Her tiara was giving her a dreadful headache, and it was all she could do to keep smiling and making light conversation.

Sir Jeremy came to her rescue with a glass of punch and an offer to escort her to view their hostess's prized new Titian painting. She moved away on his arm, waved on by her aunt and uncle.

It was only much later that she remembered she had not met Lord Osborn's son, after the evening was at long last over, and Sir Jeremy was assisting her into the carriage.

"I beg you to remember your promise to go for a drive with me, Lady Emma," Sir Jeremy said, looking intently into her eyes. "I would so like to renew our old acquaintance."

"Of course I will not forget. Good evening, Sir Jeremy," she said, smiling politely.

He pressed a quick kiss to her gloved hand before the carriage door shut between them and the vehicle jolted into motion.

Emma leaned her aching head back and closed her eyes, relishing the quiet, the peace. No one was looking at her, no one expecting anything from her for the first time in hours. It was lovely.

She opened her eyes to look out the carriage window. Were all Englishmen like Sir Jeremy, she wondered? It was a fine thing she had not met Lord Osborn's son, then, for she had met quite enough young Englishmen tonight. She probably should have married a Russian while she had the chance!

Emma giggled at that thought. Who exactly would she have married? No one had asked her.

"Did you enjoy the reception, Emma?" her aunt asked.

Emma looked across the carriage to where her aunt and uncle sat, their arms linked. "Oh, yes. It was very nice."

Her uncle chuckled. "I think that is what they call a 'polite falsehood,' Emma. It was tedious for you, I know."

Emma laughed. "Perhaps just a bit, Uncle Nicholas!"

"Well, you behaved very charmingly, as always," Nicholas said. "I received so many compliments on my lovely family."

"On your lovely young niece, perhaps," said Aunt Lydia. "Emma is so admired wherever she goes. I should not be surprised if we saw Sir Jeremy Ashbey on our doorstep very soon. Perhaps even tomorrow!"

Emma smiled at her aunt and uncle, but inside she sighed.

Chapter Three

*E*mma was exhausted, but she could not sleep. She lay in the middle of her enormous bed, staring up at the embroidered underside of the canopy. Her head and feet throbbed, and her vast bedchamber was so silent that she wanted to shout just to fill it up.

Finally, unable to lie still for another minute, she pushed aside the bedclothes and climbed down from the bed. She padded on her bare feet across the floor to pull the heavy satin curtains back from the window.

Outside, it was an entirely different world. People still thronged the park across the way, laughing, dancing, chatting, moving in one great mass beneath the lights of the Chinese lanterns strung in the trees. Emma opened the sash and leaned out, listening to the strains of some sort of rough music. Snatches of song and laughter floated up to her.

She leaned her chin in her hand and watched the crowd, soaking in all the excitement, all the *life*. How she wished she could be a part of it! She would so love to dance, to laugh, to flirt with some handsome swain. Just to have a conversation that was not fraught with etiquette would be a veritable heaven.

As she sat there, her gaze darting from one scene to another, a young couple passed on the fringes of the crowd, hand in hand. The man pulled the girl into his arms, twirling her about to the tune until she giggled. He kissed her cheek, softly, tenderly, and then they vanished back into the throng, replaced by a laughing, robust husband and wife, who trailed behind them a brood of rambunctious children.

Emma almost cried. It was all so sweet, so beautiful, so—elusive. She wanted to seize all that emotion and pull it into herself, to make herself a part of it. But she knew that could never be. That park might as well be as far away as the stars.

Still, she ached for it, longed to leave her luxurious chamber behind. She leaned farther out of the window, trying to see more . . .

"Whatever are you doing, my lady!"

Emma was so startled by Natasha's cry that she almost tumbled over the windowsill. She grabbed onto the curtains and pulled herself back, looking over her shoulder at the wide-eyed maid.

"Natasha!" she said. "Don't shout so. You almost frightened me to death."

"What else should I do when I see you about to hurl yourself out the window?" Natasha rushed forward to pull Emma completely inside by the sleeve of her nightdress, then she closed and locked the window. The music and laughter were abruptly cut off, leaving Emma in satin-swaddled silence again.

"I was not about to *hurl* myself anywhere," Emma protested. "I was merely—watching."

"Without your dressing gown or slippers?" Natasha clucked disapprovingly and picked up Emma's discarded bedroom slippers. "You should be in bed, my lady."

"I could not sleep," Emma said, sitting down on a chair to put the slippers on. "I have a headache."

"You are probably hungry." Natasha fetched the tray she had banged down on the table so abruptly when she came in to find Emma on the verge of "suicide." There was a glass of milk and a plate of dainty cucumber and salmon sandwiches.

Emma's stomach rumbled at the sight of the food, reminding her of all the scrumptious lobster patties and mushroom tarts she had *not* eaten at the reception. After all, a *lady* did not make a glutton of herself in public.

"You take such good care of me, Natasha," she said, reaching for a sandwich. "You have ever since we were children."

"Someone must, my lady." Natasha busied herself finding a warm Indian shawl to drape over Emma's shoulders and smoothing the rumpled bedcovers. "You do not eat enough. You need to keep up your strength."

Emma gave an unladylike snort. "It is much too difficult to look elegant and dignified when one is cramming a lemon tart into one's mouth." She thought ruefully of all the banquets that had gone mostly uneaten in the name of elegance and dignity. "Tell me, Natasha, did you go to the illuminations tonight?"

Natasha turned away from fluffing up the bed pillows, her face all aglow with a smile. Emma sometimes forgot that Natasha was really so young, not much older than Emma herself, she was usually so fussing and motherly. But at this moment she *looked* young and carefree.

"Oh, yes!" Natasha answered. "It was—was *choo dyes nuy*, my lady. I have never seen anything like it. It sparkled like heaven must."

Sparkled like heaven. Emma sat back and closed her eyes, trying to envision it all.

"It is happening tomorrow night, too," Natasha said. "If you do not need me, my lady, I thought I might go again."

Emma opened her eyes. "Certainly you may go, Natasha. I am sure there will be some banquet or ball I must attend. I won't need you until late." She felt a twinge of envy, but she hid it quickly behind a smile. She did not want to dim Natasha's fun with her own bad mood.

"Oh, yes, that reminds me." Natasha took a sheet of paper from her apron pocket and handed it to Emma. "I saw Madame Ana in the corridor earlier, and she asked me to give you this."

Emma unfolded it, and saw that it was her schedule for the next day. She scanned the list—luncheon with the Tsar and his sister, an afternoon carriage ride in the park with some duchess, a state banquet.

She almost groaned. Her headache, gone so quickly when she watched the crowd of merrymakers, pressed down on her again. If only she could escape all that, for just one single, solitary day. She was so tired. Her entire body yearned for the freedom that could never be hers. Even if she married Sir Jeremy Ashbey or someone like him, her life would go on in much the same way, in the cocoon of politics and diplomacy and Society and correct behavior. Not even for a moment would she be free.

Unless . . .

Emma raised her head to stare outside the window. She could no longer hear the voices, but she could imagine them, could imagine the flash of the beckoning lights. There might, just might, be a way it could all be in her grasp, even if it was just for a very short while.

"Natasha," she said, in her most cajoling tone. "My darling Natasha, I need your help . . ."

"I thought the evening went splendidly." Lord Osborn leaned back against the leather squabs of the carriage, satisfaction and contentment practically flowing from him. "King Frederick William very kindly remembered me from my time in Prussia, and the Count and Countess Suvarov were everything charming."

"The countess's gown was very beautiful," Lady Osborn said wistfully. "The Russian style is so very dashing."

Jack turned from his quiet contemplation of the street outside the carriage window to smile at her. "But your gown was by far the loveliest one there, Mother."

Jane giggled happily. Her usually pale cheeks were suffused with a sunset pink color. This stultifying social life obviously agreed with her.

Her husband looked at her in a startled fashion. Apparently, both his son and his wife had the power to surprise him tonight. "Indeed, you do look very pretty this evening, Jane." Then he turned a sharp look onto Jack. "It is just too bad that you never got to make the acquaintance of Count and Countess Suvarov, Jonathan."

"I met them in the receiving line."

"That is not the same as a personal introduction. They are very important people, and they will be leaving England very soon. It is vital that the count—and therefore the rest of the Russian party—take a favorable impression of our country with them, and that the countess remembers her homeland well."

Mr. Thompson had said almost exactly the same thing at their meeting, Jack recalled. "I hardly believe that their not meeting me will alter their views of England. Rather, I think it may improve them."

His father's lips flattened into a thin line. "You may be right at that. But I am sure their young niece would have enjoyed meeting you."

"Yes, the poor thing!" Jane said unexpectedly. "It must be so difficult for her, to be always surrounded by old people like ourselves. Such a pretty girl."

Yes, Jack thought. *A very pretty girl indeed.*

But also an impossibly remote girl, like some fairy-tale maiden in an ivory tower.

He thought about Lady Emma Weston, so perfect with her snow-white skin, her wealth of dark hair and melting brown eyes. She was one of the most beautiful ladies he had seen since returning from Spain—one of the most beautiful *respectable* ladies, anyway. He had watched her from a distance all evening, as she moved across the room speaking to various people. She was always absolutely correct, perfectly charming, but Jack could tell she was not completely there in that crowded ballroom. Her gaze seemed distant, her smile frozen, as if her body was present but her mind was someplace else entirely.

No one else seemed to notice at all, not even her aunt

and uncle, or that Sir Jeremy whatever who squired her about. Jack noticed, though—because he felt the same way. Out of place, stultified—lost.

He wondered what the snow maiden would look like if she laughed, if she took off her jeweled tiara and let the gleaming mass of her hair tumble down.

"Lady Emma Weston is not married or even betrothed," his father said, interrupting these enticing visions.

Jack turned to see Lord Osborn giving him a significant look. He wondered how his father had ever succeeded in diplomacy, since everything he thought was written in his expression.

"I hardly think the exalted count and countess would think me a suitable match for their niece," Jack answered. "Or even someone suitable to take her driving in the park while she is in London."

"You are the son of an earl, just as she is the daughter of one. It would not be an unequal match for her, and it would be a brilliant one for you. Especially as you have not yet shown any preference for any other suitable young lady."

It was an old quarrel and not one Jack was interested in pursuing. This was not the right time for him to be thinking of marriage; he did not know if there would ever be a "right time" at all. Fortunately, the carriage lurched to a halt outside his lodgings even as his father spoke. Thus he was spared, at least for the time being, the usual lecture on his duty to his family, his obligation to marry well and set up his nursery.

As soon as the footman opened the carriage door, Jack leaped down onto the pavement.

"We are invited to take tea at the Russian embassy the day after tomorrow," his father called after him. "You will join us?"

Jack nodded as the door closed again and watched the carriage lumber off down the street, blessedly taking his parents with it.

Every day, it grew harder and harder to maintain his

charade. Every day, these quiet moments alone, when he could drop his facade and just be himself, grew more precious.

He rubbed wearily at the back of his neck and took a deep, fortifying breath of cool night air. It was silent on this little side street, with only the faintest echoes of the celebrating crowds floating to him on the breeze.

The tea at the Russian embassy would be a perfect opportunity for him to carry on with his task, but if he was honest with himself, he would have to admit that was not the real reason why he was going to attend. An image of Lady Emma Weston sprang to his mind. She was sure to be there, and Jack found that he wanted very much to see her again. Perhaps even to talk to her, to begin to fathom what was behind her dark eyes.

Jack laughed at himself, tilting his head back to the stars.

Probably what lay behind those fine eyes was—nothing. Only the usual things grand ladies thought of, such as gowns, jewels, parties. All his wild imaginings of her thoughts, her longings, would come to nothing. And it would serve him right, for being so obsessed with a woman he had only seen for a few fleeting moments.

He stared up at the moon, a silver sliver suspended in the cloudless purple black sky. Lady Emma was rather like that orb—pale, shimmering, perfect and unknowable.

"You are a fool, man," he muttered aloud. "You should cease standing about in the street thinking like a lovesick schoolboy and go inside and get some sleep."

After all, he had an important errand to perform in the morning.

Chapter Four

"*O*h, Aunt Lydia, I ache all over!" Emma slid down beneath the bedclothes, trying to look as pale and fragile as possible. She gave a cough just for good measure.

Aunt Lydia, her brow creased in concern, sat down on the edge of the bed and laid her cool fingers against Emma's cheek. "Oh, dear. You *are* warm."

Emma silently blessed the heated flannels Natasha had laid over her face right before Aunt Lydia entered the room. "And my throat is scratchy."

"Poor little Emma. You must have caught a chill standing about in the wind yesterday at that interminable review. Perhaps I should send for the physician."

The physician! "No!" Emma said hastily. Then, seeing the surprise on her aunt's face, she lowered her voice. "No, I am sure we need not bother the physician. I only need some rest, then I will be fine. I promise."

Natasha, who hovered in the background holding a small silver tray, said, "I have made her a cup of tea, Countess, and I'll stay with her all day."

Aunt Lydia nodded but still looked concerned. "You are an excellent nurse, Natasha, I am sure. But I would not want Emma to become seriously ill. I could never forgive myself if I brought you all this way only to have something dire happen. I promised my sister I would always look after you."

Emma took up her aunt's hand and kissed it quickly. "Nothing will happen, dear Aunt Lydia! I only need to sleep."

Lydia squeezed Emma's hand. "Very well. I will look in on you later this afternoon, though, and if you are not better I'll send for the physician. In the meantime, your uncle and I are lunching with the Tsar, then going for a carriage ride in the park. If you need anything at all, have Natasha send a message to us."

"I will. Have a lovely day."

Lydia squeezed her hand once more, then left the room in a rustle of silken skirts. Emma waited several long, tense moments until everything was silent in the corridor.

"Is it safe now?" she whispered.

Natasha put down her tray and went to peek outside the door. "All is clear, my lady!"

"Thank heavens! I am roasting under here." Emma flung back the blankets and stood up to pull her voluminous nightdress over her head. Underneath, she wore a plain gray muslin gown and white apron. She twirled around, watching the skirt flare around her legs. "How do I look?"

Natasha's expression was most doubtful. "Not very much like a maid, my lady."

"Pooh! People only see what they expect to see." Emma turned to the dressing table mirror, and twisted her long plait of hair up into a knot at the nape of her neck, skewering it with hairpins. "If I wore a crown they would expect to see a queen. Since I'm wearing an apron, they will see a maid."

Natasha just shook her head. She had agreed to go along with this plan last night, but her every movement spoke of her reluctance.

"Oh, Natasha," Emma said, in a wheedling tone. "I will not speak to anyone. I will just look around a bit and then come back. What could possibly happen?" She laughed and kissed Natasha's cheek hastily before grabbing up a gray knitted shawl and an old reticule. She hurried from the room, with only a quick smile tossed back over her shoulder at Natasha.

The back staircase of the hotel was blessedly deserted, and it was only a moment before she was out on the crowded street, her heart singing as it never had before. Her very fingertips and toes tingled with excitement!

Emma moved seamlessly into the flowing mass of people, borne away on their surging tide. She was swept through the gates of Green Park, surrounded by waves of laughter and good cheer. She soon found herself laughing along with them, laughing until her sides ached, even though she had no idea what the joke might be.

Someone pushed a tall tankard of some foamy, amber-colored liquid into her hand. "Here y'go, love. Compliments of the Prince Regent."

"God bless Prinny!" another man shouted, then downed his own tankardful.

Emma took a long gulp of the mysterious liquid and promptly gagged on the sour taste. "God bless Prinny, indeed," she murmured, then almost clapped her hand to her mouth in consternation. She had promised Natasha she would speak to no one, for fear someone might comment on her accent.

But the people around her did not even notice. "Now, that's the finest ale to be had in London," the man who had given her the tankard said.

Ale, hm? Emma looked down at the stuff with new interest. She had never had ale before. Her aunt said only English peasants drank it, just as only Russian peasants drank rough, homemade vodka.

This is a day for doing things you have never done before and will probably never do again, she told herself. *So, drink up!*

She tilted the tankard for another sip and found that it improved on closer acquaintance. By the time she finished it all, it even tasted rather good. Not like champagne by any means, but not so bad.

Perhaps she ought to try one of those sausage things the man over there was selling. . . .

His errand complete, Jack stepped out of the servants' entrance to the Pulteney Hotel and into the fine summer's day. The hand-off of the documents had gone very quickly. Jack had just handed them to a secretary while Count Suvarov, writing at a nearby desk, had hardly glanced up. But even though he seemed not to pay attention, Jack had the distinct sense the man missed nothing. Nothing at all.

He took a deep breath and looked around him. The weather was perfectly ordered for a time of celebration, with a blue sky, studded only with the tiniest and puffiest of white clouds, and bright sunshine. Crowds hurried past him, jostling. They bumped right up against him as he walked down the street and turned past the park. No one paid him any heed, as he was dressed simply and cheaply today, as Mr. Thompson had instructed. If he had been Viscount St. Albans, people would have given him a wide, respectful berth. As plain Jack, though, he warranted no such consideration, which suited him just fine. There was something exhilarating in just moving along, being part of this extraordinary day.

And his plain attire did not deter the flirtatious glances a redheaded shopgirl was sending him. Jack grinned and leaned back idly against the brick wall of a shop. His errand was accomplished, after all, and he had the whole day ahead of him.

Then he heard a scream coming from a nearby alleyway. He went from idleness to motion in an instant and broke into a run.

Chapter Five

$\mathcal{E}$mma had never had a more splendid time in all her life.

She walked and walked, down streets and courts crowded with people. Sometimes the traffic was so thick that she couldn't pass, but she did not care. She was too enthralled by all the wonderful, marvelous life around her—and by the ale she had consumed—to care about much of anything.

Usually, when she went to the shops or the theater, she was surrounded by servants and escorts so that no one dared come close to her. She always felt that some invisible wall protected her from the touch of other people, from ordinary conversation.

Today, it was not that way at all. She was jostled on all sides by people, people of all sorts, and she rather liked it. Servants, tradesmen, soldiers, even well-dressed ladies and gentlemen pressed together in the streets, all united in the joy of the downfall of Boney and the union of the allied monarchs. For the first time in her life, Emma felt a part of the world and not set above it, gazing down in sad wistfulness.

She drank more ale when she became thirsty, ate sausages and a meat pie and cakes purchased from street vendors, and stopped to peer into the shop windows. She ogled gloves and slippers, books bound in rich leather, boxes and bottles of scents and powders.

Munching on a paper full of hot roasted almonds, she

stopped to examine a modiste's colorful display. Swaths of silks and satins were draped together in a rainbow of richness. Her gaze was caught by a violet-colored velvet, and she thought idly that it would make a lovely pelisse, perhaps trimmed in sable against the harsh Russian winter.

Then she realized that she did not have the coins to buy such a fabric, and the mantua-maker would hardly be likely to extend her credit in her current guise. In fact, she would probably be quickly bundled right back out the door if she dared set foot in there!

Emma laughed. It was a strange and delicious sensation to know that the polite world, a world that bowed and scraped before Lady Emma Weston, had no use for her now. It was enormously liberating. She could do anything she wanted, anything at all, and no one would notice. No one would frown in disapproval or whisper about her behind their fans. No one would even care.

She grinned in delight. It was a most amazing sensation to be completely unimportant.

"It's pretty, isn't it?"

Emma looked over to see a young woman standing next to her. She wore a plain blue muslin dress and a pert straw bonnet set back on her head and tied with cherry-colored ribbons. Emma quite admired her cropped red gold curls and reached up to touch her own heavy knot of hair. It would be so delicious to be free of its weight! If only her aunt wouldn't notice that her hair was missing . . . "Very pretty," she agreed.

"Cor!" the girl said, her eyes widening at the sound of Emma's faint accent. "You aren't English, are you?"

Emma felt her cheeks flood with warm, chagrined color. Once again, she had forgotten her promise not to speak to anyone! "I—no. Not really. I am a maid to a— a Russian lady. One who is with the court of the Tsar."

"Really? What a treat! My sister and me were wanting a glimpse of that Tsar. A handsome cove, ain't he?"

Emma had never heard His Highness referred to as a "cove" before, handsome or otherwise. She almost giggled. "Oh, yes. Very handsome."

"Well! Fancy my meeting someone who has met the Tsar. My sister will be ever so jealous."

Before the girl could say anything else, a new wave of people surged past them, carrying her off. Emma pressed back against the shop window until everyone passed, then she turned and went the other way. Her almonds were all eaten, and she was feeling a bit dizzy from the unaccustomed ale. If she could just find a place to sit down for a while, a bench or a low wall, she would feel much better.

She ducked into a quiet, narrow alleyway between two shops and leaned briefly against the rough bricks to catch her breath. The walls of the buildings on either side were so close that it was quite dark, and it didn't exactly smell like a rose garden, but it was deserted. Emma's head was spinning with all the excitement, and she was glad of the sudden silence.

Pulling her shawl closer around her shoulders, she walked further down the alley, the click of her shoe heels on the cobblestones the only sound.

Suddenly, a rough hand snaked out from a recessed doorway and snagged her arm. "What's this, then?" a deep, hoarse voice said.

Emma gasped, shock and outrage flooding through her, paralyzing her with cold, as a short but heavyset man pulled her closer. His breath was hot on her face, reeking of onions and ale.

"A pretty pigeon, eh, landed right in me own nest," he snickered, leering at her. His hand tightened on her arm, an iron clasp that bruised her soft skin.

"How dare you!" She yanked hard on her arm, trying to pull away. Her mind felt covered in some haze, quite unable to move from the joy of her day of freedom to *this*. No one had ever *grabbed* her in all her life! If they had, her uncle would have shot them.

But her uncle was not here now. She was all alone, deep in a dark alley with a ruffian. Emma had never before felt so foolish.

"Release me at once, you—you *pla-hoy*!" she cried

out, using a word she had sometimes heard Natasha say in moments of frustration.

"Ooh, a foreign pigeon," the man said with a nasty laugh. "And I wager that the pretty pigeon has a pretty purse, too." He pulled her closer, ever closer.

Emma realized there was only one thing left to do. She filled her lungs with air and screamed. She screamed and screamed, as loud and as long as she could.

The man swore and clamped his dirty hand over her mouth, but it was too late for him. There was a quick blur of movement in the corner of Emma's eye, and her attacker landed flat on his back, torn away from her by some unseen force. A tall figure loomed over him and delivered the coup de grâce of a right uppercut to the jaw.

The vile man's eyes rolled up inside his head, and he lay still. He'd hardly known what had happened to him.

Emma stared down at the violent scene, dizzy with the speed of it all. One moment she had been utterly terrified, and then—rescue. Just in a second. She was giddy with the fear, the relief and the heady violence of it all. She pressed her hand to her mouth to hold in an hysterical laugh.

Her rescuer stood up and turned to face her. "Are you quite all right, miss? Did this villain hurt you?"

Emma stared up, and up, into the bluest eyes she had ever seen, and suddenly her giddiness felt—different. Her head spun, and she fell back against the wall, unable to stand upright an instant longer. Her legs felt like water.

"You *are* hurt!" the man said, his voice rough with concern. He caught her arm to support her. "Only say the word, and I'll kill the ruffian here and now. Not a quick death, either, but a slow and painful one."

She just gazed up at him. She knew she must appear the veriest lackwit, but she could not seem to help herself. All the poise and grace that had been trained and drilled into her since she was a tiny child fled when she saw him.

He was handsome enough, to be sure, tall and fashionably lean, with rich, dark brown hair that waved over his sun-browned brow and those very blue eyes. Yet mere handsomeness surely could not account for her strange reaction to his presence. She saw handsome men every day. Sir Jeremy Ashbey was a veritable Apollo, and of her own station besides. This man was obviously a tradesman of some sort, as he was dressed in a rough tweed coat, brown woolen trousers and a loosely-tied white neckcloth.

Yet, everything she had hoped to feel for Sir Jeremy and did not seemed to move through her when she looked up at her rescuer. A rich, wonderful warmth like the thickest cup of chocolate flowed over her, into her very veins, bringing a soft flush with it. She felt dizzy, as if she had just drunk a great quantity of champagne—or cheap ale. She wanted to laugh, to cry, to put her arms around him and bury her face in his neck. Her fingers quivered to touch his glossy hair, the dimple in his square, shadowed chin.

It was ridiculous, absurd! Quite unreal. She had just met him, had not even spoken to him. Indeed, all her powers of conversation seemed to have vanished. All she could concentrate on was the feel of his hand on her elbow. She knew that if he did not hold onto her, she would fall onto the filthy cobblestones.

"Are you hurt, miss?" he said again, his voice gentle.

"Oh, no," she managed to gasp. "Not at all. How can I ever thank you, sir? You have surely saved my life!"

He tilted his head to one side, a puzzled frown suddenly forming between his glorious, sky-colored eyes.

Why was he looking at her so oddly all of the sudden? Had she spoken Russian or French instead of English? Was her face dirty, her dress mussed after her misadventure? She reached up to her hair, trying to push vagrant strands back into the plaited knot.

His brow cleared as suddenly as it had creased, and he smiled at her. It was like the warmth of the sun breaking from behind gray clouds at the end of a long Russian winter.

She smiled, too, and even heard a giggle break free from her lips. "Yes. I am *very* well."

It *was* she. Jack could scarcely believe it, but there could never be two such ladies in all the world. Yet, what was she, a lady, a fair flower protected by the Russian court, doing in a dirty alleyway, dressed like a housemaid and, apparently, all alone. His mind reeled with the possibilities and came up empty, until he remembered his own apparel.

Perhaps the same sort of thing a viscount is doing dressed as a servant, he thought.

Lady Emma Weston, out for a bit of spying? Absurd! But if not, what was she truly up to? He glanced around to see if she was truly alone, or if her guards were with her. There was no one. He really ought to keep an eye on her—heaven only knew what could happen to a lady alone.

He just opened his mouth to ask her what in Hades she was up to, but she stopped him by reaching for his hand and cradling it tenderly in her two small, soft palms.

"Oh!" she murmured, bending her head to examine his hand closer. She stood so close that he could smell the lilac scent of her hair. "You are hurt."

Jack was so bemused by her nearness that he scarcely heard her words, let alone felt any pain. "Hm?"

She looked up at him, her dark eyes wide, soft with concern. "Your hand is bleeding." Her faint accent flowed over him like warm brandy or—or vodka.

Yes. Sharp, hot Russian vodka.

Jack grinned at his own flash of whimsy. He just couldn't seem to help it; he was so rarely whimsical. This sprite of a snow princess must bring it out of him.

A small frown formed on her heart-shaped face as she saw his smile. "Are you—how do you say?—*unhinged* by the pain, sir?"

His grin widened. She was just too adorable. "I don't feel any pain, miss."

"How can you not? You are bleeding!" She bent her head again to examine the wound, a loose strand of her black-satin hair brushing his skin like the lightest, sweetest caress.

But the moment was spoiled when the ruffian at their feet moaned and stirred. She glanced down at him, her expression of tender concern transformed to one of deepest distaste. The ice maiden had returned. She turned to walk out of the alleyway, pulling Jack with her.

"Come," she said. "We should be leaving now."

"I certainly agree," he answered, going along most willingly. "Where do you propose we go?"

"We must see to your hand." She looked around until she saw an empty bench and drew him over to sit down beside her. Then she dug about in her reticule until she found an embroidered handkerchief, which she proceeded to wrap around his scraped knuckles.

Jack enjoyed her ministrations in silence for a long moment, listening to her soft, foreign murmurings. She was every bit as lovely as she had been at the reception, but without the trappings of her formal gown and rich jewels, she was no longer as remote as the moon, as he had fancied her. Her simple hairstyle and plain gray dress had much to do with that, of course, yet there was more. Her eyes, her skin, her very demeanor were transformed—they glowed and sparkled with life, with energy. But for all that, she still exuded a regal quality that could not be hidden.

How she thought she could fool everyone with her erect posture, her embroidered handkerchief, and the dainty kid half boots that peeped out from beneath her rough hem, Jack could not say. She was just fortunate that he was the one who had discovered her masquerade and not someone else—someone who would not scruple to reveal her. Or use her for his own ends.

He remembered how Mr. Thompson had emphasized how important it was that nothing happen to the foreign monarchs or their retinues while they were in England. It filled him again with a burning anger that someone would dare attack Lady Emma—and even an anger with Emma herself, for putting herself into such a vulnerable position.

These thoughts were quickly obscured by other sweeter ones, though. She was close to him, so close that he could lean his head the merest inch and take a surreptitious breath of her scented hair, brush his hand on her arm.

Delicious.

She finished tying off the knot in her handkerchief and gently patted his hand. "There!" she said, with a great air of satisfaction. "That is much better." She peeked up at him through her sooty lashes, still keeping his hand in hers. "Thank you again for coming to my rescue. You were so very brave!"

For one moment, Jack was completely taken aback. She looked at him as no one had in a very long time, if ever—as if he had done something completely *right*, something courageous and fine. In his careful guise of carelessness, he had become so accustomed to his family and his old respectable friends looking at him with disapproval that he wasn't quite sure how to respond to her.

He had just done what his instincts told him to do, what his years on the battlefield had taught him. It was all so automatic; he had heard her screams, and his senses leapt into battle mode. But when she looked at him with her shining eyes, he felt maybe he *was* brave. Even if only for a moment, only for this one woman.

"It was nothing," he answered. "I heard your scream, and I could hardly just stand there and let that villain attack you."

"But other people must have heard me scream. You were the only one who came."

"I was only the first to hear, I suppose."

She shook her head adamantly. "No. You were brave, and I will not hear otherwise. You saved me! I only wish I could reward you properly."

Properly? "Sitting here with you is all the reward I need," he said, half-truthfully. A kiss added to the "reward" would not have come amiss, but since that seemed out of the realm of possibility, sitting here with her would have to suffice.

She gave him a smile, more brilliant than any of the diamonds in her tiara had been. "Really?"

"Really."

"I am so glad. This has been the very best day of my life, and it would have been ruined if not for you."

Jack leaned back on the bench, laying his arm along its rough wooden top until he could just feel the warmth of her shoulder on his fingertips. The endless crowds still streamed around them, a sea of merriment, yet he saw none of them. He saw only the woman beside him. "The best day of your life, eh? You must have a very dull existence, then, La . . ." He almost called her "Lady Emma," but that would have been a great mistake. He wanted her to go on with this strange masquerade, to see what she would do with it. "—Lovely lady."

She smiled at this compliment but then sighed and leaned back on the bench. "Sometimes my life is unimaginably dull."

"Are you a lady's maid, mayhap?" he asked. "Or perhaps you work in a milliner's shop?"

"I"—she looked away from him, her slim fingers plucking at the edge of her shawl—"I am a maid. To one of the visiting Russian ladies."

"So you are a Russian?"

"*Da.*" She flashed him an impish grin. "I fooled you with my so perfect English accent, didn't I?"

Jack laughed. "Your accent is lovely. What is your name?"

"My name?" she said warily, her grin fading.

"You must have one. Even Russians have names, so I'm told."

"I am"—her gaze darted past him, as if she was thinking quickly—"I am Tonya."

"Tonya," he murmured, wondering where she had come up with such a name. It was probably the name of some friend or servant of hers, but it felt soft and smooth on his tongue, like the strange strains of a gypsy violin. Tonya. It suited her. "That's a very pretty name."

"Thank you, sir. And what is your name?"

"My name?"

"Yes. Even Englishmen have them, I think."

He laughed again, because she had trapped him with his own words. Truly he had laughed more in five minutes in her presence than he had in the last five years. "I'm Jack," he told her, not wishing to place another falsehood between them. He could at least give her his true name.

"Jack," she said slowly, as if trying out the name in her mouth, as he had hers. "I like that. It is very— resolute. And strong."

"That's me. Resolute Jack." He thought that after all her years in Russia, she might not have the firmest grasp on the English language. But "resolute" was a far better adjective than any his family or friends—or enemies— might choose for him.

"And what do you do, Jack?" she ask.

"Do?"

"Yes. I am a lady's maid, and you are . . ."

What *was* he? He wished he knew. He *did* know, however, that he didn't wish this game to end, as it surely would if he told her the truth. "I am a—secretary."

"This is your day off from your duties?"

"This day is—mine to do with as I wish." And he found he wished only to share it with her, duty or no. If he were truly dutiful, he would march her right back to the Pulteney Hotel, but he could not. Not just yet.

"That is how I feel about this day, too," she said. "It is mine to do with as I wish."

A vendor went past them, carrying a huge tray and calling, "Fruit pies! Meat pies! Fresh and hot!"

Jack saw Lady Emma—or Tonya—give the tray a longing glance. "Would you care for a pie?"

"Oh, yes!" she said happily. Her face lit up at the offer of a pie as his former mistress's would have over emeralds. "I want to try everything today."

He stood up from the bench and offered her his arm. "Come along, then, Miss Tonya, and we shall see what the good man has to offer. Would you care for chicken or beef?"

"Both! And perhaps fruit, if he has some." Her small hand slid neatly into the crook of his elbow, as if it was meant to go just there. "I am so glad we have met, Jack," she said softly.

"So am I, Tonya. Indeed, so am I." And he was. He had met the ice princess; now he saw the excited butterfly, ready to spread her wings.

Chapter Six

*E*mma chewed happily on her pie and studied her escort surreptitiously from the corner of her eye. She tried to be subtle, not to stare in a blatant or rude manner, but it was the hardest thing she had ever done in her life. Jack was quite the most extraordinary—and puzzling—man.

He said he was a secretary and indeed he looked the part, in a well-cut but unstylish and faded tweed coat and plain neckcloth. His boots were polished yet worn. But Emma was trained to observe people, to be a perfect hostess and anticipate people's needs. And though she sometimes tended to daydream at dull receptions and balls in order to survive them, she was also very well trained indeed.

Something about Jack rang false.

He did not appear like any servant she had ever seen, at least not any Russian one. His bearing was erect and strong, his shoulders straight, like the officers she had watched in the military review. He looked around them, always watching, always alert, his sky-blue gaze sharp. His light touch on her arm as he eased her through the crowds was steady, perfectly polite yet safely there in case she needed him.

She wondered about him. No, she more than wondered— she burned with curiosity. She wanted to know more about him, wanted to know *everything*.

But for now she was happy with what she had. Jack

was quite handsome, and his smile made her insides feel warm and fluttery. He was willing to walk with her through the glories of the day. He treated her like an ordinary woman, a woman who could enjoy talking and flirting. It was what she had longed for, prayed for. She was not about to toss all that away by asking foolish questions. This time would be over all too quickly. She intended to enjoy it, to wring the last tiny bit of fun from it.

Emma ate the last bit of her pie, savoring the buttery taste of the crust on her tongue. Jack held out his handkerchief for her to wipe her fingers on.

"Thank you," Emma murmured, taking the square of linen from him. It smelled of some sharp, grass-like cologne, and her fingertips touched the raised embroidery of a "J" worked in white thread.

After her fingers were clean, she slid it secretly into her apron pocket.

"Did you like your pie?" he asked, a hint of laughter in his voice.

Emma wondered if he was amused by the fact that she was happily consuming every bit of food in sight. She decided she did not really care if he was, even though she wanted so much for him to think her attractive and elegant. For the first time in—well, in as long as she could remember, her stomach was happily full.

She gave him a blithe smile. "Very much. English food is so delicious."

Jack laughed. "That is the first time I have ever heard *that*."

"Do you not care for English food?"

"It is, er, filling, I suppose. But not what most people would call fine."

Emma thought of the dishes her aunt's supposedly French chef produced, covered with sauces, smothered with creams and wines. She would prefer a chicken pie any time. "I do not care. I like it."

They had reached the edge of a small pond, where couples rowed across the still water and small children launched toy boats from the shore. Emma leaned back against the rough trunk of a tree to watch them, and Jack stood beside her, one arm braced near her head. The sunlight filtered through the leaves, casting a lacy pattern on his dark hair and the sharp planes of his face.

"Tonya," he said, but Emma did not really hear him. "Tonya!"

"Hm?" she asked, puzzled. Then she remembered she had impulsively given him the name of one of her aunt's parlormaids. "Oh! Yes?"

He gave her a crooked little half-smile. "I hope the food isn't the only thing you have found to enjoy in England," he said.

Scarcely, she thought. The people, especially the men— especially *one* man—also had great appeal. "Oh, no. I have enjoyed many things. It's very different from St. Petersburg."

"Is this your first visit to this country?"

"No. I was here once before, when I was a very small child. I—I had family here." She closed her eyes for a moment to try to recall those long-ago days. Somehow, she had hoped that being here again, after so many years, might bring back those memories again. It had not, of course. She had only those same very few, very precious memories that she had possessed before. The deep laugh of her father, the rose perfume of her mother, the wide twining staircase of their country estate. That was all.

But now she had some new ones to add to them.

"Really?" Jack said, his tone revealing only mild curiosity. "Are you going to see them while you are here?"

"No." Emma opened her eyes back to the sunny day. "No, they are dead."

He touched her arm. His fingers were light, but the warmth spread through the cloth of her sleeve, into her very skin. "I'm sorry."

"I still have family," she said. "I have been happy." Then she added, more softly, "I have." She turned slightly to him, looking up at him, as if somehow seeking his reassurance. "Have you?"

He looked at her, a small frown between his extraordinary eyes. "Have I what?"

Emma wasn't sure what they were talking about, what she was seeking from him. She felt dizzy, confused.

She reached out to hold onto his sleeve, to try to right herself. "I hardly know," she said with a laugh. "I only know I would like to know you better, Jack."

His frown cleared, and he drew her closer. "I would like to know you, too, Tonya. I have a feeling there is something quite fascinating about you that is hidden away."

Emma startled. His words were all too close to the truth. She stepped back a bit. His clasp on her loosened, but they were still close. "Hidden?"

Before he could answer, Emma felt an object strike against her legs and was pushed closer to Jack. She caught at his jacket to steady herself and had to resist the strong urge to lay her cheek against his chest. Instead, she looked down and stepped back. A small child, whose hoop had been run into Emma's skirts, smiled up at her shyly.

"I'm sorry, miss," he said.

"That's quite all right," Emma answered breathlessly. As lovely as it had been to be held by Jack, she was rather grateful for the interruption. She did not want to talk about what was "hidden," either in her life or his.

And it would not have been a fine idea for her to give in to her urge to throw her arms around him and kiss him, either.

She bent down to pick up the hoop, which she handed back to the child.

"Thank you, miss," he said, and continued on the pathway.

Emma turned to the view of the pond and ran her hand over her warm face. Despite the temperate day, she felt warm all over. The greenish-bluish water looked so very cool. She wished she could walk into it, could swim through it and feel it lapping at her hair and skin.

That would never do, of course. No one went swimming in a public park, not even ladies who had thrown off propriety for the day!

But perhaps they could do the next best thing.

She looked back at Jack. His frown, the glow of his blue eyes as he asked about her "hidden" life, had faded. He looked merely affable and good-humored.

"Could we take one of those boats out on the water?" she asked.

"Of course," he answered. "Whatever you like, Tonya. I think we can hire one over at that boathouse."

He held his arm out to her, and she slid her hand into the crook of his elbow. It felt natural and ordinary, as if they were a true couple, one who promenaded like this so often it was second nature.

It felt—right.

Jack watched Lady Emma—no, Tonya, even though she could not always seem to remember that name—as he rowed them to the center of the pond, carefully avoiding the other merrymakers in their boats and punts. She stared around her, her dark eyes wide with wonder, her head swiveling to and fro to take in everything around her. She laughed in delight at the sun-dappled scene, clasping a hand to her lips as the giggles bubbled and flowed from her.

She made him want to laugh, too, despite the true seriousness of the situation. As he looked at her, he forgot that she was a fine lady on the loose, the cherished niece of important foreign nobility. For one fleeting, precious moment, she was just a pretty girl, seated so close to him in the tiny boat that their knees almost touched. And he was just a secretary having a day out, enjoying a flirtation.

Even if the object of that flirtation evaded all his attempts to ask questions of even a vaguely personal nature.

He decided that for the time they were in this boat,

stranded on the water, he would cease trying to discover what had driven her from the Pulteney Hotel and just *be* with her.

She leaned her elbows back on the cushioned seat and smiled across at him. "It is wonderful out here! The loveliest thing I have ever seen."

Jack rested on the oars and grinned at her in return. "You are very easy to please, Tonya."

"Easy to please?"

"You seem as happy about a row on a park pond as most women would be if presented with rubies. This, and a chicken pie, appears to make your day complete." He remembered her as she had been at the grand reception, all ice and diamonds and pearls. Then he saw her as she was now, strands of dark hair loosening from the simple knot, sunlight casting color on her alabaster cheeks.

He much preferred this laughing girl, he decided. *Much.*

She twisted her head a bit to one side, as if considering his words. "Life was not easy at my home in Russia these last years. Not easy at all."

Jack grew somber as he recalled the horrors he himself had seen in the last few years. "The war has been terrible. I cannot imagine what it must have been like in Russia, an invaded land."

"I was away from most of the worst of it. I lived in the country. But it was lonely there in the quiet, sometimes even frightening. We had only vague rumors and wild, horrible stories to tell us what was happening." She turned her face to watch the people around them again, turning to the warmth of the sun as if seeking its protection from the coldness of her memories. "I like rubies as much as the next woman, I am sure, but this is far finer. People and laughter, so much happiness—it makes me feel all that is behind me now. There are only fine days ahead."

Only fine days. Jack hoped she was right, that all the war and death were behind them now. When he was with her, he could almost believe it. Almost believe that the days of battle, of heart-stopping suspense, of pretending he was something he was not, could be over.

Almost.

She turned back to look at him and smiled. "Oh, but here I have made you solemn! That will never do. Today is a day of celebration!"

"The best day of your life?" he teased, echoing her words back to her.

"Yes!" she cried. "Indeed it is. Even better since I have met you." Then, as if she feared she had been too bold, rose pink color flooded over her high cheekbones.

"And my day has assuredly improved since I met you. I've seldom been graced with such lovely company on my days off."

She laughed again, easily, as if familiar with such honeyed words. "Flatterer!"

"No, indeed!" he protested. "I am always the soul of honesty."

One raven brow arched "Always?"

He grinned at her again. It felt rueful even to himself. "Almost always."

"I thought so." She rested her hand on the edge of the boat as he turned them around a narrow bend. "Where did you learn to row this way? Were you in the navy?"

"The navy?" he exclaimed, one hand releasing the oar and covering on his heart in mock horror. "No, madam! His Majesty's army. I learned to row at school, many years ago. It has been so long since I've been on the water that I feared I had forgotten how."

"Some skills never leave us, yes?"

"Important ones do not."

"Ones such as rowing?"

He laughed. "Among others! There are many more important skills than rowing, you know." Of its own volition, his gaze went to her soft, pink bow of a mouth and could not seem to move for several long moments.

She blushed again but did not look away. "Oh, yes. I do know." She leaned back and stretched her feet out along the bottom of the boat until they barely touched the edge of his boots. "Do secretaries always go to school, Jack?"

He really had no idea if they did or not. The only secretary he really knew was his father's, and he had never had much conversation with him. But since the die was cast, he nodded decisively and said, "Of course. How else do we learn to be secretaries?"

"Hm. I wish *I* could have gone to school." Her mouth twisted wistfully.

"Do lady's maids not go to school in Russia?"

The sudden widening of her eyes was most telling. She had spoken without thinking, just as he had. "Of course not. That is why we are still lady's maids."

She shot him a long glance, as if challenging him to question her. The slight tilt of her chin was most regal.

Not like that of any maid *he* had ever seen.

His gaze was trapped by hers, by the golden tinge to its brown depths, the uncertainty and the hauteur that shimmered there. So enthralled by watching her was he that he did not even realize his grip had loosened on one of the oars. Not until it had slipped its casing and fallen with a splash into the water.

"Oh!" Emma cried, and leaned over the side to watch it float on the green-blue surface. "Are we stranded? Can you row with only one oar? Or did they not teach you that in the school?" The last was said with a distinct laugh.

"Very clever, miss," he retorted. He also leaned over to peer at the oar, as it drifted leisurely away from them. In fact, he did *not* know how to row with only one oar. He was doing well to remember how to row at all. "I will get it."

"What?" she said, looking from the oar to him and back again. "How?"

"By reaching for it, of course." He took off his coat and handed it to her.

"Are you certain?" she said, taking the garment and holding it against her. "It is quite far away."

"It has hardly floated off to China! It is right there."

She pursed her lips, still looking doubtful. "Very well."
She sat back and looked at him, waiting like the ice
princess she had once been for him to perform his chore.

He had done far more perilous things on the Peninsula, Jack thought. Things like slipping documents past
the French lines and rescuing English prisoners. Retriev-
ing a little oar was nothing.

He leaned over the side of the boat, rising up on his
knees and reaching for the errant slab of wood. Unfortunately, while he was arguing with Lady Emma, the
blasted oar had drifted even farther, and he misjudged
his reach. For one brief instant, he felt the center of
his balance shift, but it was not long enough for him to
right himself.

He pitched headfirst into the pond. As the murky wa-
ters closed over his head, he heard Emma scream and
call his name.

The pond was not very deep at all. Indeed, he could
almost have stood on the slimy floor of it and peeked
his head above water. He quickly surfaced to grasp the
boat and looked up into her shocked face.

All the happy color had faded from her cheeks, leaving
her as snow-pale as she had been at the reception. As
pale as a marble angel.

She saw him and screamed again.

Jack winced. "For heaven's sake, woman! Don't shout
in my ear. I hardly fell into the great Atlantic. Help
me up."

"Oh, yes! Of course." Muttering strange Russian
words, she reached for the remaining oar and held it out.

For such a tiny thing, she was surpassingly strong. Jack
used the oar she held to brace himself and hauled his
body up over the gunnel and back into the boat.

Only when he was solidly seated again did he become
aware of the people in the other vessels watching him.
Some laughed; some looked away politely. One child, the
one who had earlier run his hoop into Emma, rudely
pointed. Jack scowled at them all until they turned away,
leaving him alone again.

Alone with Emma, who leaned over him, cooing and murmuring and wiping ineffectually at his grimy self with her apron. She was grace personified, while he—well, he probably looked like a muddy water gnome. In front of the only woman he had truly wanted to impress in such a very long time.

He laughed at the sheer ridiculousness of it all. Emma gaped at him as if he had suddenly gone delirious, which, he supposed, he really had.

"You will catch such a chill!" she said, wrapping his discarded jacket around his shoulders. "You should not be wearing these wet clothes."

He laughed even harder. "Do you suggest I strip down right here? Shocking, madam! Shocking."

"Jack!" she protested, sputtering. "Of course not. There must be someplace we can go where you could get dry garments."

"Or I could escort you home, and we could call it a day," he suggested, even as all his senses screamed a protest. He did not want this time to be over—not at all. They were only just beginning.

She looked as horrified as he felt. She could never be the diplomat her uncle was. "No! That is, not yet. I do not want to go home yet. Surely there must be *some* place. You cannot walk about with wet clothes, and I cannot go home."

Jack tipped back his head to look at her. There were his own rooms, of course, not far from here. They were a bachelor's lodgings, dark, temporary, shabby. Nothing there to betray that he was a viscount, not a secretary. He could change quickly and then sweep her back out into the celebratory day.

It would be highly improper, quite unthinkable to take Lady Emma Weston to his rooms. Foolish in the very extreme.

But, of course, she was *not* Lady Emma Weston. Not today. And he was not a viscount.

"There is some place," he said. "Yet I fear we are still trapped here with just one oar."

She laughed, the sound like silver bells in the warm air. "Oh, never fear! I have rowed before. There was a lake on the country estate where I lived. I'll get us to shore."

Jack also laughed, laughed until his sides ached. He wasn't sure how many more surprises he could survive with this woman. "Minx! You are the veriest Russian minx."

She smiled blissfully and settled back with the oar balanced carefully in her hands. The boat smoothly turned back to shore. "Oh, Jack. That is the nicest compliment anyone has ever given me."

Chapter Seven

$\mathcal{E}$ mma looked about avidly as she followed Jack up a narrow staircase, which no doubt led to his lodgings. They passed two landings, both with doors leading off them to the right. The faint scent of sugary baking drifted through the air, and the scratch of a violin played behind one of the doors.

It was all very mysterious and illicit-feeling, everything about it from the dim light to the faded red carpet under their feet. Emma felt breathless, her stomach aching with a mix of excitement, trepidation, too much ale and, above all, astonishment at herself. She had never been alone like this with an unmarried, unrelated young man. Not ever, and yet she had *wanted* to come here with Jack, had wanted to see if her attraction to him could possibly grow stronger if they were alone, or if it was merely a product of the day's party atmosphere.

But now that they were really here, in the quiet of a rooming house, it seemed as if a thousand trepidations overtook her. What if she was wrong about Jack? What if he became like that awful man in the alleyway? Was she being a terrible fool? Was she becoming a "wicked woman," like the ones she sometimes read about in novels? They always met terrible ends to pay for their sins.

Her steps slowed as she stared at Jack, who led onward, oblivious to her lagging. His dark hair was a bit overlong, waving over his damp, dirty tweed collar, and somehow that gave him a boyish touch of vulnerability despite the strong width of his shoulders. He hummed some low, carefree tune under his breath. He was obviously completely at ease.

No, she thought. Jack might be mysterious, but he was not like the man in the alleyway. He would not hurt her. She could not have said why she felt so very certain about that, but she did.

He stopped at a door on the third landing and dug a key out from inside his coat. He glanced back at her, and one brow arched when he saw her hovering at the head of the staircase.

"Would you like to wait out here?" he asked her quietly. "I will only be a few moments."

Emma smiled at him and hurried across the landing to his side. "Oh, no. I would feel so awkward if one of your neighbors came out and saw me."

He smiled in return, yet she could see a flicker of uncertainty in his eyes. Could there be something in there he did not want her to see, something he had just recollected?

"They are probably all at the celebration," he said. "All but Mr. Bright, the violin player. But if you are sure you want to come in . . ."

"I do."

Jack turned the key in the lock and pushed the door open, holding it for her to walk in ahead of him. Emma pulled her shawl closer about her shoulders and slid past him. She wondered what she would see. Red satin cushions? Silk-draped walls and low tables, as in a drawing she had once seen of a sultan's palace? Surely a bachelor's residence could hold any number of exotic items!

To her great disappointment, she found herself in an ordinary sitting room. Plain brown draperies hung at the windows, drawn back so the light came in and illuminated the sturdy, simple furnishings. More brown upholstered the chairs and settee, and books were piled on the two round tables. The only spot of ornamentation was a vase of some Oriental design in rich, deep green and blue porcelain, which sat in solitary splendor on the fireplace mantel.

Jack also looked about as if he had never seen this room before, or as if he was assessing now it might appear to her eyes. Emma ran her hand over the back of a chair and said, "It looks very—comfortable."

"Oh, yes," he answered. "It is that. I should offer you some tea or something, but I fear I have none about. Not even a tin of biscuits."

"I am quite all right, thank you." Emma felt very strange and formal all of a sudden, as if she had been transferred from Jack's sitting room back to the hotel. She smoothed down her skirt and looked around again.

Jack seemed to feel the same tension. His hands were clasped behind his back, and he rocked a bit on his heels. "Well, then," he said. "I will just go and wash up. I won't be long."

Emma nodded and watched as he opened another door and stepped into the room beyond. She just had a quick glimpse of a large, high bed draped in plain dark red curtains before that door closed again.

That glimpse was enough to make her feel oddly warm and tingling all over again. That bed was where Jack must—must . . .

"He *sleeps* there, of course, you ninny," she told herself aloud, albeit quietly, so he would not hear her. She was a green girl indeed if the merest glimpse of a bed was enough to overset her!

Even if it *was* the place where Jack laid his handsome body down at night. Perhaps even *naked*. *Oh, dear heavens*.

Emma laughed at herself and her fancies and sat down on one of the armchairs next to the largest round table. There were lovely, inviting piles of books there, and she reached for one.

Unfortunately, it was in Spanish. And the next one was a dull political treatise, but she leafed through it anyway. She put her feet up on a low footstool and leaned back in the chair, putting the book across her knees.

It must be very nice to live like this, she thought. In nice, cozy rooms, where one could do anything one wanted, with no Madame Ana coming in with lists. Instead of stultifying banquets, there would be evenings by the fire with a book. Or maybe supper and a card game with friends—*friends*, not "important personages."

What she would not give to have a dwelling place like this. She never would, of course; it was just another of her impossible daydreams. But right now, she could pretend that it was true, that this was her home.

And if this *was* her house, she would make a few changes, just to make things cozier. All of this brown would have to go and be replaced with— with blue, perhaps. Yes, blue, with some pictures, some ornaments for the mantel and shelves for the books. A carpet on the floor to warm the smooth wood on chilly evenings . . .

These whimsical musings were interrupted when the bedchamber door opened again and Jack came out, giving her one more small glance at that bed.

"I hope I did not take too long," he said, easing his arms into the sleeves of his coat and smoothing down the dark blue cloth. He smoothed it again, and it seemed an uncharacteristic gesture of uncertainty. Even in the very short time Emma had known him she had come to sense he was seldom uncertain about anything. When she had called him resolute, she meant it.

"Not at all," she answered, and sat up straighter in her chair, moving her feet from the stool. "I was enjoying your, er, book." She looked down at the volume in her hands. She had forgotten it was there.

Jack took it away and examined the lettering on the spine. "I did not know you enjoyed Montesque."

Emma had never even heard of the man, but she was not about to admit her ignorance to him. She shrugged and said, "You cannot truly know a great deal about me, since we have only known each other for about three hours."

He laughed and sat down in the chair next to hers. "A very *eventful* three hours, I would say! I almost fear what might come next."

Emma laughed, too. It had been a most eventful three hours indeed, more eventful than any three normal *days* ever were. But she longed to know what might happen next. "I promise I will not lure you into any more ponds or force you to rescue me in any alleyways I have no business being in."

Jack glanced down at the book in his hands. "Those are not the things I would fear," he muttered, almost to himself though she heard him.

Emma longed to know what he meant by those words, but she felt she should not press him to be more serious. She did not want to do anything that might make him take her back to the hotel and end their day.

It would end far too soon, anyway.

She looked over at him and noticed how his hair curled damply against his temples. She wanted to smooth it back, to feel if it was satin-soft or wiry or coarse.

Yet she knew what touching that dark hair would lead to wanting, at least for her, a kiss, a touch. All of them forbidden. She had no idea if Jack could possibly want the same things. He was so kind to her, so funny and dear, but always polite. She did not have the experience to tell if a man found her truly pretty. Men flattered her and complimented her, but that was Lady Emma Weston. Not Emma the woman.

It was that uncertainty that kept her hands folded in her lap. That and the knowledge that she had gone to the very edges of boldness just by being here. She dared not go further. Certainly not yet.

"What should we do now?" she said brightly.

He smiled at her and tossed the book back onto the table. "Should you not be going home soon?"

Emma glanced at the plain little clock hanging on the wall. It was afternoon now, but surely her aunt would not be back yet. "Not for a while. What else is there to see?"

"We could try to catch a glimpse of the foreign monarchs," he suggested. He peered at her closely as he spoke, almost as if to gauge her answer.

"I—no," she said. Seeing someone she knew sounded like the very last thing she wanted to do. "No, there must be something more *fun* to do."

"Oh, of course. You probably see the Russian Tsar and his sister all the time."

Emma turned to him, startled. *Did he know? Had he just been teasing her all along?* He looked back at her with guileless blue eyes. "I—what?"

"Since your employer is a lady of the Russian court."

"Oh. Yes. Of course." Her tale of being a lady's maid.

"Perhaps we could go and take a look at Carlton House without seeing any royalty. It is quite a sight," he suggested.

Emma remembered Natasha's tales of the glorious illuminations. "What about the illuminations? I have heard they are wondrous! Like—like heaven."

Jack smiled. "So they are. But you can't see them until it is dark."

"Oh. Yes." Emma sank back in her chair, feeling foolish. Of course illuminations could not be seen in daylight. And she would have to return home long before night fell. "Perhaps some luncheon, then?"

"You are still hungry?" he asked, in a most surprised tone.

"I am, a bit." And she was. She had thought she would never be hungry again after the pie, but her stomach felt rather hollow. She didn't know if it was hunger or knowing that the day was drawing to a close. "Shall we go find something to eat, since you don't have even tea and biscuits here?"

"Certainly." Jack stood up and offered her his arm. "This is *your* day, Tonya. Your wish is my command."

After a flash of uncertainty about who he was speaking to—why, oh why, hadn't she picked a name closer to her own?—she smiled and slid her hand under his arm. As he led her to the door, she glanced back over her shoulder at the cozy room. For all its brownness, it was lovely, and if she could have one wish, it would be to stay here for the rest of the day.

And maybe even into the evening.

Jack held the door of the public house open for Emma as she stepped past him into the dark, crowded room. Her skirts brushed against his boots, and he could smell the sweet lilac scent that always seemed to cling about her, like springtime. He knew he would never be able to smell that light, fresh fragrance again without seeing her in his mind. Seeing her as she laughed, as she did now, giggling behind her hand at some silly joke he had told her. Seeing her rapt face as she watched ordinary, everyday life flow around her.

Seeing her in his very own sitting room, looking so much at home with her small feet on his stool and his book open on her knees.

He had known as soon as he opened the door to the sitting room—no, before that, as soon as he suggested that they go to his lodgings—that it was a mistake. The sight of her there, in those intimate, familiar surroundings, had awakened feelings that could more easily be kept at bay in public. She was a beautiful woman. No, more than beautiful. The lady at the reception had been beautiful, like a porcelain doll or a painting.

Emma was full of color and life. And there, in his own room, he had wanted to take her in his arms and kiss her, kiss her until they fell to the floor in sighs and heat . . .

He rubbed his hand across the back of his neck, acutely uncomfortable. He had been just so ever since he had seen her glance at his bed. What he needed now was ale. Or something stronger. *Much* stronger.

He held a chair for Emma at a table in a quiet corner.

"This is a fascinating place, Jack!" she said, folding her hands demurely on the scarred tabletop and looking around at the dim, smoky environs. "One time my unc—

that is, some obscure relatives, took me to a dining establishment in St. Petersburg, but it was nothing like this."

"I would imagine not." He gestured to the barmaid for drinks and a platter of food. The Rose and Thorn was not the sort of place a fine lady would ever frequent. But it was comparatively quiet and close to his lodgings, and the food was cheap and plentiful. He had a feeling, after watching Emma consume her pies, that that would be a consideration.

Also, he was not likely to run into anyone he knew here.

"Is this what they call a public house?" she asked.

Jack laughed. "Where did you hear that phrase?"

"I read." She watched as the maid put a tall tankard of ale in front of her. Jack would have wagered she would be done with ale after her earlier dizziness, but she just picked it up and sipped at it without comment. "I have learned many, many things from books."

"Including public houses?" Jack took a long swallow from his own tankard.

"Oh, yes. I never thought I would actually get to *see* one. It looks just as I imagined."

She examined the platter of food the maid plunked down on the table, piles of bread, fruit, cheese and cold roasted beef. And Jack, in turn, examined her.

For just one second, he wished this was not a game. He wished they were truly just a young couple out for a treat, that they could walk down the street hand in hand, and not know that this would all end so soon.

He was proud of his life, proud of what he had done and was doing, even if he could not say he was happy. He had almost everything a man could want—family, title, wealth, a job he felt was important. But right now he wanted to be someone else entirely. He wanted *her* to be someone else.

She popped a bit of bread into her mouth and speared a piece of meat on the end of a fork. "You are not eating, Jack! Are you not hungry?"

He leaned his chin on his hand and grinned at her

lazily. "I am just enjoying watching you, Tonya. You are very pretty."

She frowned doubtfully. "Pretty when I am stuffing myself like a pig?"

"Always pretty." He reached for a slice of fruit and munched on it.

"You are rather pretty yourself. Or should I say handsome?" she said, but her soft voice made the bold words sound shy. She looked down, toying with her tankard. "Tell me more about yourself, Jack. We have been together for hours; I have even seen your lodgings. But I feel I know nothing about you at all."

Wariness moved like a cold wind over his whimsical contentment and futile wishes. He sat back in his chair, away from the enchantment of her perfume. "What would you like to know?"

She still moved her tankard about with the tip of her finger. "I don't know. Anything you want to tell me. You were in the army?"

"Indeed I was. In Spain."

"I did not see anything of it in your sitting room, aside from that one book in Spanish."

That was because he had pushed everything he could—uniforms, swords, citations, letters—into a trunk and shoved it beneath the bed long ago. Where he did not have to see it every day, even though he always lived with it in his mind. "It was a very—different time." And it was not yet over. Not by a long shot.

Emma nodded. "You do not want to be reminded. I understand. There are many things I would rather not be reminded of, too. But I know people who hang swords and battle colors on their walls and talk all the time of the glories of battle."

Jack snorted. "Glories!"

"Exactly so." Emma was silent for a long moment, staring down at her hand as if she, too, was remembering scenes best forgotten. Then she looked up at him with one of her bright smiles. "I have made us so solemn again, when this is meant to be a day of joy! All that is behind us now. Gone." She snapped her fingers. "Like that! And I need more ale."

As Jack turned to summon the maid, he saw what he had come to this out-of-the-way place to avoid—someone he knew. Bertie Stonewich of all people stood in the doorway, sunlight behind him, a petite blond woman in a vivid red gown on his arm. Jack slumped down in his chair, but it was too little too late.

Bertie had seen him.

"Jack!" he called happily, the joviality in his voice a clear signal that he, too, had been "celebrating." "Jack, old man, imagine running into you here." He made his way over to their table, the woman trailing beside him, her steps unsteady.

Jack had no choice. He stood up, giving Bertie what he hoped was a warning glance. "We were just having a quick meal. Bertie, this is Tonya, a visitor to our country. She is lady's maid to a member of the Russian court."

"Tonya. What a lucky devil my friend here is, to have found such a lovely companion," Bertie said, with a roguish grin. Emma held out her hand to him in an automatic imperious gesture, and Bertie bowed over it. "And this is my friend Lottie. Meet my other friends, m'dear."

Apparently Lottie, and presumably Bertie, had been imbibing freely in celebration of the day. Jack only wished he had been, too. It would make this whole absurd situation more bearable. Maybe even laughable.

The odd thing was, he was not so much afraid that Bertie might expose his and Emma's mutual masquerade as he was angry that Bertie interrupted his precious time alone with Emma.

"Won't you join us?" Emma asked. She moved her chair over to make room for them. "There is still some bread and cheese left."

"I *am* feeling a bit peckish," Lottie said, sliding into a vacant chair and reaching for a piece of bread. She gave Bertie a flirtatious smile. "I wouldn't mind a spot of ale, either, dearling."

"Say no more. I will go order some directly. It would

be quicker to fetch it from the bar than wait for the serving maid," said Bertie. "Perhaps Jack will join me." He raised a brow inquiringly at Jack.

Jack wondered what his game was. He was tempted to just sit down by Emma again, try to resume their day and ignore Bertie, but he knew he couldn't. He had to talk to Bertie. "Certainly. Tonya, is there anything I could get for you?"

She gave him a small, distracted smile. She was obviously busy examining Lottie's bright gown and pink, rose-trimmed bonnet. "Some tea, perhaps, if there is any."

"I'm sure there must be some tea to be had." Jack followed Bertie to the long, grimy bar and joined the crowds clustered there waiting for their ale. It was noisy and jostling—the perfect spot for secrets.

"What game are you playing, Jack?" Bertie muttered, all traces of tipsy buffoonery dropped away. He gave a silly little wave to Lottie, but his gaze was steel blue and serious when he looked back at Jack.

"Game?" Jack said. He and Bertie had been friends since their earliest days in Spain. They had worked together in so many things; Jack had always felt Bertie was the one person he could tell anything to. Now he was at a loss for words.

How could he explain what was happening with Emma when he wasn't certain himself? He told himself that he was doing his duty, protecting the lady. Yet if that was true, he would have taken her back to the Pulteney Hotel posthaste, not squired her around the city and into common public houses.

"Do not think I don't know who that lady is," Bertie answered. "That plain dress does not disguise her a bit. What in Jove's name are you doing with someone like Lady Emma Weston in *here*?"

Jack glanced about to see if anyone heard Bertie's softly spoken words. No one paid them any heed at all; they were all far too busy clamoring for their drinks and food. "It is a long story."

Bertie crossed his arms over his chest. "I have time. Lady Emma and Lottie are obviously enjoying their own chat."

Jack looked over at Emma. She was indeed deep in conversation with Bertie's "friend," her head tilted in rapt fascination at whatever Lottie was saying. "I found her this morning in a deserted alleyway being accosted by a cutpurse. She was dressed in this fashion and has not even given me her true name. She made up this absurd story about being a maid. I thought it best that I keep an eye on her, until she is ready to tell the truth or go back to the hotel."

Bertie did look surprised at that. "A runaway, eh? Is she intending to leave her family permanently, do you suppose?"

Jack had not even thought of that. "I have the distinct impression that it is a temporary thing. A mere lark."

Their turn came at the bar, and Bertie moved away to procure his ale. "Lottie and I are going to view the illuminations this evening. You and—Tonya, is it?—are welcome to join us. Then, if she proves reluctant to go back to the Pulteney, I will be on hand to assist you. It is of course necessary that she be returned to the bosom of her family as soon as possible, lark or no."

Returned to the bosom of her family. Jack had known all along that that would come to pass. But he could not have known how much that thought would pain him.

Emma listened raptly as the blond-haired Lottie told her where she had procured her extraordinary red gown. Emma had had numerous conversations with other ladies about fashion before—it was a standard polite topic, and she loved gowns. But it had never been as interesting as this before.

". . . and I got these boots especially to go with this dress," Miss Lottie was saying. She displayed a pair of purple half boots embroidered with tiny red flowers. "They're adorable, aren't they?"

Emma nodded. They were indeed "adorable," and she

wished she could have a pair just like them. Then she imagined the look on her aunt's face if she appeared at, say, an official military review in an ensemble like Lottie's. It was not an encouraging vision.

But a girl could still dream. Emma thought of a lavender-colored gown that would be lovely with those boots, topped with a violet-colored spencer made from the velvet she had seen in a modiste's window earlier that day.

As Lottie prattled on, telling Emma about the shop where she had purchased her bonnet, Emma glanced over to where Jack and his friend Bertie still stood by the bar. It was obvious that the two men had been friends for a long time; they talked together in an easy, albeit serious, manner. But Bertie, though hardly dressed in the first stare of fashion, wore expensive, well-cut garments. His dark gold hair was precisely cut, and his pale gray waistcoat was made of silk. Their friendship did not appear to be that of an employer and employee, so Emma wondered where they knew each other from.

As she watched them, Bertie turned his head and caught her staring. For one instant, the expression of bored fatuousness he had worn since entering the pub dropped away. He seemed hard and very serious as he looked at her—almost frightening. It was quickly replaced by his former jaunty grin, and he laughed at something Jack said.

Disconcerted, Emma turned to Lottie and tried to focus on what she was saying about hairstyles. She felt strangely discomposed, though, and could not help but wonder about this Bertie person and his friendship with Jack.

Soon, the two men returned with more tankards of the dark brown ale and a small pot of tea. Jack slid into the chair next to Emma's and casually laid his arm lightly along her shoulders. Emma leaned into him, grateful for the warmth, the security, of his touch.

She could have sat there, just like that, forever.

"Bertie and Lottie have invited us to go view the illuminations with them, Tonya," he said. "What do you think?"

Emma smiled at him. She had really hoped to have him to herself for just a little time longer, but a party had appeal, too. And they could always slip off alone for a moment or two. "I think it sounds splendid!" she agreed, even as she knew it would be impossible. She had to go home, but she was too caught up in the enthusiasm of the moment to say that yet.

"Excellent," Jack said. He pressed a quick kiss to her temple. "Drink up your tea, then, and we'll be off to secure the best vantage point before dark."

"Bottoms up!" Lottie said cheerfully, and swallowed her tankardful of ale almost whole.

Emma raised her cup of tea. "Salut," she replied. As she sipped at the strong liquid, she saw a quick, almost imperceptible glance pass between Jack and Bertie.

But she decided to simply ignore it, to ignore everything that was at all disquieting. Her wonderful day would come to an end soon enough, and she intended to enjoy every last second of it.

Chapter Eight

*E*mma watched as the sun sank lower and became brighter in the sky, turning the low hanging London clouds into great puffs of pink and orange and pale lilac. It was undoubtedly beautiful, but it filled her with dread. It might as well have been her heart, disappearing forever below an invisible horizon.

Her day of freedom, which had proved to be more marvelous than she could even have dreamed, was coming to an end.

Her eyes itched with unshed tears, and she closed them against the sight of the gathering evening.

Behind her, Jack, Bertie and Lottie went on laughing and talking, drinking their newly procured bottle of rough wine and making plans for the night ahead. They were tipsily oblivious to her distress.

Or so it seemed. But then Emma felt a gentle touch on her arm, and she opened her eyes to see Jack right beside her. He still wore a half-smile on his lovely mouth, a remnant of the joking, but his eyes were dark with concern as he looked at her. His hand tightened on her arm, and she reached up to cover it with her own. It was warm and strong, and she wanted to cling to it.

"Are you all right, then, Tonya?" he asked quietly. "Do you feel ill?"

Emma forced herself to smile. *Now* she was finally used to hearing that blasted made-up name Tonya! Now, when she had to shed it and forget it and try to pretend that she never even wanted to live another's life. "No, I am quite well. But I must be going soon." She had already stayed far too long. She could not linger longer and be found out. Natasha would get into trouble.

Jack's smile fled altogether, and he nodded. "You must return to your—duties?"

Duties. That was certainly all too true. "Yes."

"But you said you would see the illuminations with us!" Lottie cried, leaning unsteadily against Bertie's shoulder. "They are the best part. And there is music and dancing!" She grinned up at Bertie, who grinned back. "So romantic."

Bertie smiled back at her, but said, "If Tonya needs to go home, we should let her."

Emma allowed herself to imagine it for just one moment. She saw in her mind the night sky lit up by the glow of a thousand candles, heard the strains of music. Not the formal cadence of a stiff, old-fashioned minuet, but a wild swirl, accented with laughter. Best of all, she imagined Jack's arms around her, holding her, twirling her to that glorious music.

It would be paradise. It would be a night to last in her memory for the rest of her life. If only she could! If only there was some way . . .

"I—I would have to send a message . . ." she began uncertainly. No sooner were the words out of her mouth than Jack handed her a scrap of paper dug from inside his coat, and Lottie produced a stub of a pencil from her reticule.

She took the pencil and stared down at it for a moment, almost as if she had never seen paper and pencil before. Dared she? Could she? Her heart pounded.

Could she not?

She would surely be caught out. But her aunt was not wholly unreasonable. If Emma threw herself on her mercy and swore that Natasha had naught to do with it, then she would have only herself in trouble. She might be locked away in her room until the day they either returned to Russia or she married Sir Jeremy Ashbey, but it would be worth it.

It would be so very much worth it. She could see the illuminations, maybe have a dance, a last ale . . .

Jack held his hand out to her with the paper laid invitingly on his palm, beckoning her on to more adventures.

She took the paper, laid it across her knee and began to write.

"Are you certain you know what you're doing, Jack?" Bertie whispered, with no sign of his former silliness in his voice. Jack thought, not for the first time, that his friend ought to be treading the boards. No one had ever played the buffoon better.

Only Jack was the one who truly felt like a buffoon now, as he watched Emma slip inside the servants' entrance of the Pulteney Hotel, her shawl drawn up over her hair. If he had an ounce of sense, he would have sent her home hours ago, not encouraged her even further in her dangerous game. She should be in the care of her relatives, getting ready to go to a grand ball; he should be going on about his own business, free of her care.

Instead, all he could think about was being with her! To see the grand illuminations through her eyes, to dance with her and maybe have one more chance to sit together, this time alone and undisturbed.

He had to live his life under an iron control, yet he knew that with her in his arms, in the velvet, dark intimacy of the night, that control could crack.

The day had begun as a lark, a joke. Now it felt serious. *Too* serious. It had gone beyond seeing what his ice princess would do next, beyond protecting her. Emma was something he could have never imagined before, a woman who lived life so fully, so wholeheartedly, and made him want to live it that way, too.

Bertie was still talking to him, in his low, urgent voice, but Jack had not heard his words. He shook off his thoughts and looked at his friend. "I beg your pardon?"

Bertie's gray gaze, usually so affable and seemingly empty, narrowed. "I said, are you sure you know what you are doing?"

"Bertie, my friend, I have no idea what I am doing." Jack laughed. Even to his own ears it was a humorless sound. "No idea at all." Or perhaps he was very sure of what he was doing—he just did not know *why*.

Bertie studied him for a moment before he turned to watch the passersby. He scuffed his boot across the pavement in studied casualness. "This is not just about keeping an eye on her so that she does not come to grief in her escapade, is it? There is more to it."

Of course there was. But Jack could hardly say that to his friend. He could not even say it to himself. He just shrugged, and they fell into silence.

Where was this all going, Jack wondered, as he watched the door Emma had disappeared beyond. If he was with her in the darkness of night, if he held her hand and looked again at the sweet wonder of her face as she beheld the celebrations around her, surely he would be lost. He would want to live in this sweet lie forever and never return to his old life, his old ways.

Perhaps it would be better if she never came back through that door. He could only come to care about her more, and he could not afford to care about another person, not until his work was truly finished. Perhaps not even then. And if she *did* happen to discover the truth of his identity, she would surely hate him and even hate the memory of this day.

Yes. It would be better if she did not come back. But Jack found himself wishing, as he had never wished for anything before, that she *would* come. That he could have her with him for just a little while longer.

Before she opened the door at the servants' entrance to rush back outside, Emma paused, her hand on the knob.

Natasha had been very glad to see her but not so glad when she heard that Emma wished to go back out again.

Aunt Lydia and Uncle Nicholas had not yet returned to the hotel and had even sent word via Madame Ana that they were running behind schedule and would prepare for the ball at the home of their hostess, so as to save time. Madame Ana, Aunt Lydia's maid and Uncle Nicholas's valet had already departed with their mistress's and master's evening attire in hand. So Emma was lucky and safe—at least for a little while longer.

But Natasha had shaken her head, looking very worried. "Oh, Lady Emma! I do not like it," she had said, crossing herself as she always did when faced with a dilemma. "I feel that something bad will happen."

Emma paused in tidying her hair and dabbing on fresh lilac scent to turn and stare at Natasha. Something bad? No—almost only good things had happened today. "What do you mean?"

Natasha glanced quickly about, as if she feared being overheard, even though they were all alone in the bedchamber. "Maria, one of the countess's kitchen-maids, you know, sometimes reads the cards. She read them this afternoon, and they tell of a dark force, a man with bad intentions, who lurks over our lives, just waiting until we are vulnerable. I am sure he waits out there for you tonight!"

Emma's hand stilled on the stopper of her enameled scent bottle. Even though she had been raised and educated by her thoroughly modern aunt and uncle and a French governess, she, like Natasha, secretly harbored a superstitious streak, bred in the Russian countryside where she had grown up. She had listened to Maria's readings before, and sometimes they did come eerily true.

A dark force? A malevolent man? Emma shivered. Surely it could not be . . . No. It was not Jack. There was no malevolence about him at all.

She shook the feelings away. If the cards *were* true, they only spoke of the man who had attacked her in the alleyway this morning.

"Do not worry, Natasha dear," she said. "I will not be out late. I only want to take a peek at the illuminations, and I am with some lovely new friends I have made. They will keep me safe."

She remembered those words now, as she prepared to open the door back onto the outside world.

Jack *would* keep her safe. She was certain of it.

She pushed at the knob and stepped out into the dying sunlight, blinking at the dazzle of it after the gloom of the back stairs. For a second she could see nothing, and she feared Jack had left her.

Then she rubbed a hand over her eyes and saw that he was there. He pushed away from the wall where he leaned and held his hands out to her with a glorious smile, as if he had always been waiting just for her.

Emma ran to him with a glad cry and caught his hands in hers like they were her only lifeline in a sinking world. "It is all right," she said, as much to reassure herself as him. "I can go."

He drew her closer, his cheek coming to rest, just for one sweet instant, against her hair. Emma closed her eyes. "I am so happy, my Tonya," he said. "So very happy."

She wished she could hear her name, her *true* name, in his voice. Just once. She imagined his rough whisper. "*Emma. My Emma.*"

But of course, he never could call her Emma. He could never even know it was her real name, or else this fantasy day would collapse about her like a house made of cards. He would hate her if he knew how she had deceived him, had used him. As well he should.

She had been given this day, and it was a greater gift than she could ever have imagined. She would take it and be grateful, and not wish for things she could not have.

Like having Jack call her Emma.

She opened her eyes to see that Bertie and Lottie were standing together nearby, looking away from her and Jack in a pointed attempt at tact. She also remembered that they still stood right outside the Pulteney Hotel, where someone she knew might spot her. She drew away from Jack with a self-conscious little laugh.

"We should be going, so that we can find a good place to have our supper before dark," she said.

Jack laughed and tucked her hand into the crook of his elbow to lead her onwards. Bertie and Lottie fell amiably into step behind them. "Of course you *would* be thinking of supper, Tonya!" he said.

Emma smiled ruefully. She *had* been thinking of her stomach an inordinate amount today. But it was better than thinking of other impossible things—like kissing Jack. "Of course! First things first."

After today, she could say farewell to pies and ale. It would be back to dainty cucumber sandwiches. She just hoped her gowns would still fit after all her self-indulgence.

"I hear the best illuminations are at the Bank of England," Bertie said. "I know a fine coffee house near there. We can eat and then find the best spot from which to view the show."

"That sounds pleasant," said Emma. Lottie giggled in presumed agreement.

Jack threw his friend an unreadable glance over his shoulder. "You just have all the answers, don't you, Bertie?"

Emma looked up at him, puzzled by the flash of steel beneath the jovial words.

Bertie just laughed. "Someone has to, Jack, m'boy. Someone has to."

Chapter Nine

The illuminations were all that Emma could have imagined. They were indeed as "heaven must look," just as Natasha had said. Or like a fantasy from the Arabian Nights. On their way to view the Bank of England, they had passed houses and shops whose windows were full of transparent, glowing images of landscapes, allegories and famous heroes. They shone blue, green, red and gold in the night.

But the enormous Bank building was truly the masterpiece. More than fifty thousand lamps were arranged in rows and columns around the windows and pediments. In the center was a huge transparency of a woman in classical draperies, one hand on the bust of a man, the other supported by a helmeted figure.

Emma stood in the midst of the crowd, staring in awe at the spectacle, her hand clasped in Jack's. All around her flowed murmurs of astonishment, cries of surprise and bursts of laughter.

"It is beautiful," she said, tightening her fingers on his as if he might escape her in the throng.

Yet, he did not appear to want to escape or to be anyplace else at all. His fingers squeezed hers in return, and he smiled down at her. "Oh, yes. Very beautiful."

Emma smiled back at him. By the flickering lights, his eyes shimmered with blue fire. "But what is it meant to be?"

"To be?"

"The figure." Emma pointed at the figure.

"It is the genius of France reviving."

"The genius of France?" Emma looked back to the classically draped woman. "How can you tell? I would have thought it was Athena or Aphrodite or some such."

"I read about it in the papers. See the bust? That is King Louis, and the other figure is Britannia."

"Oh. I see." Emma thought it had been more interesting before she knew that.

"Terribly stuffy, isn't it?" Jack said lightly.

Emma laughed. "A bit, yes."

"Let's go look at some of the other lights," he suggested. Emma nodded, and they turned away, weaving past the knots and gatherings of people. Bertie and Lottie stayed on the bench where they had seated themselves when they first arrived, giggling and whispering.

All around them were strung paper lanterns, which cast a fairy-tale light over the city. All dirt and darkness was expelled for this one night.

Just as her life was full of fun and light—for this one night.

Emma twirled around in a sudden fit of uncontrollable glee. The lights whirled giddily in a blur of blue and red. "It is *so* beautiful I cannot bear it!" she cried. "Nothing could ever be more beautiful than this."

Jack laughed and caught her around the waist to lift her into the air. "Nothing could be more beautiful than *you*," he said. His voice was hoarse and serious.

Suspended in midair, Emma looked down at him and reached out to touch his cheek. It was rough with late-evening whiskers, but satin-smooth beneath and very warm.

All day he had been a merry companion, engaging, full of talk and laughter. Now the bar of golden light that slanted over his cheekbones revealed a new intensity and seriousness. He looked at her, held her, as if she was the most precious jewel he had ever beheld. Not because she was Lady Emma Weston or the niece of

Count Suvarov, but because of what she was. Because she just was.

It made her feel so nervous and scared and exhilarated.

He slowly lowered her to her feet, but his hands stayed at her waist, holding her close. Emma linked her hands behind his neck and leaned back to look at him.

"Do you mean that?" she whispered. "Am I beautiful?"

"You are more than beautiful," he answered her. "I have never met anyone like you before. Never."

"And I have never met anyone like you. How could I? There *is* no one like you." Emma wished she could tell him what this day, what knowing him, had meant to her. She wanted to tell him everything, all about her life and her fears and wishes, all she had dreamed of for years. She wanted to place all that she was into his hands, for she felt, deep in her heart, that she could trust him.

But more than that, she did not want him to hate her. She did not want to lose that look in his eyes. And it would certainly vanish if she told him who she truly was.

She had only this night. Surely it could not be wrong for her to hold onto what little she had.

He gave her a heart-stopping, crooked little smile. "I am quite ordinary. You could find a man like me every day of the week."

"Oh, no! I am sure I could not." She remembered the men she knew—men like Sir Jeremy. Jack was as unlike them as the sun was unlike the moon. She slid one finger along his jaw and the tiny dent in his chin and rested it on his lower lip. It was surprisingly soft under her touch.

Jack ducked his head to kiss her finger. It was so light, almost tickling, but it sent tiny sparks down her arm to her very heart.

"Jack," she whispered. "I do so wish . . ." Her words trailed away, for how could she even articulate what she was feeling, what she longed for, what could never be?

He drew her even closer, until she went up on tiptoe

and could rest her cheek on his shoulder. "What do you wish?" he murmured.

She made herself laugh, to push away those gloomy feelings and revel in the moment. She heard distant music, a lively, danceable tune. "I wish we could dance!"

Jack kissed the top of her head. "Perhaps we can."

"We can?"

"Do you not hear that music?" He stepped back and took her hand in his. "Where there is music, there must be dancing. We just have to find it!"

Emma laughed in relief that the strange, tense moment had passed. Yet, beneath that laughter, there was also a small touch of chagrin—chagrin at her own cowardly lack of boldness. She followed him willingly back into the crowd.

The setting for the dance was as far from a grand ballroom as could be imagined. There was no polished parquet floor. There was no floor at all, just a clear space with a rough wooden platform at one end for a group of musicians to sit upon. There were no gilt chairs along the edges, where well-dressed matrons could sit and watch their young charges. No chandeliers, no flowers, no jewels. Just a lovely tune and laughing couples twirling about in the glow of the illuminations.

Jack watched Emma as she took in the whole scene, her beautiful rosebud lips parted in astonished joy. He thought she must have attended many balls in her life, danced many dances. It was easy to picture her in a ballroom, clad in silk and pearls, but she fit here, too. Her feet bounced up and down in time to the music, her skirts swaying.

She swung their clasped hands between them and smiled at him. "This is wonderful! Did you know this was here, Jack?"

He smiled, too, and put his free arm around her waist to sweep her close to him. "Not at all. It was—serendipity."

Her brow crinkled a bit. "Serendipity?"

"A fortunate chance. May I have this dance?"

She tilted her head back and laughed. "Of course you may!"

They stepped out into the flow of the dancers, their steps blending into the bounce of the lively schottische. Emma was a graceful dancer, just as Jack knew she would be, but at first she felt a bit uncertain in his arms. Stiff, as if she was not entirely sure of this style of dancing. Yet, as they moved and turned, their bodies learning the rhythm of each other, her back and shoulders relaxed beneath his hands, and her steps became more certain.

She giggled delightedly as he spun her about, giving her an extra twirl. "Why do people not dance like this all the time?" she said, raising her voice above the music and the voices of the other people. "It is marvelous! Not like some staid old gavotte."

"Oh?" Jack thought she had obviously forgotten her charade. But he did not care. He only cared about holding her for as long as he could. "Do you often dance a staid gavotte?"

She seemed to come back into herself and remember her masquerade. Her gaze dropped, and a pink stain spread across her ivory cheeks. "I—no. But I have watched them. They do not look very merry. Not like this at all."

The lively music ended. Couples drifted around them, breaking apart, re-forming, but Jack and Emma stood still, their arms around each other. They stood there, watching each other, as a slow, uneven waltz began. It was obvious that the musicians were quite amateur, but that did not matter at all. Jack thought it was sweet music, angelic even.

Slowly, their feet shifted to the rhythm. Emma leaned into him, much closer than any ballroom waltz could properly allow. Jack slid his hand further along her smooth, slim back and rested his cheek against her hair.

"You are truly like no one else I have ever known," he said.

"Mmm," she whispered, her breath cool on his neck

as she tilted her head back to smile at him dreamily. "And you are like no one I have ever known. Completely."

"I would like to know more about you," he said. It was true. Surprisingly so. He wanted to know more about her life in Russia, about why she had seemed so very far away at the reception. What she hoped and wished for, what had driven her from her home today. He didn't want her to vanish back into her Lady Emma world, with his Tonya never to be seen again.

He wanted more time with her. Even though he knew very well that that was impossible. She had her family and duties, just as he did.

And if she knew the truth, that he had known of her masquerade all along, that he was not who he said he was, she would be so angry. Even though her surface was so ladylike, he had seen temper and anger flash in those dark eyes when the ruffian had accosted her in the alleyway.

She might even hate him, might flash that temper in his direction, if she discovered the truth.

He didn't want that. He wanted her to remember this day, and him, with fondness and happiness. The best day of her life, just as she had said.

"You would like to know more about me?" Emma stepped back a bit to look at him. "You already know me better than anyone else." There was a sad, solemn truth in her tone.

Jack folded her hand more securely in his as they turned a corner in the dance. "Do I? We have only known each other this one day. Surely you must have family, friends . . ."

"I have people who care about me, as I care about them," she interrupted. Her earlier laughter had faded into intensity, as if she longed to persuade him of something. The fingers that rested on his shoulder reached until she touched his neck softly. "But I cannot show them all the things I would like to. They are far too busy; they have many important things to do. I wish . . ."

She paused and looked past his shoulder as if she feared to say too much.

Jack wished for things, too. He wished that they did not have these ridiculous constraints between them, that they could speak freely.

But his feelings, feelings that were new and odd, ran free. As did his body, which came warmly to life whenever she brushed against him.

"What do you wish, Tonya?" he asked hoarsely, asking her this again. Some time, she would *have* to answer.

"I wish this dance could go on and on, never end."

"I wish that, too."

Emma gave a small, half-hysterical laugh. "But nothing goes on forever, does it?"

"No. It doesn't." Even as he spoke, the music crescendoed and stopped, and the air was filled only with the laughter and voices of people who, for this night, had no cares in the world. Jack and Emma came to a stop in the shadows at the edge of the clearing. "But the memories can last for all time, if you want them to."

"I want them to!" She went suddenly up on tiptoe and pressed her lips against his, her arms twining about his neck to cling as if she would never let go. Jack caught her against him, and he feared he was clinging in much the same way. As if he could not let her go.

Her kiss was unpracticed, her lips hesitant, parted slightly, but it was very, very sweet. He tilted his head to better take all of her in, parting his own lips. She trembled under his hands, like a delicate, exotic bird who could take wing and fly away at any moment. He did not want to frighten her, did not want to lose her embrace, but her kiss was more intoxicating than any brandy. More arousing than that of any courtesan.

He reached out carefully with the tip of his tongue to touch the softness of her lower lip. She gasped and trembled harder but did not push him away. Instead, she moved closer, parting her lips for his intimate caress.

Jack felt his body harden in a way that could prove most embarrassing in a public place, even if they *were* in the shadows. His mind was full of such enticing images, like drawing Emma even closer, lowering her to the ground, kissing her throat, her shoulders, her . . .

A cough and a loud giggle from behind him made all these visions burst like a translucent soap bubble. Most reluctantly, he drew his lips from Emma's and looked back over his shoulder.

Bertie and his lady friend stood there, the girl laughing tipsily behind her hand. Bertie, with his arm about her waist, gave every evidence of the same drunken casualness, but he frowned severely at Jack for the merest instant before he covered it in a lopsided grin.

That one reminder was enough. Jack recalled, like a dash of cold stream water, who he truly was. Who *she* was. Emma was no lightskirt to be kissed at a public dance. She was Lady Emma Weston.

And he was a damned fool.

He gently took Emma's arms down from his neck and drew her behind him, deeper into the shadows, away from the view of the curious. She looked most startled, her eyes wide, her lips parted, as if she was not quite in the reality of the moment yet. Then her lips snapped together, and her blush deepened. She opened her reticule and pulled out a handkerchief, which she used to dab at her lips and cover the pinkness of her cheeks.

"It is getting late, old man!" Bertie said. "I'm going to take Lottie home in a hansom. Can we take you and— Tonya anywhere?"

Jack glanced at Emma, who gave a small shake of her head. "No, we will leave here soon and walk home."

"Good." Bertie gave him one more hard look before taking Lottie's hand and turning her away. "I will see you tomorrow, then, Jack. We have a great deal to talk about."

"Indeed." Jack watched his friend stroll away, he and Lottie whispering and laughing together. He dared not look at Emma, not just yet. What could he say to her? What could he do? If he saw her, he would only want to kiss her again.

There was a rustle, a waft of lilac scent, as she tucked away the handkerchief and straightened her skirts.

"You have—have been friends with Bertie for a long time?" she asked in a quiet voice.

Jack turned back to her but did not touch her. She looked composed again, back to her Lady Emma self. Only the slight disarray of her hair betrayed what had happened between them. She gave him a small, tentative smile, urging him to follow her change of topic. Very well. If she did not want to discuss their kiss, they would not discuss it.

"Yes," he answered. "Since we were at school together. We were also in the same regiment." And now they worked together. But Emma did not need to know that.

"It must be very nice, to have someone you have been friends with for so long." Her tone was wistful.

"It is. But, then again, it can be difficult to have someone who knows me so well."

"It is far better than having no one who knows you at all," she said softly.

Jack did not know what to say. Any reassurances he made, any comfort he offered, would only sound hollow. In the distance, church bells chimed. It was growing very late.

"Shall I take you home now, Tonya?" he asked. Really there was nothing left to say.

She gave a smile that was really more of a mere twist of her sweet lips. "Yes. I suppose that would be best."

Chapter Ten

$\mathcal{T}$he door to the servants' entrance of the Pulteney Hotel *looked* ordinary, painted, bound in iron hinges. But Emma knew it was not. It was the portal of doom.

Well, she thought grudgingly, maybe not *doom*. It just meant the end of her special, wonderful day, and that felt enough like doom at this moment. Once she passed that door and went up the stairs to the corridor where her chamber was, Tonya would be gone forever. She would be Lady Emma Weston again.

Her hand tightened on Jack's, clinging as if he could hold her back from her own life, keep this magic from ending. He could not, of course. He didn't even know she wanted to be held back from anything, thanks to her masquerade. Her fiction of Tonya, the Russian lady's maid, had earned her this time of freedom, yet it had also prevented her from true intimacy with Jack—or anyone. If he did not know the truth of who she was, how could she really get to know him, or anyone?

Perhaps that was all for the best. Jack could remember her just as a charming maid he had met and kissed once. And she would remember him—how?

As a man she could have cared for, even come to love. If life were different. If *she* were different.

She turned to Jack quickly, before she could lose her nerve, and kissed his cheek. She inhaled deeply of his clean, soapy scent, memorizing everything about this moment to take with her when she left. She felt the weight of his hand in hers, heard the soft sound of his breath.

For a second, she had the wild thought that she could run off with him now. She could just walk away from the hotel, go to live in his rooms, be Tonya forever. Yet she knew, even as the image of the two of them cozy before his grate flashed through her mind, that she could not. Her aunt and uncle counted on her, loved her. She had duties and obligations, and if she deserted them, she could never be truly happy—even if she had Jack.

She gave a choked little laugh. Here she was, creating air castles in her mind, and he had not even asked her to come away with him! How silly she was. Just as silly as she had been when she threw herself on him and kissed him at the dance.

The memory of that glorious kiss made her face burn. At least it was dark here, and he could not see her blush.

"Tonya," he said, in an oddly strangled voice.

"I wish you would not speak," Emma answered, resting her forehead against his chest. "This day has been so perfect. It should end in silence. Words would only spoil it."

She felt his hand on her hair, moving very softly, as if he feared to muss it. "But I must tell you, I—I want to see you again."

So there it was. He *did* want to see her again. It changed nothing, of course, but it was sweet to hear nonetheless. "That cannot be," she said. She was surprised her voice sounded so steady, when her chest ached as if her heart were truly broken. "We had a glorious day. You gave that to me. Now, I must go through that door, and you must go home."

Emma knew that if she did not leave now, she never could. She stepped back, onto the shallow step that led to the door, and reached up to touch Jack's cheek. In the very faint light from the moon and the faraway illuminations, his face appeared carved of marble it was so expressionless. But his eyes burned.

"I have to tell you . . ." he began.

Emma laid her finger over his lips, silencing him. Whatever he was going to say, she did not, *could* not, want to hear it. It was best to leave the memories as they were. "Good bye, Jack," she said. Then she spun around, pulled open the door and dashed inside. The portal of doom slammed behind her, shutting out the life of the streets.

She leaned back against it and pressed her hand to her mouth. She wanted to cry, to wail, to scream, to curse the unfairness of it all. Her eyes and throat ached with the unshed tears, but she dared not let her emotions run free. The belowstairs area of the hotel was quiet; most of the servants were either waiting on their masters and mistresses or clearing away supper or maybe having their own hurried meals.

It was late, and she might be found out, yet somehow she did not care. Her initial desire to have a temper tantrum was fading away, leaving her tired and numb. She wanted to crawl into her own bed and stay there for days and days until she had no desires at all anymore.

Emma wiped at her eyes and made her way to the narrow, twisting staircase that led to the lavish front rooms of the hotel. She passed two hurrying footmen, who gave her scarcely a glance. Her plain dress was still a great disguise, for all the good it did her.

The lamps were turned low in the corridor, making the gilt picture frames and brocade chairs gleam in dull magnificence. It was all so very different, this silent grandeur, from what she had seen today. She might almost have flown to the moon and back, so unsettled did she feel.

She quietly opened the door to her own chamber and slid inside, already loosening her hair in anticipation of her bed. As she dropped her shawl onto a chair, she became aware that she was not alone in the room. She heard Natasha's choked sobs coming from the shadows.

Oh, no! Had something terrible happened while she

was gadding about? An accident or . . . ? "Natasha? What has happened?"

Emma turned to see Natasha sitting by the bed, crying into her apron. Next to her, straight-backed and stern in a thronelike velvet chair, was—Aunt Lydia.

Jack stood in the street, staring at the door Emma had disappeared through, for a long while. People moved past him, a few even giving him curious looks, but he noticed this only in a peripheral way. He looked at the door, and all he really saw was her standing there, bidding him farewell.

What had come over him, telling her he wanted to see her again, almost giving the charade away? He would almost have said he was foxed, yet he had drunk nothing stronger than ale, and that hours ago. They had spent only a day together, shared a few dances, one innocent kiss, and he had felt in that moment as she slipped away that he was losing something precious, something vital to his life.

He had never, ever felt this way before. His work demanded that he be clearheaded, free of emotional encumbrances. There had been women he was fond of before but never one who made him feel as completely off-balance as he did now. He did not understand it. It must be simply the enchantment of this strange day, the mummery they had both indulged in. If he saw her in her own conventional surroundings again, gowned and jeweled at a ball, it would not feel this way.

He rubbed at his eyes and turned away from the hotel, walking off into the crowd. What he needed now was his bed, sleep. All would be clear in the bright light of morning.

But Emma was wrong when she said they were parting forever. They *would* meet again, and soon.

If only she did not hate him when the truth was revealed.

Chapter Eleven

Oh, no. She was really in trouble now.

Aunt Lydia was still wearing her ballgown of stiff gold satin and her necklace, earrings and tiara of diamonds and topaz. Her long kid gloves had been removed and folded across her lap, beneath her hands. She was so still and pale and glittering, so rich after Emma's day among ordinariness, that she could almost have been a mirage.

Except for the way her lips pursed and flattened.

Emma looked wildly from her aunt to Natasha, who sobbed even harder into her apron. "It was not Natasha's fault!" Emma cried. She wanted to throw herself on her knees before Aunt Lydia, but she feared that might appear *too* dramatic. She contented herself with clasping her hands before her. "I—I forced her into it. I *made* her do this!"

Lydia drew in a deep breath, her nostrils flaring delicately. "I am perfectly aware whose doing this was, Emma. Just as I knew whose idea it was to let the kitchen milk goat into the house during the supper party for Prince Yulanov."

Emma gaped at her aunt, completely taken aback by this seeming change of topic. The goat? "That was when I was nine years old, Aunt Lydia."

"Yes, and you see how little things have changed. You are still persuading people to assist you in wild schemes." Lydia relented just a bit and relaxed her shoulders before she said, "Natasha, you may retire now. I will help my niece into her nightdress. We will talk about your penalty tomorrow."

Natasha peeped cautiously over the edge of her apron, her gaze darting between Lydia and Emma. "Do—do you mean I'm not to be dismissed, Countess?"

"Certainly not. You are a fine lady's maid, and I would hate to have to instruct someone else now. But I will have Madame Ana keep stricter vigilance over the two of you from now on," Lydia said, and waved Natasha away.

Natasha bobbed a curtsy and rushed from the room with great alacrity, shutting the door behind her.

Emma was not sure what to do in the fresh silence. She folded her arms over her suddenly queasy stomach and stared at the carpet beneath her feet. She had been so scared of what might happen if she was discovered, had braced herself for tears and shouts. She hated this disappointed smile more than any recriminations.

Of course, she should never have expected shouts. Aunt Lydia had never once raised her voice, not even after the incident with the goat.

Lydia sighed. "Sit down, Emma. Tell me where you have been."

Emma moved to the nearest chair, feeling like her feet were moving through thick water. She had forgotten how tired she was until she sat down, tucking her weary feet beneath her. She wove her fingers through her loosened hair, freeing the hairpins to scatter onto the floor. She still didn't look at her aunt. "I wanted to see the celebrations."

"You wanted to see the celebrations? Whatever do you mean? Your uncle and I would have taken you to see anything you liked. Why, we rode in an open carriage through the park just this afternoon. The celebrations were all around us!"

"I don't mean like that! With everyone staring and bowing. I wanted to see what it was *really* like. Just this once," Emma cried out. Much to her chagrin, she burst into tears. The emotions of parting with Jack, her exhaus-

tion and probably all the food she had eaten that day all
flooded into those tears. She could not stop. She buried
her face in her hands and wished she had an apron
like Natasha.

A soft hand touched her shoulder, and she looked up
to see Aunt Lydia holding out a handkerchief.

"Oh, Emma," she said, in a gentle, tired voice. "My
poor child. Stop crying and wipe your eyes."

Emma obeyed her, mopping away tears and blowing
her nose most inelegantly as her aunt sat back down. "I
am truly sorry if I disappointed you, Aunt Lydia," she
said soggily. "I never wanted to hurt you. I just . . ."

"You just wanted some fun," said Lydia. "And who
could blame you? You are young, and you have always
been so spirited. This visit cannot have been very exciting
for you. But I was very worried when I found you gone,
and Natasha did not know where you were. Anything
could have happened, Emma! You are a sheltered young
lady. You cannot know what waits out there. You should
never, ever have gone out by yourself."

Emma thought of the cutpurse Jack had rescued her
from and shuddered. Her aunt was right. She could never
have imagined that *either* of those things—the thief or
Jack—waited out there for her.

"Yes, Aunt Lydia," she said.

Lydia shook her head. "I promised your dear mother
faithfully that I would look after you as my own if anything happened to her. I have certainly loved you as my
own daughter, but I have not given you an easy life."
Her voice dropped almost to a whisper, an uncertain
murmur that Emma had never heard from her before.
"Did I fail my dear Lizzie? Do you hate your life with
us, Emma?"

This caused a fresh flood of tears. Emma slid off her
chair onto the floor next to Lydia and buried her head
in the satin of her aunt's skirt. "No, no! I love you and
Uncle Nicholas. No one could have been better parents
to me than you have been. I do not know what came
over me today. I just wanted to see something different."

"My dear child." Lydia laid her hand against Emma's hair, smoothing the long strands back. "We will only be here for a few more days, and I am sure we can make those days more interesting for you. Tomorrow, for instance. We must take tea at the embassy with Countess Lieven, but afterwards that young Sir Jeremy Ashbey would like to take you for a drive. You would be free of us old folk for an hour or so. Would that not be nice?"

No! Emma wanted to shout. She did not want to see Sir Jeremy—or any other man—after knowing Jack. She did not want to sit next to him in a carriage, making polite conversation. Knowing that, for whatever reason, her aunt and uncle had "expectations" of Sir Jeremy. She couldn't, not while her dreams of Jack were so fresh and clear.

But she couldn't bear to disappoint Aunt Lydia any further. She nodded against the gold satin, then immediately felt terrible for smearing tears on the expensive fabric.

Lydia didn't seem to notice, though. She patted Emma's head and said, with smiling relief in her voice, "Good. You will enjoy that. But you must promise me that you will not go slipping away again."

"I promise."

Lydia leaned down and kissed the top of her head. "You must be so tired, dear. Let me help you into your nightdress so you can go to bed. Unless you are hungry? I could send to the kitchen for some supper."

Emma's stomach lurched. "No, I am not hungry." She would probably never be hungry again after all she had eaten today.

Feeling as if she was in a trance or a dream, Emma let her aunt help her out of her borrowed dress and into one of her embroidered nightgowns and tuck her into bed. It reminded her of her childhood days, when Lydia, if she was not off on official duties with Uncle Nicholas, would brush Emma's hair and read to her before she went to sleep. It was comforting, after all the tumultuous emotions of the day, soft like an eiderdown quilt tucked around her shoulders on a cold day. Yet, at the same time, it made her feel like she *was* a child again, thrust back into her cocooned world when she had only just had a glimpse of what it was like to be a free woman.

She turned her face into the pillow, so weary that her entire body ached with it.

Lydia kissed her gently on the cheek. "You do look so tired, dear. Sleep now. Perhaps tomorrow you will want to tell me everything that you did today?"

Despite the gentle words, there was a certain steel in that last sentence. It was an order, disguised as a question.

Tell everything that she had done today? Emma feared she could not ever find a way to begin. She was not sure herself what had happened to her. But she could tell her aunt an abbreviated version, excised of ale, thieves, Lottie and her red gown and the most important part of all—Jack.

She would never speak of Jack, not to anyone. He was hers now, hers alone, or at least his memory was. She would keep him safely locked away in her heart for the rest of her life.

"Yes," she said. "We can talk about it tomorrow."

Aunt Lydia nodded and stood up to leave. She extinguished all the candles in the room, save one on the dressing table. "Good night, Emma," she said, and shut the door softly behind her.

Emma waited until her aunt's footsteps faded away down the corridor, then she slid out of bed and padded over to the window in her bare feet. She pulled back the draperies and looked down onto the street.

Despite the lateness of the hour, crowds still gathered there, as noisy and boisterous as ever. Behind the thickness of the glass, they moved in seeming silence, but Emma knew how they really sounded in the mad cacophony of unbridled joy.

For a brief time, she had been part of it.

She laid her hand flat against the window in farewell. There was a click behind her as the bedroom door opened again. She looked back, expecting to see her aunt returned and braced for a scolding about being out of bed. But it was Natasha. The maid had washed her tear-stained face and smoothed her hair, leaving no trace of earlier storms and quarrels. She held a pot of tea and a dainty china cup on a tray.

Emma couldn't help but smile. It was as if nothing at all had happened.

"I thought you might like some tea, my lady," Natasha said, with a tentative smile of her own.

"Thank you, Natasha. It seems just the thing to help steady my stomach." Emma took one more long look at the crowd outside before pulling the draperies closed. "Natasha, I want to say how very sorry I am I got you into trouble. I never would have stayed out so long if I thought that Aunt Lydia and Uncle Nicholas would come back early. I wish . . ."

"No, my lady. I didn't get into very much trouble. The countess was stern, but kind enough. I just feared what might happen to you."

"Aunt Lydia was kind to me as well," Emma murmured. She sat down and took the cup of tea Natasha offered. The sweet, milky liquid did help to settle her stomach a bit and was warm to her suddenly chilled heart. "So, we can begin again? I promise you I will never ask you to help me in such a prank again. From now on, I will be perfectly ladylike."

Natasha giggled. "I hope not perfectly, my lady! It would make my job so much more dull." She picked up Emma's discarded "Tonya" costume, shook it out and folded it neatly. "Tell me, my lady, did you see the illuminations?"

"Mm, oh, yes." Emma smiled at the memory, closing her eyes and seeing the sparkling multitude of lights as if they were still there before her. "And it was as you said—just like heaven."

Lydia expected only her maid and maybe Madame Ana to be waiting for her when she returned wearily to her own suite, her head aching beneath the weight of her tiara. But Olga was not there to help her out of her gown, nor was Madame Ana there to take notes on the next day's engagements. Only her husband waited in the sitting room.

Nicholas sat slumped in an armchair by the fireplace, the white and gold tunic of his uniform half-unfastened, as if he had been too tired to go any further. Almost always he looked as young and dashing as he had on the evening when he, a young officer visiting London from Russia, had swept her off her feet at a ball. Tonight, though, he looked weary, pale even, his dark hair iced with gray, purple shadows beneath his eyes.

Well, she was no longer the young miss who had danced all night with him at that long-ago ball, either.

We are getting old, she thought, with some surprise. Too old to be all of Emma's family, perhaps. She needed young people around her, a social circle of her own.

A family of her own?

When the door clicked shut behind her, Nicholas looked up and smiled. It was the same roguish smile as ever.

Perhaps they were not so old, after all.

"Lydia, my darling," he said, rising from his chair. He came across the room and kissed her cheek. "Is Emma still ill?"

Lydia leaned against his shoulder, grateful for his strength. "No, she is better." She had seen no reason to worry Nicholas with Emma's little escapade, not unless it had proved necessary to call out a search party, which mercifully it had not. "She will be able to join us for tea at the embassy tomorrow."

"That is excellent news!" he said, his tone most relieved. "I fear we had exhausted our little *koshka* with this journey."

"She *was* tired, I think. But a day of rest has done her a world of good."

"You look as if you are in need of rest as well, my darling. Come, sit down. I will ring for Olga."

"Thank you, dearest." Lydia sat down on the settee near the fire, sighing as she tucked her aching feet up on a footstool. It had been a very long night indeed.

She watched as her husband went to ring the bell. It was so nice to have this quiet time together, and such a rare luxury. She did love Nicholas and had never regretted marrying him. None of her English suitors could have held a candle to him. Truly, though, she could have wished for more time together. They had spent perhaps three months together in every one of the twenty-five years they had been married.

It was the price she paid for being married to a diplomat. Did she really want Emma to pay that price, as well?

Lydia looked into the crackling flames, mesmerized by the red and gold dance. She had hoped that on this visit Emma would make a match. It would have pleased Lydia's sister so much to see her daughter marry an Englishman, perhaps even return to her own English estate. Despite the pangs Lydia felt at the thought of losing Emma, she had thought it the best thing. Despite how very Russian Emma so often seemed, the truth was that she was an English lady.

Sir Jeremy Ashbey appeared to be the answer. He was well spoken of, young and handsome, with lands near Emma's own. And he seemed to greatly admire Emma. Nicholas liked him. But—Sir Jeremy was embarking on a diplomatic career of his own.

What was the right answer? Lydia feared she did not know.

She rubbed her hand over her eyes. "I thought you would still be with the Tsar," she said, as her husband rejoined her. He held two glasses of sherry, one of which he pressed into her hand.

"I was, until a short time ago," Nicholas said. "He went on to another ball. Can you imagine?" He laughed. "Were *we* ever that young?"

Lydia sipped at the deep golden liquid, savoring its bracing warmth. "Tonight I feel as if I was never young."

Nicholas frowned in concern. "Are you feeling unwell, darling?"

"I am quite well. Just a bit tired. Certainly not up to dancing all night!" She drained the glass. "I have been thinking about Sir Jeremy Ashbey."

"Yes. He seems a most admirable young man, and so admiring of our Emma. But there is something about his family, his mother perhaps, that is not quite right."

"Something alarming?"

"I am not sure. I have not yet discovered the details." Nicholas's quiet, hard tone promised that he soon would. "In the meantime, I see no reason why he should not spend time with Emma. Properly chaperoned, of course."

"Of course. She has agreed to go driving with him tomorrow after the tea."

Nicholas nodded. "That would be an excellent time for them to get to know one another better."

"Yes," Lydia murmured, staring down into the empty depths of her glass. "An excellent time."

Chapter Twelve

"Tell me, Lady Emma, how are you enjoying your time in London?" Countess Lieven asked.

Emma watched as the countess sat down next to her on the settee, a china cup and saucer balanced perfectly in her hand. Just as at the reception, Countess Lieven looked elegant and poised, her salmon-colored gown and embroidered spencer in the first stare of fashion. And just as at the reception, Emma felt like a little mouse next to her. She put down the plate of cake she held and carefully smoothed the skirt of her own blue-sprigged muslin afternoon gown.

"I am enjoying it very much, thank you, Countess Lieven," Emma answered politely. "London is a lovely city."

"But not as lovely as St. Petersburg, is it?" The countess gave a wistful sigh and made an adorable little moue with her red lips. Emma wished she could learn how to do that without looking ridiculous. "I do so miss my home sometimes. But that is why I am so happy all of you are here! It is almost like being in Russia again. I so seldom get to talk with my own countrywomen."

Emma remembered all she had heard of the countess's active social life in London. She imagined the lack of Russian women to talk with did not really make a great deal of difference, when one was a patroness of the fabled Almack's. But she just smiled politely and nodded.

That was really all she had been doing all day. It was all she had the strength to do.

She was still so tired from her grand adventure of the day before, tired and hollow feeling. There seemed to be a cold core right in the center of her chest that would not melt, no matter what she did. She tried to forget, to concentrate only on what she must do today—be polite and pretty.

She had thought that if she could have a short time away, she could come back to her real life refreshed. She had been wrong. It only made things harder. Now that she knew there was another way, how could she face another interminable tea party again?

Her face felt so stiff from smiling that she feared it might crack. She ground her back teeth together and feared everyone must hear the horrid squeaking sound.

Countess Lieven didn't appear to notice anything amiss with Emma's smile, though. She laid her slender, beringed hand lightly on Emma's sleeve in a friendly, sympathetic gesture. "I was so very sorry to hear you were ill and could not be with us at the ball last night. Are you feeling better today?"

"Oh, yes, thank you, Countess Lieven," Emma managed to say, releasing her teeth from their death's grin.

"Travel is so very rigorous. I hope you will be up to joining us at Lady Hertford's ball tomorrow?"

"I am sure I will."

"It will be quite a crush." Countess Lieven leaned forward a bit and said in a confiding tone, "I am sure there will be one gentleman in particular who will be eager to claim a dance. Or two."

Emma felt that dreadful tightness at the back of her jaw again. "I am sure I cannot know who you mean," she said, even though she feared she *did* know. Sir Jeremy Ashbey had sent her a huge bouquet of pink roses that morning, with a note expressing the ardent wish that she would still be able to join him for a drive this afternoon.

"Sir Jeremy Ashbey, of course!" the countess said. "He seems to admire you so much, Lady Emma. And he was so desolate at your absence last night. None of the pretty young misses could make him smile! Today, though, he is all smiles."

Emma and Countess Lieven both turned their heads to peer discreetly at the gentleman in question. He was indeed smiling as he talked with Emma's uncle near one of the high windows.

Emma had to admit he was handsome. His golden, perfectly arranged hair gleamed in the sunlight. He was stylishly attired in a well-cut bottle green coat and buff pantaloons, his ivory cravat beautifully but not ostentatiously tied.

He could not compare with Jack, though. No one could.

There, she had broken her promise to herself not to think of him today. It could not be helped. Watching Sir Jeremy or almost any other man just invited comparison with Jack. She looked at Sir Jeremy's elegant appearance but saw Jack, with his windblown dark hair, his suntouched skin and brilliant eyes that laughed down at her.

Not even the most cleverly tied cravat could compare with that.

But Sir Jeremy *had* been most attentive to her, greeting her when she first arrived at the embassy and making certain she had a comfortable seat. He had brought her cakes, made light conversation with her, even told her a joke or two. And, of course, there were the roses. It was all very proper, very flattering.

Yet, there was something almost disquieting about his attentions. Something almost—almost grasping or possessive. They had only spoken perhaps two dozen words together, which made this feeling harder to understand. She *didn't* understand it—he had not made one single gesture to her or said one word that could be construed as improper.

Emma gave her head a tiny shake. Just because Sir

Jeremy was not Jack, that did not make him a bad person. He was just—different, and once they had a chance for more conversation, she would surely like him.

"He is handsome," Countess Lieven said, with another of her theatrical sighs. "We are very fortunate that he is to work here in London from now on. I hear that all the young ladies at his former post are pining."

Emma laughed, picturing multitudes of young ladies falling prostrate upon the ground, sobbing, because Sir Jeremy was gone. It felt good to laugh again, even for so silly a reason.

"You are a fortunate girl," the countess went on. "And I am sure that these tales of Sir Jeremy's mother are nothing but tittle-tattle. You would not believe the gossip idle minds can produce!"

Sir Jeremy's mother? Emma could not recall ever hearing one word about the woman, whoever she might be. What tales could be going around about her? She opened her mouth to ask but was interrupted by the arrival in their little corner of Lord and Lady Osborn.

Countess Lieven turned to them with a glad greeting and held her hand out to Lord Osborn. Emma smiled at them and added her own greeting. She remembered them from the reception. Lady Osborn had seemed then a sweet little sparrow, her husband a bit loud and rather full of his own consequence, as aging statesmen sometimes were, but generally pleasant.

Nothing changed her impression today. Lady Osborn wore a well-cut but not very dashing gown and pelisse of gray silk with a pale blue bonnet, which seemed to fade into the wallpaper along with her die-away little giggle. Lord Osborn was all smiles and bluff heartiness as he bowed over Emma's hand.

"Lord Osborn, Lady Osborn," Emma said. "It is very good to see you again."

"The pleasure and privilege are entirely ours, Lady Emma!" Lord Osborn answered. "We were sorry to hear you were not feeling well yesterday evening."

"Thank you, Lord Osborn. I am quite recovered now."

"Travel can be so *difficult* on one's system," Lady Osborn said, with a delicate flutter of her handkerchief. "I remember . . ."

"Quite, my dear," Lord Osborn interrupted. "Quite. Well, I do hope we shall see you at Lady Hertford's ball tomorrow night, Lady Emma."

"I hope very much to attend," said Emma. She tried to smile at Lady Osborn, but the lady was now staring at the floor.

"Good, good," Lord Osborn said. "I hope we may have the honor to present our son, Viscount St. Albans, to you there. He was meant to accompany us this afternoon but was unhappily prevented."

"I would be happy to meet Lord St. Albans tomorrow," Emma answered politely. Lord Osborn had mentioned his son at the reception, too. Emma wondered why he was so very keen for her to meet him. Probably the viscount was yet another spoiled young Englishman, like so many of the ones she had met in the embassy drawing room today, concerned only with horses and their clubs and the cut of their coats.

Ah, well. Surely she could stand another introduction and perhaps a dance with this Lord St. Albans.

She did not have long to speculate on the Osborns' son, though. She saw that her uncle and Sir Jeremy were walking toward her. It was time for her drive.

"What do you think of London thus far, Lady Emma?" Sir Jeremy asked.

"Hm?" Emma murmured absently. Her aunt would have been very disappointed in her lack of manners, but the truth was Emma had not really been attending. She had been watching the people gathered in the park. Just as she had thought they would, the people on foot backed away from Sir Jeremy's elegant phaeton, bowing respectfully.

It was nothing like when she had been here just yesterday, going for a row on the pond.

Emma sighed and turned to Sir Jeremy with a polite

smile she hoped apologized for her lack of attention. "I am so sorry, Sir Jeremy, but I fear I did not hear your question."

He smiled at her, too, the indulgent sort of smile one might give a rather slow child. It irritated Emma to no end, and she felt a sudden urge to slap it off his face. She tightened her gloved grip on the carved handle of her open parasol.

"I merely asked what you thought of London, Lady Emma," he said.

Hadn't he already asked her that? Oh, no. That had been Countess Lieven who asked her a similar question, along with a dozen other people.

And she gave the same answer she always gave. "I think London is charming."

He smiled at her again. "A charming setting for a charming lady."

Ugh. "You are far too kind, Sir Jeremy. We have truly not had enough conversation for you to know if I am charming or not."

Sir Jeremy tugged on the reins, turning the carriage so that they ran along a path beside the pond. Emma tried not to look at the happy couples in their rowboats. She turned her parasol to block the view.

"I know you quite well enough to know that you are very charming," Sir Jeremy said. He looked down at her for a moment before turning his gaze back to the path, suddenly unsmiling. "We have met before, you know, Lady Emma."

She frowned in puzzlement. "Of course we have. At the reception . . ."

"No, I mean before that. When you lived at Weston Manor."

"My parents' home?" Emma studied him a bit more closely, hoping a closer look would somehow nudge her memory, but of course it did not. She had been six when she left to live in Russia, and Sir Jeremy would have been not a great deal older. It was perhaps possible that they had met then, but she had no recollection of it. "I am sorry, I don't remember. I was very small when I lived there."

"My family's estate marches with Weston Manor, as I am sure you know. My parents sometimes attended social functions there, and once I came along for a picnic. I was twelve, home for a school holiday." Sir Jeremy still looked at the path, but it was obvious his thoughts were far away, in another time. A time Emma had shared but could not recall.

"A picnic?" she said.

"Yes. It was a beautiful day, summertime. All bright and warm, with flowers everywhere. Weston Manor had such splendid gardens," Sir Jeremy said, going on in that same distant voice. "And you were there. You wore a yellow frock, and you offered me lemonade and a cake." He suddenly turned to her, his previously flat gray eyes wide with the remembrance. "You were the loveliest thing I had ever seen, Lady Emma. You are still—lovely."

Something in his expression, in his manner, made the fine hairs on Emma's neck prickle. She edged back on the seat until she felt the hard wall of the phaeton against her back. This was not just a casual reminiscence of a childhood afternoon, she sensed. But she did not know what it *was*. She did not even know how their dull, conventional afternoon had turned so confusing. So—so menacing.

She wanted to jump down and run back to the hotel, but even as she thought of it, she knew it was foolish. Even if she did not injure herself in the leap, she would cause an on-dit.

They were in a public place, she told herself, so she was safe. And besides, he had hardly threatened her. He was just making conversation—albeit rather odd conversation, to a woman he had just met.

She tried to laugh it away. "It sounds a most charming day! I wish I could remember it."

"I have always remembered it. All these years."

Emma cast about in her mind for a way to answer

that. "You—you said your family used to visit mine. Do your relatives still live on your estate?"

Sir Jeremy's jaw tightened, and the misty light of remembrance lifted from his eyes, leaving them empty again. "Only my mother and sister. My father died several years ago, leaving the estate to me."

"Your mother? Does she ever come to London?"

"No. She is not suited to town life," he answered shortly.

Indeed? Emma thought. A very curious description to offer of his mother. And Emma remembered now that Countess Lieven had said something about Lady Ashbey. She wondered what could be so wrong with her.

But Sir Jeremy now no longer spoke to or looked at her, and she did not intend to change that by pursuing the subject. She settled down to get what enjoyment she could out of the rest of the drive and determined to tell her aunt and uncle that she did not care for Sir Jeremy as soon as they returned to the hotel. She wasn't certain what their motives had been in promoting him as a desirable suitor, but she knew that they would not insist that she continue the acquaintance.

She stared out over the park. They had left the pond behind and now followed a carriage path that ran parallel to a pedestrian walkway. Several people strolled there, couples, families, nurses with their charges, ladies with dogs on leads. There was even a child with a hoop who reminded Emma of the one who had bumped into her yesterday. She smiled at the little memory.

Then her gaze was caught by a man who hurried along past all the strollers, obviously intent on his own destination. He was very well-dressed in a beautifully cut coat of burgundy-colored superfine and dark trousers, his boots so highly polished the sun glinted off them. A tall hat was set rakishly atop perfectly styled dark hair, and he carried a carved walking stick.

It was not the man's sartorial splendor that captured her attention, though. It was the way he walked, the set of his broad shoulders that spoke of boldness and confidence. The—familiarity of that walk.

Emma leaned forward, clutching at the handle of her parasol until it bit into her hand, pressing the lace of her glove against her palm. Was it—could it be . . . ?

Her heart beat so loudly she could hear it drumming in her ears, feel it pounding against her bodice. She longed to jump from the carriage again, but in joy this time rather than trepidation.

She nearly called out Jack's name, just to see if it was he. But the man turned a bend in the path, out of her view, and Sir Jeremy turned the carriage toward the hotel.

Emma fell back against the seat, her heart still fluttering like a wild trapped bird. She was so disappointed she could cry. "Oh!" she sobbed, before she could stop herself.

Sir Jeremy turned to her, his face all polite concern, his earlier intensity vanished. Emma was glad; she did not think she could face it right now, not when she was so close to tears anyway.

"Are you ill, Lady Emma?" he asked, in great solicitude.

"I—just a touch too much sun, I fear," Emma murmured. "I think I need to go back to the hotel."

"Of course. We are going there now."

Emma smiled at him weakly. When he turned his attention back to the horses, she craned her neck to try to catch a glimpse of the man again. It was in vain, though. Whoever he was, he had quite disappeared.

Jack ducked quickly around a turn in the path and stood plastered flat against a tree. He felt rather foolish, especially when a couple with a small child paused to look at him quizzically. He gave them a quelling gaze in return—hadn't they ever seen a man hiding behind a tree before?

Obviously not. They moved off with a laugh, and he

leaned his head back against the rough bark. Indeed, he had never *had* to hide in the park before. But—blast!— who would have expected Emma to be driving here right when he decided to cut through the park on his way to Bertie's lodgings?

He peered cautiously around to see that she was driving away from him. Being driven by that bloke who had been escorting her at the reception, too, Sir Jeremy Ashbey.

Damn his eyes.

Jack knew he should not be staring at her, not when he was dressed in his own expensive clothes. He was not quite ready to reveal himself to her yet; that was why he had made his excuses to his parents for the embassy tea. He needed to plan this carefully.

Yet, he could not help but stare at her. She looked like summertime today, in a pale blue-sprigged muslin gown and butter-yellow spencer. The blue and yellow ribbons on her chipped straw bonnet fluttered in the breeze, past the lace-trimmed edge of her yellow parasol.

Suddenly, that parasol tilted, and she looked in his direction. Jack ducked back behind the tree.

He waited for a few moments, until he could be certain they were out of sight, before he continued on his way. He was already late; he and Bertie were meant to call at Mr. Thompson's headquarters, and that was not something one could be tardy for. Jack was usually quite punctual—it was the army in him; certain things became engrained. Today, though, he felt almost as if he was walking underwater. Everything around him seemed in a haze. It was probably because he had not been able to sleep last night after he returned to his rooms; not until dawn was already lighting the sky.

He had never expected the feelings that filled him yesterday. He had felt young, lighthearted, as he had not since—well, since long before he had joined the army. Emma had made him laugh, really laugh, not just a fashionable, cynical chuckle. She had made him see the world, the city he had always lived in, in all new ways.

She had made him want to see everything like that, through her wide, dark eyes.

He slapped his walking stick hard on his leg as he climbed the steps to Bertie's lodgings. There was no time for that now. He had to be at Mr. Thompson's meeting, and he had to focus absolutely on everything that was said. The security of the society they had fought to protect on the battlefields of Europe for so long was still very precarious. They still had work to do.

And protecting Lady Emma Weston was no longer his task.

He pounded his stick on Bertie's door. The wood opened, and his friend stood there, every dark gold hair in place, cravat impeccably tied in complicated whorls. He looked focused, alert, serious, despite the fact that he had no doubt been awake late with Miss Lottie.

Bertie was Jack's best friend, but sometimes he hated the man. He was a consummate actor, and nothing ever distracted him from his work.

Once, Jack had thought he could say that about himself as well. Now he knew he could not.

That just soured his disposition further.

"You are late," Bertie said. He tipped his own hat onto his head and stepped out onto the pavement.

"Then you should have gone on without me," Jack answered shortly, and strode off.

"I wanted to talk to you before we got to Thompson's." Bertie kept stride with Jack, unperturbed. "Did you deposit Lady Emma safely back at the Pulteney?"

"Safely, yes. She was no doubt tucked up safe as a little lamb in her own chamber long before midnight."

"Indeed." They walked along in silence for a moment before Bertie added, "Lady Emma is a most intrepid young lady. Very–unexpected."

"Yes," Jack answered shortly. *Quite unexpected.*

Chapter Thirteen

*E*mma watched listlessly in the dressing-table mirror as Natasha lifted a wreath of pink rosebuds from the florist's box and pinned it in Emma's upswept hair. Every flower was a perfection of pale pink color and sweet perfume, entwined with a strand of pearls that matched her mother's necklace and earrings. The jewels, jewels she usually loved to wear because they made her think of her mother, lay waiting in their cases. Her pink silk gown, freshly pressed, was spread across the bed like the lightest sunset cloud.

Emma saw none of this splendor. She didn't even really see her reflection in the mirror. She kept going over and over the memory of that man she had seen in the park. Had it been Jack? Or was her mind leaving her, making her insane so that she saw Jack in every dark-haired man she passed? It was probably just wishful thinking. She would never see him again, and even if by some miracle she *did* see him, what could come of it? Her aunt and uncle would never allow her to marry a secretary.

One thing she *did* know was that, Jack or no Jack, she could not wed Sir Jeremy Ashbey. Their brief encounter in his phaeton, that look on his face when he told her of their childhood meeting, had frightened her. She had thought perhaps there was nothing behind his perfect, polite, handsome exterior. Now she knew that there *was*, but it was not something she wished to know further.

Anyone who could be so intent over a meeting that took place twelve years ago between two children was just—odd.

Now, Jack would never have done such a thing . . .

"No!" she cried aloud, slamming her palm down on the dressing table. The hairbrushes, pots and bottles rattled. Rice powder spilled in a shimmering fall. She could *not* think about him any more.

"My lady?" Natasha said in alarm. She lifted her hands from the wreath she was still pinning and stepped back. "Is something amiss? Do you not like your hair this way?"

Emma closed her eyes and took in a deep breath. Now her perplexity, her foul mood, was affecting everyone around her. It had to cease. "No, Natasha. It looks lovely. You are always so clever. I just—I am tired."

"You do look a bit pale." Natasha opened one of the small cases on the dressing table and rummaged about until she came up with a little silver box. "Do you want to use some rouge tonight?"

Emma's interest was piqued. "I did not know I had rouge! Does Aunt Lydia know?" Glad of a distraction, no matter how small, she opened the box and dipped her fingertip into the sticky pinkness. "It is just like Lottie wore."

"Who is Lottie, my lady?" Natasha asked curiously.

"What? Oh, no one. Just someone I met once."

Natasha's eyes widened. "Someone who wears rouge all the time?"

"I don't know if she wears it *all* the time," Emma said.

The bedchamber door opened and Aunt Lydia stepped inside, just in time to hear those words. "I should hope you do not know a woman who always wears rouge, Emma," she said. She stepped behind her niece, so Emma was faced with her full reflection. Her pale gray satin gown and sapphire jewels flashed and sparkled, making her more the majestic Countess Suvarova than the stern but affectionate Aunt Lydia of the night before.

"No, of course not, Aunt Lydia," Emma answered.

Natasha came back at a gesture from Aunt Lydia to finish Emma's hair and fasten her jewelry.

"But perhaps you *could* use a touch of it this evening," Lydia said, straightening her long kid gloves over her arms. "You seem quite pale. I hope you are not truly becoming ill!"

"I feel quite well," Emma answered. "I do need to talk to you, though. About Sir Jeremy . . ."

"Later, my dear. There will be plenty of time for that later. Right now, you must finish dressing, or we will be late for this ball."

"Yes, Aunt Lydia. Of course." Emma faced her reflection full on again, watching Natasha put the finishing touches on the wreath.

Lydia suddenly bent down and pressed a careful kiss to Emma's cheek. "You look lovely tonight, Emma. Your uncle and I are so proud of you."

Emma smiled weakly. "Thank you, Aunt Lydia."

The grand ballroom at Lady Hertford's mansion was decorated to look like a forest, albeit one where hothouse roses and orchids grew. Thick, glossy greenery lined the walls, entwined with sweet smelling pastel flowers. Tall branching candelabra stood everywhere, casting their glowing light and wispy white smoke into the crowd. And since Lady Hertford was Prinny's current mistress, that crowd was considerable. Everyone of any importance in Society, or anyone who *wanted* to be of importance, was gathered there, listening to the orchestra hidden behind a wall of palms, sipping champagne, exchanging *on-dits*.

Everyone except Tsar Alexander and his party.

Jack stood with his parents near a set of tall glass doors that opened onto a moon-washed terrace, half-listening to the conversation his father was having with one of his old cronies.

He took a slow sip of his champagne, studying the room over the edge of the crystal flute. A country dance was forming on the floor, and he saw Bertie leading an elegant redhead to their places. Sir Jeremy Ashbey, the insufferable man that Jack had seen driving with Emma that afternoon, stood across the room. He was talking with Lord Castlereagh, but he, like Jack, watched the door with stealthy interest.

What an insufferable prig the man was, Jack thought, taking a deeper swallow of the champagne.

He turned away from Sir Jeremy and thought about the meeting with Thompson this afternoon. It had been brief, but rather unsettling. There had been word from their agents in France that all was not as stable as the allies might wish. Not by a long way.

He should be thinking of that, not Emma. But somehow, he knew he just had to set things right with her. How he was to do that, though, he did not know.

He hoped he would know what to say when he saw her. And that would be—now.

The ballroom doors opened, and Tsar Alexander and his sister stood there, a picture of contrasts, he in his white and gold uniform, she in her black satin and lace gown. The entire congregation fell into a hush; even the music stilled. Everyone dipped into bows and curtsies, and Prinny and Lady Hertford hurried forward to greet the latecoming guests of honor.

As the Tsar and Grand Duchess moved into the room, the people who stood behind them became visible. Count Suvarov, in a dark green uniform, had his wife on one arm, his niece on the other.

Jack almost choked on the champagne he had just swallowed. She was so preternaturally lovely, in a gown of pink silk trimmed with white satin ribbons, a wreath of flowers threaded in her dark hair, her double-strand pearl necklace gleaming against her skin. Her gloved hand rested lightly on her uncle's sleeve, and her head inclined at a regal angle as Lady Hertford greeted her.

But she did not look like *his* Emma. She looked as she had the first night he saw her, at the reception. Her smile was polite yet fixed, her face a pretty mask. She seemed to be staring into herself, at something no one else could see.

Jack wanted to rush to her, to take her in his arms and hold her until all her coolness melted, to tell her a silly jest and make her laugh, to make her come back to him.

He took one step in her direction, but that blasted Sir Jeremy was quicker. As Jack watched, the other man stepped to her side and gave her a bow, saying something to her.

It seemed to startle Emma. Her eyes widened as she saw Sir Jeremy, and she took a tiny, almost imperceptible step toward her uncle.

Count Suvarov glanced down at her and gave her an indulgent smile. He patted her hand and urged her toward Sir Jeremy. After a small hesitation, she nodded and gave Sir Jeremy a quirk of her lips that could be construed as a smile. As Jack watched, she moved to the dance floor with Sir Jeremy, to take their places in the set that was just forming.

To all outward appearances, Emma seemed perfectly poised and at ease. She made an elegant curtsy to Sir Jeremy, then held her gloved hands out to him. Jack, though, knew her. He saw the stiffness of her shoulders, the white cast of her face. As Sir Jeremy turned her in a slow circle, Jack noticed that she leaned back slightly, her grasp straining at Sir Jeremy's.

She was miserable, and Jack could not bear it for another minute. He put his empty glass onto a passing footman's tray and, ignoring his parents' bewildered questions, set off across the ballroom.

Why, oh why, had she agreed to dance with Sir Jeremy? After their drive, after all her determination to tell her aunt and uncle she did not care for him? She should have refused, should have said she did not intend to dance tonight, but she had not. And here she was, with her hands caught in his.

She turned and moved around the next couple, remembering the little skipping steps only from instinct. As sometimes happened at these grand galas, her mind wanted to drift away to more interesting places, leaving just her body to move through these oft repeated pleasantries. Unfortunately, tonight her mind would not drift far enough to allow her to imagine that it was *Jack* she was dancing with.

The figures of the dance brought her back to Sir Jeremy. As they clasped hands again and moved closer together, he said, "I so enjoyed our drive today, Lady Emma."

"Mm," Emma murmured, and gave him a polite, vague little smile.

"It is always good to meet an old friend again, after such a long parting. I feel so fortunate that you came back to England now." His gray gaze was bright as he looked down at her and strangely anticipating, as if he expected a certain reply from her.

Emma wasn't exactly sure what that reply should be. And—*old friends*? She didn't think *that* was true. She just nodded.

"I would be honored if you would allow me to escort you to Carlton House the day after tomorrow," he said, his hands tightening on hers.

Carlton House? Oh, yes, the Prince Regent's home. They were meant to attend a grand supper party there. She was actually looking forward to it, she had heard such extraordinary things about it. But she certainly did not want to attend with Sir Jeremy.

He did not seem to expect a refusal or indeed any reply at all. He gave her a charming smile, as if all was decided.

Emma glanced over to where her aunt and uncle stood, but they were conversing with Lord and Lady Osborn and paying no attention to her. She was entirely on her own, in a ballroom filled with dozens of people.

"I think my aunt and uncle have already made plans," she managed to say through her dry throat.

His smile widened, taking on an indulgent, confident air that she found particularly unpleasant. "I am sure they will not object to your attending the supper with me."

Emma wasn't sure what to say. It wouldn't be the thing at all to start a quarrel in the middle of a dance, but she could not let Sir Jeremy go on thinking of her in—well, in whatever way it was that he *did* think of her.

Fortunately, she did not have to say anything just yet. The dance separated them again, and she moved around the next couple in line. As she skipped and twirled, her gaze scanned the people who stood around the edges of the dance floor, talking, laughing, drinking champagne. *They* seemed as if they belonged here; they seemed as if they had no cares in the world, beyond perhaps a snagged hem or dancing pumps that pinched.

She wondered if she could possibly trade places with one of them, just for a while—much as she had traded places with an imaginary lady's maid.

Then she saw him, threading his way through the crowd to stop just outside the periphery of the dancers, not six feet away from her. He wore an exquisite evening coat of midnight blue velvet and pale gray satin breeches. His white-as-snow cravat fell in perfect folds over his cream-colored satin waistcoat, anchored with a sapphire stickpin. But Emma saw all this, took note of it, in only a peripheral fashion. She could see only his eyes, bluer than the sapphire stone. Eyes that stared right into hers.

Jack. It was truly Jack. It could be no one else. It could not be her imagination, as the man in the park today had been. She saw him so very clearly, his jaw working as if he tried to say something. Her heart pounded painfully, and she could scarcely breathe.

If she took just a step or two, she could even reach out to touch him.

She stumbled over her feet, the trim satin slippers feeling suddenly as big as boats. She would have fallen if the man next to her in the dance had not grasped her arm and drawn her back to the proper position. She took his hand and performed the turn, looking back over her shoulder at the first opportunity.

He was not there.

She scanned the crowd again, searching for any sign of him. He seemed to have vanished. Yet, she had seen him! She was certain of it. Her daydreams were never that vivid.

She clasped hands with Sir Jeremy again and turned. As she moved to face the crowd, Jack mercifully reappeared, moving from the group to the edge of the floor, closer than before. He gave her a crooked little smile.

Jack. A sudden joy leapt from her heart into her throat, a warm rush of feeling unlike anything she had ever felt before. She had been in such despair these past two days, had felt she had lost something so infinitely precious, something that could never be replaced.

Now here he was! Right in front of her, not a figment of her dreams. She wanted to run to him, to throw her arms around him and never let him go.

Her social training was too deeply engrained, though. She could not quite bring herself to make a scene. But as soon as this dance, this *dratted* dance, was over, she would go to him. Her very fingers and toes tingled with impatience.

When Sir Jeremy reclaimed her to lead her down the line of dancers, she could not stop herself from giving him a wide smile of pure joy.

He looked startled, then gave her an answering smile. She did not even truly notice.

As she automatically performed the final steps, her thoughts whirled. Jack was here. *Here.* Her happiness overflowed within her. Yet even as she bubbled with anticipation, one question rose unbidden to the back of her mind.

What was a secretary doing in Lady Hertford's ballroom? Dressed in the first stare of fashion, apparently accepted by everyone around him?

She shook her head. He surely had a proper explanation for it, for everything. Maybe he was in disguise, just to get to see her. If she could only get out of this dance and hear it from him!

The final notes of music sounded at last, and Emma dropped into a curtsy to Sir Jeremy. As she rose, he offered her his arm.

"Shall I escort you back to your aunt and uncle, Lady Emma?" he asked solicitously.

"No!" Emma cried out without thinking. She could never look for Jack with Aunt Lydia's sharp eyes on her. She saw Sir Jeremy's startled expression, and modified her tone. "I—I have to go to the ladies' withdrawing room first."

As she expected, he flushed at this and averted his gaze. "Oh, er, of course, Lady Emma. Shall I escort you there, then?"

"Oh, no, that won't be necessary. I know the direction." She disengaged her hand from his arm and bobbed him another quick curtsy before hurrying off into the enveloping crowd. She did not even look back.

She walked as quickly as she could without running in an unseemly fashion around the edge of the room, standing on tiptoe to peer over shoulders, giving distracted greetings to people who spoke to her. She tried to avoid her aunt and uncle, who would not let her stray from their sides again without a good reason.

But she could not see Jack anywhere.

As she passed the half-open doors to the terrace, a breeze moved over her shoulders and neck. She paused there to plot her next move, to peer very carefully around her.

"Psst!" she heard. Was the breeze picking up, whistling noisily past the doors?

"Psst!" it came again, more insistent. It did not sound like the wind this time. It sounded like—a voice.

She pushed the door open wider and slipped out onto the terrace. The shadows out here, beyond the glow of the ballroom, were deep. She peered around, staring past potted plants and marble statues.

"Hello?" she called softly.

A hand reached out and caught hers, pulling her behind a tall, potted topiary. She gasped in surprise, but the sound was swallowed when a pair of lips pressed lightly against hers. Her hand reached out and encountered the lushness of a velvet coat, the warmth of hard shoulders beneath. A familiar soapy, spicy scent crept into her senses.

After a second of startlement, she knew the truth. This was Jack who was kissing her; Jack who was in her arms.

His lips slid from hers. Emma did not open her eyes. This *seemed* real, but if by some chance it was another dream, she wanted to hold onto it for as long as possible. She opened her eyes only when she heard him give a rueful laugh, felt the rumble of it under her palms. He looked down at her, that half-smile on his face, his eyes as blue and warm as she remembered. She curled her hands into his coat.

"Hello—Tonya," he said.

Chapter Fourteen

Emma reached up to touch Jack's face, to assure herself that he was real. His skin was warm through the thin kid of her gloves, the line of his jaw and cheekbone strong.

He *was* real!

He was right here in front of her, illumined by a strong, pale beam of moonlight that silvered his dark hair. He had never looked more beautiful than at this moment.

"Jack!" she cried, and flung her arms around his neck to press close to him. "How did you find me? What are you doing here? You could get into such trouble if you are discovered!" The questions rushed from her lips before she could stop or even slow them.

His arms tightened on her waist but only for a moment. At her words, his hands slid to her shoulders to hold her away a bit. "Trouble?"

A small, cold finger of uncertainty touched the back of Emma's neck. She had just assumed that Jack had come to the ball in disguise to find her, but now the simple perfection of that assumption began to show its frayed edges. She had told him she was a maid—how would he know to look for her here? He did not seem at all surprised to find her in her gown and jewels. And he seemed completely at ease in his grand attire, surrounded by grand Society.

What was happening here?

Emma stepped away from him, careful to remain in the shadows of the terrace. Her confusion was better hidden in the dimness. "In trouble for being here without an invitation," she said, in the wild hope that her suspicions were unfounded. "Perhaps your employer is even here and will see that you have borrowed his clothes! I would not have you lose your position because you came here to see me. And how did you know where to find me?"

Jack rubbed his hand across the back of his neck and gave her a rueful smile. "Well, it is really rather a humorous story when you think about it in a certain fashion."

Emma took another step back. The cold spread across her shoulders and down her back. She did not know what he was going to say, but she was pretty certain she did not want to hear it. "Humorous?"

"Yes. You see, I am not truly a secretary." His smile widened, became cajoling.

Not a secretary? Perhaps that was not so bad. Her cold muscles relaxed. She, after all, was not a lady's maid. "Then what *are* you?"

He stepped toward her, his face turning wary and guarded. "I am a viscount."

That she was not expecting. "A—viscount?"

"Viscount St. Albans, at your service, my lady." He gave her an elegant bow, as if they had just been introduced in the ballroom.

"You are the son of Lord and Lady Osborn!"

He nodded slowly.

"But I met them at Lady Bransley's reception." Emma felt trapped in a very strange dream, her thoughts spinning as she tried to adjust to this new reality. Her Jack was not a secretary; he was a viscount, the son of people she knew. She remembered Lord Osborn saying she should meet his son, and she *had* met him. He was Jack.

Had he seen her at the reception? Had he planned to meet her, to somehow deceive her?

She glanced over her shoulder, through the glass doors into the ballroom, seeking escape. Even as she looked, though, she knew that no escape would be found among those blithe, bejeweled dancers. She was trapped here, with this Jack who was not Jack, her cold feet rooted to the marble terrace. She remembered what Natasha had said about Maria's card reading, the dark man who would disrupt their lives. *Could it be—Jack?*

She turned back to Jack, who watched her, perfectly expressionless. It was as if he wore a mask over his handsome features, one that was just as attractive but totally void.

"Then you knew all along who I was," she said. She had wanted to shout, but her voice came out as a murmur. She was only able to conjure up one explanation. "You were sent to spy on me."

Jack flinched. "No, Emma . . ."

"You know my name. But then, you knew it all along. Who sent you to spy on me? My uncle?" Her voice rose to a higher pitch.

Jack shook his head, a flash of something like consternation peeking from behind that mask. "Of course not. No one sent me. I was not spying on you."

"You lied to me!"

"You lied to me, as well—Tonya. But I would never accuse *you* of spying on *me*."

Somewhere, deep in Emma's mind, she saw the rationality of that. She *had* lied to him. But she was just too confused and hurt to acknowledge that voice. The beautiful charm of her perfect day with Jack had been snatched from her, leaving her bewildered and pained, faced with the wealthy lord her handsome secretary had suddenly become.

"That doesn't matter!" she cried. "How can you come here now and—and . . ." Words failed her. She had none to express what she was feeling. She stepped away again, pressing her hands to her queasy stomach.

"Emma, please, listen to me! This is not what you think. Sit down on this bench here, and listen to me." He moved toward her, his hands outstretched, reaching for her.

Emma didn't want him to touch her, not right now, not like this. "No!" She took another, larger step back. Unfortunately, she had forgotten the potted topiary behind her. She barely felt the edge of its stone container at the back of her knees before she toppled backward into its sharp, leafy embrace.

The clatter of the stone, the sharp sound of rending fabric filled her ears, and pain shot from her arm when it collided with the terrace. She screamed, startled.

"Emma!" Jack shouted, his voice echoing as if coming from a long way away. He knelt beside her, gathering her into his arms. "Are you hurt?"

He half-pulled her to a sitting position. She felt a rush of cool air against her leg, bare where the skirt had torn. She looked down and saw her white silk stocking and pink garter.

"What has happened? I heard a crash!"

Emma twisted around in Jack's arms and saw their hostess, Lady Hertford, standing in the open doorway to the ballroom. Her face was shocked but also somehow—thrilled.

Other guests crowded in behind her to see what was happening. Emma felt frozen, unable to move, unable to think, unable even to comprehend the depth of what was happening. She was sprawled across the terrace in Jack's embrace, her gown torn, in front of everyone who mattered, both here and in Russia. And all she could think was that Natasha would be unhappy that her careful coiffure was ruined.

As she looked, an arm in a green uniform sleeve reached out and gently moved Lady Hertford to one side. Her Uncle Nicholas stepped to the front of the crowd.

Emma had seen her uncle stern, had heard his infrequent lectures. Despite his affection for her, he had never been one to let her little contretemps go without punishment, as Aunt Lydia sometimes did. Yet she had never seen him as he was at this moment, completely expressionless, his face gray. Like a statue—a vengeful statue.

Emma's frozen limbs were finally able to move. She struggled to stand, hardly aware of Jack's touch as he helped her. "Uncle Nicholas! I never meant to . . ." she began. But her throat closed when he merely flicked her one glance before turning the full force of his glare onto Jack.

Nicholas's right hand reached for his left and pulled off his glove. He flung the white kid into Jack's face.

Jack flinched, but he did not turn away from Nicholas, nor did he move. He still stood there, his arm around Emma.

The crowd gaped in rapt silence.

As did Emma. She found her mouth was open in shock, but her mind could not command her muscles to close it. This whole scene was moving from bad to horrible, and she did not know how to stop it. She was glad of Jack's arm, or surely she would have fallen.

"You have insulted my niece," Nicholas said, his voice icy. "My seconds will call on yours."

A duel? This could not be! "No, Uncle Nicholas!" Emma cried. She tried to step forward, but Jack's arm tightened.

"I will meet you, Count Suvarov, if that is your wish," Jack said. Emma wondered wildly how he could sound so very calm in the midst of a disintegrating world. "But I feel I must tell you that I have just asked Lady Emma to be my wife, and she has consented. We were on our way to seek your permission, when unfortunately Lady Emma lost her balance and fell over this plant. I am sorry for the awkward circumstances, but we are very happy and beg for your consent."

Nicholas's stony expression cracked just a fraction. He turned to Emma. "Is this true, Emma? Have you consented to marry this—young man?"

Jack bowed. "I am Viscount St. Albans, Count Suvarov. I am sorry we have not truly met before."

Nicholas did not look away from his niece. "Well, Emma?"

Emma hardly knew what to say. Marriage? To Jack?

She stared wildly from Jack to her uncle, trying to find words, *any* words.

They had all fled, though, and all that came out from her throat was, "Um—argh."

The crowd parted a bit, and Aunt Lydia swept through, her head held high. She stopped next to her husband, her gaze sweeping over the assembled players. Beside her were Lord and Lady Osborn. Lady Osborn seemed horrified by the attention focused on her family, but Lord Osborn seemed—triumphant. Even though he tried to hide it with a suitably stern expression.

"Well," said Lydia, placing her hand lightly on Nicholas's arm. "What is this I hear of a betrothal?"

Jack looked out boldly at all his audience, his arm tight around Emma's shoulders. He tried to appear cool and disdainful, as if he had planned this entire scene and things were progressing exactly as he wished. As if he had meant all along to become betrothed tonight.

The truth, of course, was that he had had no idea what would happen when he saw Emma again. Usually he greatly enjoyed designing plans and stratagems, as he had when he was in the army, but tonight all he had known was that he must see her again. Nothing beyond that. Nothing like what was happening to them now.

He had thought he would never marry, or at least not for a long while, after the situation England was in had stabilized and he was no longer needed for Mr. Thompson's work. But standing here now, with Emma at his side, facing the world together, felt so very *right*. It felt the way things should be, as strange as that was.

Jack tightened his hand on Emma's shoulder and felt it tremble as if she was chilled. He glanced down at her and saw that her face reflected none of his own surprised gladness. She was as white as her pearls and stared at her uncle with an unreadable expression.

Jack frowned and looked at Count Suvarov. The man appeared a fraction less infuriated after Jack's announcement of an engagement but no less stern or unbending.

His wife also watched the scene with narrowed, suspicious eyes. She seemed poised to swoop in and rescue her niece from his evil clutches.

He would not let that happen. Now that he had seen Emma again, he could not let her go. They could make a betrothal, a marriage, work. If he only had time to think of a plan.

If only he could talk to Emma alone.

That was not going to be possible just yet, though. "Countess Suvarova," he said, bowing to Emma's aunt and giving her what he hoped was a charming smile and *not* a pained grimace. "It is true that I have the great honor of begging for your niece's hand in marriage."

"Do you, indeed?" the countess said coolly. "And who might *you* be?"

Jack's father stepped forward with a jovial laugh. "This is my son, Countess! The Viscount St. Albans."

"The son you have been telling us such glowing tales of?" Countess Suvarova said, with a disdainful little sniff that said exactly what she thought of *those* tales.

Jack thought it best if this little farce ended. He slid his hand down to Emma's elbow and led her closer to her uncle. She moved stiffly, like a marionette, still not looking at him.

"Count Suvarov," he said, "is there someplace where we might have a more private conversation?"

"I think that would be in order," answered the count.

"You may use the library," Lady Hertford offered. Her face was shining; this ball was obviously turning out to be even more exciting than she had hoped. "I will show you the direction, and my servants will make certain you are not disturbed."

"Thank you, Lady Hertford." The count followed her into the ballroom, not glancing back to see if Jack followed.

Countess Suvarova took Emma's other arm and drew her, gently but inexorably, away from Jack. Emma went to her with that same dreamlike stiffness. "Come with me, Emma," she said. "We will find the ladies' withdraw-

ing room and see what can be done to repair your skirt."
She turned her basilisk stare onto Jack again. "I believe
my husband is expecting you—Lord St. Albans." Her
tone managed to be polite yet convey doubt that that
was indeed his name.

"Of course, Countess." He bowed to her again and
watched as she led Emma into the house. Jack's own
mother trailed behind them, her hands fluttering
uncertainly.

His father stepped up to him and clapped him heartily
on the back. "Congratulations, m'boy! I knew that given
time, you would find the right lady."

Jack gave him a quelling look and went to follow Count
Suvarov. Just inside the ballroom doors, a cold prickle, just
like the tip of an iceberg, touched the back of his neck.
He had often had that feeling, that inkling of some sixth
sense, in Spain. It meant that something was not right.

He touched the chill spot on his neck and glanced
over his shoulder. Standing near the glass doors, halfway
behind one of the flower arrangements, was Sir Jeremy
Ashbey. And he stared at Jack with a coldness and a
hatred Jack had never encountered before, not even in
battle when he stood bayonet to bayonet with a French-
man. Jack's hand reached instinctively to his side, feeling
for a sword that was not there.

Jack wondered if the man was mad. Anyone would be
angry at losing a woman like Emma, of course, but that
stare spoke of something more, something unfathomable.

Sir Jeremy took a step back and melted away into the
milling crowd. The chill faded from Jack's skin, but he
still felt unsettled deep in his gut.

There was nothing he could do right now about Sir
Jeremy, though. He had to settle a betrothal. He turned
away and moved out of the ballroom into the silent darkness of Lady Hertford's library.

Count Suvarov waited for him there.

Betrothed!
Sir Jeremy Ashbey stared after St. Albans and Lady

Emma as they left the terrace, surrounded by shocked and titillated crowds. He would have followed, too, but he felt frozen in place, unable to move an inch or even arrange his facial expression into suitably bland and uninterested lines.

That—that bastard had announced he was engaged to Lady Emma. Yet, that could not possibly be! She was engaged—or as good as engaged—to Jeremy. She had been meant to be his ever since they were children! He had waited patiently for her these many years, had laid the careful groundwork by attempting to befriend her powerful uncle.

Now someone else, someone who could have known her for only a day or two, had swooped in and stolen her from beneath Jeremy's very eyes.

Stolen her.

How come fortune smiled so on men like St. Albans and left steady, faithful men like himself behind? First his father's death, then his mother's illness and now this. Emma had been so close to his grasp. On their drive in the park, he had seen the fondness in her eyes before perfect maidenly modesty made her turn away. They had been so close until *this*.

It could not be borne. It *would* not be borne!

His feet unfroze at last, and he whirled about to follow St. Albans into the house.

Chapter Fifteen

The ladies' withdrawing room was blessedly empty when Aunt Lydia shepherded Emma into it. All the chattering, primping young women had fled to the ballroom, to dance, talk—and giggle over the sensation of Lady Emma Weston's very sudden betrothal.

Lady Emma Weston herself would like to have had the time to consider that betrothal, she thought, but that would have to wait until she was alone in her own hotel chamber. Right now, she had to face her aunt.

Emma sank down onto a white satin settee and watched as Aunt Lydia locked the door behind her. She strode over to one of the mirrors and proceeded to straighten her skirt and her sapphire necklace, her movements jerking. Emma *hated* this suspense. It made her stomach churn and her palms itch. What was going to happen? What was her aunt going to say?

Was she *truly* betrothed to Jack, who suddenly was not just her Jack but a *viscount*? And how did she feel about that? Was she still angry at his ridiculous deception?

Was she—happy about it?

The uncertainty made her stomach churn even more. For something to do, so that she would not have to look at her aunt, she stripped off her gloves and laid them over her lap, smoothing them and folding them.

The silence stretched on and on, thick in the perfumed, candlelit air. It startled Emma so much that she dropped

her gloves when Lydia said, "What happened, Emma?
And how do you know this Lord St. Albans so—
intimately?"

Emma, who started to reach down to pick up the
gloves, snapped up straight. She opened her mouth, then
closed it again. She did not know what to say. Should
she make up some tale? What could it be?

"Do not try to tell me that you just met him this evening, because that will not wash," Lydia said. "I saw the
way you watched him. Yet Lord Osborn says his son
rarely accompanies them to social events. *Respectable*
events."

Emma stared down at the now crumpled gloves and
swallowed hard past the dry lump in her throat. "I met
him when I—went out the other day."

"What?" Lydia whirled from the mirror to stare directly at Emma. "Why did you not tell me you had a
titled escort that day? Why did you not introduce him
to your uncle and me? I would have thanked him for
keeping my heedless niece safe!"

Emma shook her head. "It was not like that! I did not
know he was a viscount. I thought he was . . ."

"Was what?" Lydia asked, when Emma faltered.

"A secretary," Emma whispered. She peeped up at
her aunt carefully.

Shock froze Lydia's elegant features. "Do you mean
to say that this young man was out on the streets masquer-
ading as a *secretary?*"

Emma nodded. Now all the truth was out—or most of
it, anyway. Her aunt was sure to forbid the betrothal.
Emma was still mad at Jack, to be sure, but she did not
necessarily want their connection severed. Not until she
had had time to think, time to speak with him again,
alone. Time to sort through all her jumble of strange
feelings.

She almost expected her aunt to scold or shout. She
did *not* expect her to burst into laughter, yet that was
exactly what happened. Lydia covered her mouth with

her gloved hand, but still the laughter came, a great, rushing river of mirth.

Emma stared at her in utter amazement. She had been working herself up to defend Jack, to argue for giving him a chance. But she did not know how to respond to laughter. She did not even know *why* her aunt was laughing.

Or when she would stop.

Finally, Lydia's laughter faded to giggles. She dabbed at her eyes and came to sit down on the settee beside Emma. "Ah, my dear," she said. "You do look surprised. I confess, I am surprised myself."

"Then why are you laughing, Aunt Lydia?"

"Because, from your tale of Lord St. Albans's masquerade, I suspect he may be a perfect match for you. Or very close to it."

Emma had not thought it possible for her shock to increase, yet so it did. A perfect match? She stared speechless at her aunt.

"Oh, I am not saying he is *definitely* the man for you," Lydia continued. "We will have to talk to him further and be certain this is right. But I had begun to fear you would never meet anyone who could understand your flights of fancy, could appreciate your true worth." She laughed again. "It sounds as if Viscount St. Albans has his own—flights of fancy. Do you like him?"

Like him? Emma was furious with him, but . . . "Oh, yes. I like him."

"Yes. I can see that you do." Lydia reached over to take Emma's hand.

"I know that you had hopes for Sir Jeremy Ashbey," Emma said.

Lydia squeezed her hand. "He seemed nice and very suitable. Your uncle and I would never have pushed you into a match you did not care for, and I saw rather quickly that Sir Jeremy was not right for you. The viscount is just as suitable, certainly, but I do want to speak to him before anything is definitely decided. And you must do some careful thinking as well, yes?"

Emma nodded.

Her aunt sighed. "It is just too bad we have so little time. We must return to Russia in just a few days."

Just a few days—and her life would have to change, no matter what she decided. She pressed her hand to her throbbing temple.

"Poor Emma. You look so tired," Lydia said. "Well, you do not have to get married tonight. First things first. We should find some thread to sew up your skirt."

A soft knock sounded at the door, so quiet that they almost did not hear it.

"Yes?" Lydia called.

"It—it is Lady Osborn," a tentative voice answered. "I came to see if perhaps you needed some—assistance?"

"Your future mother-in-law, perhaps?" Aunt Lydia whispered teasingly, before she went to unlock the door.

Emma gaped at her. Her aunt was many things, but a tease was seldom one of them. Could this evening possibly grow any more odd?

Lady Osborn slipped into the room like a tiny, pale green silk-clad ghost and closed the door behind her, shutting out the staring girls who lingered in the corridor. "Is everything—quite all right?" she asked. Her blue eyes, so very like her son's, were wide as she looked from Emma to Lydia and back again.

"Oh, yes, Lady Osborn, quite all right, indeed. I was just finding some thread to repair my niece's skirt." Lydia linked her arm with Lady Osborn's and led her over to the settee. "I am so glad we have this opportunity to get to know one another."

After the tumult of the party, the crowds of people, the stares of avid scandalmongers, the library seemed to hold the dark hush of a temple—or a tomb. Only one lamp was lit. Placed on the desk, it threw the rest of the high-ceilinged room into flickering shadows.

Jack stood with his back against a shelf, out of habit not leaving himself vulnerable. He liked to see everything before him. Obviously Count Suvarov felt the same. He seated himself behind the desk, quite as if he owned it, and stared at Jack across the expanse of the room.

The silence was dense, thick as a London fog, but Jack was reluctant to be the one to break it. He had the sense that this situation was very delicate, and he feared doing the wrong thing, bringing an erroneous conclusion to the situation. That he did not want to do.

Now that the initial shock of the idea of matrimony had worn away, he knew the idea of having Emma Weston as his wife was a far from repugnant one. In fact, it was quite the opposite.

He knew his family and Society always expected him to marry. Yet, it had been impossible for him to envision marriage fitting into his life, his work. With Emma, he *could* see it. All too easily, despite the difficulties. Those would have to be worked out later, of course. Right now, all he could see was this particular obstacle.

Emma's uncle—who looked as if he would prefer to run Jack through with his sword rather than see him married to Emma.

Jack wondered if he knew anything of his niece's adventures as Tonya, the lady's maid. He rather doubted it, for if the count *did* know, then surely he, Jack, would no longer be breathing.

He decided that perhaps his best course was simply to wait. He did not have to wait for long.

Count Suvarov folded his hands atop the desk and said, "So, Lord St. Albans. What exactly happened this evening?"

Jack folded his own arms and answered, "Lady Emma's gown tearing was a complete accident, Count, I assure you. She fell over the plant, and I was helping her up when—well, when everyone found us there. I would never insult your niece. I hold her in great esteem."

"Do you, indeed?" The count's face was utterly expressionless. "That esteem could not have been of long duration."

Jack thought fast. "No. I met her at the reception at Lady Bransley's, and then in the park. I have not had as much time with her as I would have liked, which is why I welcomed the chance to talk to her on the terrace this evening. But I do assure you that my regard for her is genuine."

"So genuine that you proposed to her as soon as you saw her on that terrace?"

Jack hesitated at that, and the count saw it. "The proposal, then, came *after* your discovery together," he said.

"Yes," Jack admitted. "But that makes it no less sincere. I would be greatly honored if Lady Emma would be my wife."

Count Suvarov studied him very closely for a long, silent moment. Seemingly satisfied at whatever he saw there, he nodded and leaned back in his chair. "Her aunt and I did have some hopes that she might meet someone suitable here in England. She is English, you know, and my wife thought her late sister, Emma's mother, would prefer her to have an English husband. But you are not exactly what we had in mind."

"I realize this is quite a surprise . . ."

The count snorted. "Surprise, indeed!"

Jack couldn't help but grin. Despite the acute discomfort of the situation, he found he rather like Count Suvarov. It was obvious that the man cared for Emma as he would have his own daughter. "But I do have my own credentials. I am a viscount, and one day I will inherit an earldom. My family is wealthy, we have many estates and Lady Emma would be able to live anywhere, in any style she chose."

"And you fought very bravely, some might even say recklessly, in Spain."

That *did* surprise Jack. He stared at the count.

Count Suvarov shrugged. "I know a great deal about many people, especially people involved in the military. We were fighting the same enemy in Russia, you know."

"Yes," Jack answered quietly. "I know."

"You still have not sold your commission, yet you cavort about London like some young pup, I hear. Drinking with young Bertie Stonewich, gambling, not wearing your uniform. Curious." The count's eyes narrowed. "You also deliver papers to my office here dressed in very plain attire. Papers from a certain—Mr. Thompson."

Jack remained silent. What could he really answer to that? He had no glib lies, and Count Suvarov deserved better than that. He was a brave man, a man devoted to duty and his own work. But Jack could not tell him the full truth, either.

"Well, this is not the place to discuss these things in any great depth," Count Suvarov said. "I must think on them and speak to my niece. Yet, we are to leave in only a few days, so of course there is not much time to tarry. Perhaps you would be so good as to call on us at the Pulteney Hotel tomorrow, Lord St. Albans?"

Jack nodded warily. Was this, then, a positive outcome to his proposed engagement? Usually he was quite good at reading people, but Count Suvarov's years in imperial service had stood him in good stead. His face was a blank. "It would be my honor," Jack answered.

"Excellent. Until tomorrow, then."

Effectively dismissed, Jack left the library, daring to relax a bit only when he was alone in the corridor. Blessedly, no one waited for him. Faint strains of music could be heard from the distant ballroom, so at least people were going on with their merriment and perhaps forgetting the scene on the terrace.

At least until tomorrow, when they would be looking for the announcement of his betrothal in the papers.

Jack started to walk away from the door, only to realize that he was not alone in the dim corridor. A figure moved out of the shadows and stepped into a narrow beam of lamplight.

Sir Jeremy Ashbey. Jack remembered how the man had been seen escorting Emma about, how he would watch her with an almost proprietary solicitude. He had forgotten until this moment that Emma had had an admirer besides himself.

But he remembered now.

Sir Jeremy's expression was cool and unreadable, one could almost say impassive. But his pale eyes burned as he stared unwaveringly at Jack. He made no move once he came to a halt a few feet away, yet somehow Jack yearned for his sword.

Sir Jeremy reminded him of a French officer he had encountered once, a cold, expressionless man who would have tortured and killed Jack with no compunction at all. If Jack had not killed him first.

"I understand congratulations are in order," Ashbey said, his voice as flat as his face.

"Indeed," Jack answered shortly. He would have moved on, but Sir Jeremy slid into his path.

"My family has been friends with the Westons for a very long time. I have known Lady Emma since she was a child," Sir Jeremy said. "I hope you realize what a truly fortunate man you are and do not take that good fortune for granted."

"Of course I do not," said Jack tightly. He wondered if he was going to be forced to do battle with only one of Lady Hertford's spindly gilt chairs as a weapon.

But Ashbey moved, melting back into the shadows. Jack went on his way, still feeling the chill on his skin from that icicle gaze.

That was certainly a man who would bear watching, he thought, before he forgot all about Jeremy Ashbey in the shower of good wishes heaped upon him by the crowd in the ballroom.

Later that night, when she was at last alone with her husband, Lydia asked him what she had been aching to ask all during the silent drive back to the hotel but had been unable to because of Emma's silent presence.

"Well?" she said, pulling a brush through her loosened

hair. "What did you think of Lord St. Albans? What did you say to him?"

Nicholas gave an unreadable little laugh. "A most interesting young man, my darling. Most interesting."

Lydia sighed impatiently. "Interesting in what way?"

"Interesting in that he might possibly, just possibly, be a proper match for our Emma. They seem to share a, shall we say, impulsive nature? A foolish bravery. I have asked him to meet with us here tomorrow."

Lydia spun around on her dressing table bench to face her husband squarely. "And?"

"And—if a betrothal agreement is drawn up . . ."

"A betrothal agreement!"

Nicholas held up his hand. "I said *if,* darling. We will have to see that a very generous settlement is made on our niece and pay particular attention to her widow's portion."

Lydia was thoroughly confused. "Widow's portion? Emma is not even a bride yet!"

"It is merely a precaution. That impulsive nature, you know. It can be a grand, passionate thing. But it can also be quite dangerous indeed. It would never do for dearest Emma to find herself stranded alone in a country far from us, with no resources."

Chapter Sixteen

"Just look at the lovely flowers that came for you this morning, my lady!" Natasha said happily. She carefully placed the breakfast tray across Emma's knees.

Arranged neatly on the tray's japanned surface was a pot of chocolate, a dainty cup and saucer, a plate of toast and a small nosegay of yellow rosebuds and sprigs of dried lavender. They were bound by a wide swath of purple ribbon, under which was tucked a note.

Emma unfolded the paper and read written there, in a bold, black scrawl, "Dare I hope that you will favor me with a short walk this morning? Your uncle has granted his permission. We have much to talk about. Your penitent Jack."

She stared down at the note until the black ink blurred before her eyes, running into an endless, incoherent dark river.

Much to talk about, indeed.

Her life had changed so completely last night, so irrevocably. She had found her Jack again, yet he had not been at all what she had thought. And no sooner had she discovered that than they found themselves betrothed! Her head still spun when she thought of it. After a night spent sleepless, turning things over in her mind and trying to find a solution, she knew nothing at all. She did not even know her own feelings.

Jack wanted to meet with her. She wanted to see him, too. There was so very much she wanted to ask him,

explanations she must have. But how would she act with
him? How would *he* act around *her*? After all, despite
the wondrous day they had shared, they were really
strangers. What would Lady Emma Weston say to Viscount St. Albans?

They were supposed to be betrothed. If she had found
herself betrothed to the Jack who danced with her in
the light from the illuminations, she would be wild with
happiness. She was not so sure about the viscount. Her
anger over his deception had faded, leaving her just—
confused.

But even though her world had turned tip-over-tail,
the routine of life went on around her, seemingly oblivious to her turmoil. Natasha opened the draperies, letting
in the pale yellow light of morning, and proceeded to
open up the wardrobe and plan Emma's attire for the
day.

"Now, what would you like to wear this morning, my
lady?" she asked, riffling through the jumble of muslins
and silks. "What is on your schedule for this morning?"

"Schedule?" Emma left off her ruminations on Jack
to consider this most mundane subject. "I am not sure
what we must do today . . ."

As if summoned by that magical incantation "schedule," Madame Ana entered the chamber after a quick
knock at the door. Despite the early hour, she was immaculately dressed in her black silk gown with its narrow
white lace collar. Her dark hair was as usual drawn back
into a neat knot, her spectacles perched on her nose, a
neatly penned list in her hands.

As always, Madame Ana made Emma want to sit up
straighter and smooth her hair down. In the force of her
fierce efficiency, Emma always forgot that Madame Ana
was only a few years older than herself. No wonder Aunt
Lydia found her indispensable in organizing the family's
social calendar.

"Your aunt asked me to inform you of today's activi-
ties, Lady Emma," she said.

"Er—yes, of course." An activity list. If she had had

any doubt that dutiful life went on even in the face of surprise betrothals, the list ended them. How she hated lists! She wanted to throw them in the fire and never think of them again.

To cover her fit of pique, she carefully poured out a cup of chocolate and sipped at it.

"The morning is curiously blank," Madame Ana said. "But after luncheon there is an afternoon musicale and tea with Princess Charlotte. Then, there is a supper . . ."

And on it went. A ball, dancing with Lord So and So and Sir Something or Other, the white muslin gown and pearls. She nodded, as if paying the utmost attention, but in reality, her mind was flying free on the clouds of a daydream. If she was a married woman, she could do as she liked. She could be done with lists forever!

She envisioned a country house, with comfortable rooms and pretty gardens. Near enough to a town to have company, but not with so many neighbors that there would be a surfeit of social engagements. There could be small suppers with friends, quiet evenings with books and cards and conversations. One day, there would be children to run and play in those gardens.

It was a lovely picture. But it would truly only be complete with *Jack* to share it with.

The empty cup clattered down onto the tray as Emma dropped it in surprise at the truth she had so idly uncovered.

She could, just possibly, have a chance here to make these visions true. The Jack she had met was buried somewhere beneath the viscount. He *had* to be. Surely it could not all have been a lie. Surely not.

She had to talk to him, to hear what he thought of their odd betrothal, what he said about his deception—and hers. Only then could some of the fog lift from her thoughts and let her make a decision.

She moved aside the tray and said, "Natasha, help me up! I must bathe and dress."

"Surely there is no hurry, Emma dear," Emma heard her aunt's voice say. Lydia stepped into the room next to Madame Ana, already dressed for the morning in a pale fawn-colored muslin gown and Indian shawl. "It is still early. Thank you, Madame Ana and Natasha—may I have a few words alone with my niece?"

Natasha and Madame Ana curtsied and withdrew, closing the chamber door behind them. Aunt Lydia came and sat down on the edge of the bed, pulling the bedclothes tight along Emma's legs. "You have not eaten even your toast."

Emma looked down at the plate of buttered bread, feeling as if she had truly never seen it before and had no idea what it was for. "I am not very hungry."

Lydia nodded. "I was just the same when I first met your uncle. Never hungry at all. Are your flowers from Lord St. Albans?"

"Yes." Emma touched one of the velvety rosebuds with her fingertip.

"Very pretty. Nicholas says you may go for a short walk with him, but there is no need for you to hurry. Better to make him wait for a bit when he gets here."

Emma bit her lip. "Does that mean that Uncle Nicholas—approves of Lord St. Albans?" That title still felt odd on her tongue, like the name of a stranger.

"Well, that all depends."

"Depends on what?"

"On what you think of him, my dear. I have not told your uncle of your little adventure the other day, but I have said you might look at the viscount with a favorable eye. Nicholas seems to know a great deal about Lord St. Albans. I must say he does have some reservations, but he would not stand in your way."

"Oh, Aunt Lydia!" Emma threw her arms around her aunt's neck in an exuberant burst of hope. "I will meet with Lord St. Albans this morning, and then I will know what I should do."

Lydia stroked her hair gently and kissed her cheek. "My dear, it seems only yesterday that you were a tiny little girl, getting your frocks all dirty playing in the puddles. Now you are thinking of marriage."

Marriage. The very word was thrilling and strange, and—and frightening. Made even more frightening by the odd note of sadness in her aunt's voice. She clung to her more tightly, but Lydia just kissed her again and said, "Come now, dear. What would you like to wear this morning? The lavender muslin?"

Jack sat at his own breakfast table, the rolls brought in from a nearby bakery untouched, the coffee barely sipped and becoming cold. He was too busy making his way through the morning post to eat.

Usually he received only perhaps two or three letters, but today there was a veritable deluge. News, particularly news with the hint of possible scandal about it, traveled fast in the *haut ton*. There were notes from old friends he had not seen since coming back to England, relatives he had forgotten he possessed, all expressing congratulations. And this was just from the ones who were in London—surely the country-based relatives would write soon enough.

There was a message from his colonel and one from Mr. Thompson asking, nay, demanding, an appointment. Count Suvarov wrote with his permission for Jack to call on his niece and yet another demand for an appointment. His father asked that he bring his betrothed to their town house for supper.

Jack shuffled all the missives into an untidy pile. Mr. Thompson would have to be answered with alacrity, as would Count Suvarov and his father. The relatives who were clearly dangling for a wedding invitation would just have to be disappointed. The ceremony would be a very small affair.

The ceremony! The wedding. His wedding.

Jack groaned aloud and ran his hand through his already disordered hair. Everything had been moving at such a hell-for-leather pace that all practical matters had simply slipped his mind. Things such as special licenses, wedding trips, settlements and a place he could bring a bride to live. Here, in his rooms?

He gazed about at the plain, comfortable sitting room that had served him so well. He saw Emma as she had appeared there during their day out, sitting in his armchair, her dainty feet up on his footstool. She had seemed quite comfortable there, quite at home. But surely her aunt and uncle would insist she have a proper town house. His parents would probably want them to come and live at Howard House with them, but *that* was out of the question. Ah, well, they could decide all that after the wedding trip, if there was time for a trip. He would know more after he spoke with Mr. Thompson.

Jack laughed at himself. How quickly he had gone from thinking he would never wed to planning things such as licenses and homes. All because of a dark-eyed fairy princess.

A knock sounded at the door, forcing Jack to abandon his ruminations for the time being. "Come in!" he called.

Bertie stepped into the sitting room, perfectly turned out in his green coat and gray trousers, hat and walking stick tucked beneath his arm. "Well, good morning, Lord St. Albans," he greeted, with an ironic formality. "I understand congratulations are in order."

"Well, well. News does indeed travel quickly. I have not even met with her uncle yet to finalize the arrangements."

"I was at Lady Hertford's, too, remember." Bertie helped himself to a cup of coffee and sprawled out in the same chair where Emma had sat. "I saw the entire, er, romantic scene, albeit from a distance. The lady did not appear too happy to discover your true identity."

"She will understand, once we have had a chance to speak alone." Surely she would.

"She will, eh? Well, I wish you both happy." Bertie swallowed the last of his coffee and put the empty cup on the table next to Jack's books. "Mr. Thompson wants to see us this afternoon. Did you get his message?"

"Hm. No doubt he wants to know how the work is progressing. And to offer his own congratulations, I am sure."

"And to ask if you will be able to continue, once you are in possession of your blushing bride."

Jack gave his friend a hard glance. "Of course I will continue. Why would I not? The situation is far from secure. And Emma will know nothing about it."

He would make very certain of that. Emma would be protected, no matter what he had to do or what lies she had to be told. Once she was his, he would be certain that she was always safe, that his work could never touch her.

Chapter Seventeen

"*L*ord St. Albans is here for you, my lady," Madame Ana announced. "He is waiting for you downstairs in the small salon."

Emma's throat suddenly went dry at the message. He was here, waiting for her. She could not turn away from the mirror, though, where she watched Natasha putting the final touches to her coiffure, nor did her expression change. She was too well trained for that, now that the initial shock of learning Jack's identity had passed. "Thank you, Madame Ana. I will be there in a moment."

Madame Ana nodded and rustled out of the room again, busily going on her way to another errand. For that moment, Emma envied her. She knew where she was supposed to be, what she was meant to be doing in the next five minutes, the next hour, the next month. Emma had no idea where her own life was going. It was careening out of control like a runaway carriage, bearing her to who knew where.

She had always hated the lists. Now she almost wished she had one, one that told her how to behave, how to think, when faced with a would-be fiancé who had turned from a secretary to a viscount in the blink of an eye.

Natasha handed her her bonnet, and Emma put it on her head and tied the lavender and white ribbons in a jaunty bow beneath her left ear. That she *did* know how to do.

She left the mirror and picked up her gloves and reticule. She draped a lacy white shawl over her shoulders. Then, thinking of nothing else she could contrive to do, she moved slowly to the door. Part of her wanted to run down the stairs to him; part of her felt like she was walking to the gallows.

"I will be back before luncheon," she told Natasha.

Natasha giggled, her face suffused with delight, as if she was witnessing a romantic play or opera. Emma was glad *someone* took unalloyed pleasure in these odd proceedings. "Yes, my lady," Natasha said.

Emma nodded and left the chamber, moving along the corridor and down the staircase toward the small salon. She had the same strange dreamlike feelings that had enveloped her ever since she met Jack at the ball. Things had a slow, misty quality about them. She wondered if it was ever going to end, or if this was her life from now on—one big walking dream.

She pushed open the door to the salon, not exactly sure what to expect, Jack or the viscount. It appeared to be the viscount, fashionably clad and bearing a bouquet of more yellow roses. But the smile he gave her was entirely Jack, a wide, white, crooked slash of a grin.

It soothed her, reassured her, yet at the same time made her stomach jump in nervous anticipation. Such a paradox.

Only as she moved toward him, seeking that smile, craving it, did she see that he was not alone. Her aunt and uncle stood behind him. They were perfectly expressionless, Aunt Lydia seated in a high-backed chair with her hands folded in her lap, Uncle Nicholas standing beside her.

"Good morning, Lord St. Albans," Emma greeted, the title still sounding strange and foreign in her ears.

Jack, still smiling, came to her and lifted her hand to his lips. She had not yet put on her lace gloves, and he did not just politely bow over her hand. His kiss landed on her bare skin, warm and soft. "Good morning, Lady Emma. You are looking very lovely today." He held out the bouquet to her.

"Thank you," she managed to murmur. She took the flowers, and inhaled their sweet fragrance to give her a moment to compose herself after his kiss. She had to remember who she was, what the situation was, and not make a schoolgirl fool of herself.

"We have told Lord St. Albans he may take you for a short walk," Uncle Nicholas said. "But do not forget we have a luncheon engagement."

"No, of course not, Uncle," answered Emma.

"You can see some of the celebrations, as you have said you wanted to do," added Aunt Lydia.

"Shall we, then?" Jack offered her his arm.

Emma stared at his dark blue superfine sleeve for a second before carefully sliding her hand into the crook of his elbow. Beneath the expensive cloth, he felt just like Jack the secretary—strong, hard-muscled, warm. The sort of arm that could always support her, always keep her safe.

She handed her flowers to a housemaid who waited just outside the door and walked with Jack to the front door of the hotel. No servants' entrance for them today. They were silent as they walked, their steps perfectly matched, their movements coordinated as Emma shifted to pull on her gloves. It was almost as if they were one of those long married couples who had nothing left to talk about but who knew the rhythms of each other's walks perfectly. Who could communicate with a glance, a gesture.

Of course, though, the truth was they knew almost nothing about each other. Emma knew how his lips felt on hers, the scent of his skin, the silk of his hair. She did not know about his family, his friends, his past, his hopes for the future.

That would have to change, and soon. They did not have very much time before they wed.

As they passed through the hotel's grand vestibule, a figure suddenly appeared before them, as if materializing from the very air. It was Sir Jeremy Ashbey. His expression was everything that was polite, but his hair was, for once, not perfectly dressed, his cravat tied ever so slightly askew. And his eyes—Emma took an involuntary little step backward when his gaze met hers. She had never seen a look so very *cold* before.

Jack covered her hand with his, holding her at his side. "Sir Jeremy. Good morning." Jack's voice was also all that was polite, but there was a strength, a warning, in its brandied depths.

"Good morning," Sir Jeremy answered. His stare never left Emma. "I understand I must wish you both happy."

Emma moistened her dry lips with the tip of her tongue and flicked a glance at Jack. He was smiling amiably, yet the tense feel of his arm told her he was prepared for any eventuality. She was deeply glad of his solid presence beside her. "Th-thank you very much, Sir Jeremy," she said.

"Indeed, Sir Jeremy," Jack added. "That is very kind of you."

"Any man would be fortunate to win Lady Emma. I hope you realize the true depth of your fortune, Lord St. Albans. Such gifts are rare and fragile," Sir Jeremy said, in an odd high-pitched tone. "Very fragile."

"Oh, I do realize it. At every moment." With another nod, Jack tugged lightly on Emma's arm and led her out of the hotel into the sunshine and fresh air of the summer's morning. Emma filled her lungs with it, with the life that surged around them. Just as it had the last time they were alone in the city. Emma could feel her heart stir tentatively within her, in a faint echo of her feelings on that other day.

There must be hope for her yet.

Sir Jeremy, her aunt and uncle, Lord and Lady Osborn, they were almost forgotten in that sweet stir. Almost.

Jack shot a quick glance behind them before steering her into the ebb and flow of the pedestrians. "Odd chap, that Ashbey."

"Hm? Oh, yes, Sir Jeremy. He is. A very odd chap."

"I understand he had some—hopes of you."

Emma looked at Jack in surprise. Surely Sir Jeremy's courtship, only in its infancy, had not been as noticeable as all that. "Perhaps he did, though they were unfounded. How did you hear of that?"

Jack shrugged. "It is very hard to keep a secret here. Before you and your aunt even arrived in London, it was seen that Sir Jeremy and your uncle had struck up an acquaintance, and it was remembered that you had an estate that marches beside his family's. Then he paid marked attention to you when you got here. He seems disappointed now, though of course who could blame him?"

They turned into the park and strolled along the same pathway they had once trod as Tonya and Jack. Today, no one jostled them. Everyone moved to the side to give them a clear walkway, eyes respectfully averted. If Emma had noticed the separation, she would have hated it, but she did *not* notice. Not really. She was too busy puzzling over Sir Jeremy. "If he did have hopes, I certainly did not encourage them. We have scarcely spoken, though he says we knew each other as children. He can have no great affection for me."

"Well, you are, shall we say, a very unusual female, Lady Emma. One cannot blame him for feeling disappointed, especially if he has been dreaming of you since childhood," Jack said, in a deceptively light tone.

Emma blinked up at him, and he smiled at her as if his words were just a form of polite flirting. The smile did not reach his eyes, though, and she did not feel like smiling back. She was too nervous, too uncertain.

Their steps slowed, and they paused beneath the shade of a large tree somewhat out of the way of the bustling traffic of passersby. Nearby, a Punch and Judy show was going on, and Judy hit Punch over the head with a board, much to the shrieking delight of the children in the audience. The raucous cacophony seemed the perfect background music to the turmoil in Emma's own head and heart.

She was standing here just inches away from Jack, so close she could simply reach out and touch him. But she could not. They were as effectively separated as if there was an ocean between them. She wanted the connection, the closeness they had felt before, but she did not know how to find it. It had been so easy to relate to him when she was someone else. It was nearly impossible as Lady Emma.

Her tentative hopes for their betrothal withered inside her.

The Judy puppet shrieked and fell down to writhe on the ground of the tiny stage. Emma wished she could do the same. But that would be unseemly, of course. Most improper.

"I behaved like such a widgeon at the ball," she said, finding words to say at last. They were inadequate words, nothing to what was in her heart, but at least they were not silence. "Screaming and falling over the plant like that! What an idiot you must have thought me."

Jack shook his head, a ghost of his old smile still hovering at the corners of his mouth. "Not at all. It was my fault entirely for giving you such a shock. I should have found a better time, a better place, to reintroduce myself. I am sorry for that—and for the entire deception."

Emma placed her hand flat on the tree trunk beside her. It was rough and hard under the dainty lace of her glove, and she was glad of its solidity holding her upright. "You knew all along who I was, didn't you?"

He glanced away from her to the group of laughing children watching the denouement of the Punch and Judy show. "Yes. I saw you at the Bransley reception, though I was almost sure you would not remember me. You seemed to be—thinking of something else that evening. Something far away."

She felt her cheeks grow warm and pink at the knowledge that someone had noticed her daydreaming. "My goodness. Aunt Lydia would be angry at my impoliteness."

"You were never in the least impolite. You were always perfectly gracious. I only noticed because, well, because I *do* notice things. Alertness, being aware, is what kept me alive in the army. I cannot seem to turn that off, even at so harmless a place as a Society reception. And I have a certain tendency to drift away a bit at such functions, myself."

He gave her a conspiratorial smile, and Emma couldn't help but laugh. He looked so like a roguish little boy, caught out in some mischief.

"So, yes," he continued, the stiff set of his shoulders and back relaxing a bit at the sound of her laughter. "I did recognize you. I meant at first to tell you who I was, to escort you back to the Pulteney. But then I got caught up in your game. It was delightful; I could not help but play along."

"Did you have to, er, play along the entire day?"

"No, of course not. Yet I found myself wondering at every minute what would happen next. It was a wondrous day, Lady Emma. I think I have never had one to equal it."

Emma stared at him, astonished. She searched his face carefully for signs of deception, but all she saw was openness, a certain surprise, a trace of—was it hope? No mockery there at all. "It *was* a marvelous day," she said. "And I was fortunate that you were there to share it with me. Yet, any impropriety of that day was entirely instigated by me. You should not be punished because I chose to run away from my duties."

A tiny ripple of a frown appeared between his eyes. "What do you mean? Are you still angry with me, then?"

"No!" Emma shook her head. "I *was* angry with you at first, it is true. But the truth is, I also lied to you. My lie was the first. That is why it would be wrong of me to be angry at you. And it would also be wrong for you to spend your whole life paying for my deception."

"You are saying you do not want to marry me, then."

Oh, but sweet heaven above, I do want to marry you! Emma thought. She wanted it more than anything, wanted it in the same elemental way she had wanted her freedom on the day she ran away. It would be horrible beyond words, though, if he began to blame her for the unforeseen direction his life had taken, if they proved to be unhappy together. "I am saying that in a few days I will be going back to Russia. People here will forget all about this. It was very noble of you to offer for me . . ."

"Noble!" he interrupted, his voice a blast of indignation. He caught up her hand, pressing it between his, holding it over his heart. Even through the layers of his clothes, she could feel the beat, the urgency of it. "Damn it, Emma, I did not propose to be *noble*."

It was her turn to frown. She stared up at him, confused. "You did not?"

"No. To own the truth, that entire scene on the terrace was just an excuse I seized upon. I want you to marry me. I want to be your husband."

"You do?" Gads, her words were beginning to sound as repetitious as those of Punch and Judy, if considerably less violent. She could think of nothing else to say. A tiny white bloom of something like hope opened in her heart. Hope or maybe even something like the beginnings of love. It was all more beautiful, and more strange, than anything she could ever have imagined.

She lifted her other hand to Jack's shoulder, moving closer to him, seeking to find an answering emotion in his eyes. She saw a seriousness there and the leap of attraction when she pressed against him. It was enough— for now.

"I *do* want to marry you," he said. "But only if you want it, too. I think we could do well together, Emma. We like each other. We understand each other. And we could have a marvelous time together."

"Oh, yes," Emma breathed. "Yes. We would certainly have a marvelous time."

"Then you will marry me?"

"I will marry you, Jack."

A smile of pure delight and dazzlement broke across Jack's face, banishing the seriousness, the doubt. His arms came around her and drew her flush against him, pulling her up on her tiptoes. His lips met hers, searching, seeking, diving deep in the sudden dizzying joy of a future.

Emma reached up, her fingers moving into his hair, drawing him closer still. She knocked his hat off; it fell unheeded with a soft thud to the grass. This moment was perfect, all she could ask for, all she had ever wanted. Jack was hers, and she was his.

Applause broke out around them, and Emma stepped back from Jack. For a second, she thought the cheers were for them, but then she saw that the Punch and Judy show was ending. A few small children *did* watch Emma and Jack, and Jack scattered them with a good-natured wave of his hand and a shouted "Boo!"

Emma laughed and touched Jack's cheek with her palm. "Are we really going to marry?"

He covered her hand with his, holding her against him. "We really are. I will always try to make you happy, Emma; this I swear. And I will always be loyal to you, to our family."

Loyal? Emma would prefer faithful, but loyal would do for now. "I am happy right now. And in the future—we will just work on that when we come to it. We have so much time now, where before we had only one day!" She rested her head on his shoulder and inhaled deeply of his clean, spicy, soapy scent. "So much time."

Jack held Emma close, his cheek pressed to the top of her head. Her straw bonnet itched—it was not like the satin of her hair—but he did not move away. This moment, this pure, perfect moment, was too fleeting, and he wanted to keep it for as long as possible before it moved into the unreachable past. Soon, she would be pulled into the swirling abyss of hurried wedding preparations, the expectations of her family and his family and Society. She was his for now, though, his alone.

He had not lied when he told her he would be loyal, would always strive to make her happy. He would do everything in his power, for the rest of her life, to give her everything she wanted. There were parts of his life she could not share, could not even know about. Could never know about. He would not let that ugliness, that deception, touch the joy he saw now in her eyes. He would not let it touch their future, a future he had only just begun to hope for.

Surely he could keep them separate. He *must*.

Emma looked up at him, her eyes wide, dark-bright with the shine of tears. One had escaped and lay shimmering like a star on her cheekbone. Jack touched it with the tip of his finger, and she smiled.

"I will be a good wife to you, Jack," she said.

"I know. You will be the very best."

She nodded and rose up to kiss him again. Her lips were soft and tasted of salt, fresh air and the sweetness of hope. There was so much they needed to talk of, to plan. A wedding, perhaps a wedding trip, a place to live. But that was all far away. All they had right now, all they needed, was each other and this kiss.

It was all they ever needed.

So caught up were they in their own future, they did not notice that someone watched them, someone besides the giggling children and the now silent Punch and Judy.

Sir Jeremy Ashbey drew up his phaeton on the pathway, much to the ire of the carriage driver behind him. He had no awareness of the shouts and curses. He watched the embracing couple, listened to the faraway ring of their mingled laughter. His held his face still, expressionless, almost pleasantly distant.

But his gaze burned; his thoughts sizzled and smoked as if bathed in acid. That should have been he, holding her in his arms. She was meant to be his and had been, ever since she was a child and he had vowed to himself that he would wed her.

She was his still. The viscount would pay for touching her.

Chapter Eighteen

"Which one do you think?" Aunt Lydia asked doubtfully, fingering the hem of the gown Natasha held up, while Madame Ana took notes beside her. "Oh, how I do wish there was time to have a new gown made! But with the wedding tomorrow, I fear there is not a mantua-maker in the world who could accomplish it."

Emma stared out over the chamber from her perch on the edge of the bed. Every item of clothing from her wardrobe was spread as far as the eye could see, or at least so it seemed. Gowns, pelisses, spencers, shawls, slippers, bonnets, petticoats, even nightrails were scattered in a rainbow over the furniture and the carpet.

Of course she wished she could have a new gown, especially designed for the occasion. Of course she cared how she would appear at her wedding. Yet nothing, not even the lack of new clothes, could cloud her mood today. She felt she was walking on golden stardust, moving in a pink bubble of music. Unfortunately, this hum of contentment also meant she had a rather hard time making any decisions or even focusing on anything but airy dreams of the future.

She swung her feet and said, "I do not know. Whichever gown you think, Aunt Lydia."

Lydia gave her an exasperated glance. "You are no help whatsoever, Emma, and it is *your* wedding! Even though it is to be a small affair, we should make it as elegant as possible."

"I think all the gowns are very pretty," Lady Osborn said shyly, reminding them of her presence there. Ever since her arrival at the hotel, she had sat quietly in a chair by the dressing table, watching the proceedings from blue eyes so like her son's but without his fire and decisiveness. Spots of bright pink painted excitement on her thin cheeks. "Any of them would be lovely for a wedding."

"You are quite right, Lady Osborn!" Emma agreed. "That is why it is so difficult to make a choice."

"I wore blue at my own wedding," said Lady Osborn. "But that was so long ago. Perhaps it is not the fashion now?"

"I, too, wore blue at my wedding," Aunt Lydia answered. The militant light of plan-making in her eyes faded for a moment, replaced with the glow of remembrance. "Embroidered with pink roses. It was exquisite."

"Blue is always fashionable," said Madame Ana, always the arbiter of style, even though her own attire of black silk never changed. "And quite suitable for weddings."

Emma nodded. "Then, if you both wore blue, so will I!"

"I know just the gown," said Natasha. She reached back into the wardrobe, where only a few garments still hung, and brought out a creation of pale blue silk. It had been made to wear at a ball planned for their last night in London and had a classically pleated bodice and short cap sleeves. It was a beautiful gown and would look just right with her mother's pearls at a late afternoon wedding.

"Oh, yes," Aunt Lydia said, with an approving nod. "That will do very well. I do not know why we didn't think of it sooner. But what can you wear on your head? A bonnet with a veil would not do."

"There is my tiara," Emma said. But that did not seem terribly romantic to her. It seemed formal and stiff. If she had her way, she would marry in a meadow somewhere, with flowers tossed in her hair. She supposed the tiara would do quite well for the large drawing room in the Pulteney Hotel where the ceremony would actually take place, though.

"I brought this," Lady Osborn said, in her soft, hesitant voice. She reached into her large velvet reticule and brought out a folded square of lace. When she unfurled it, it was revealed to be a length of intricately wrought, palest ivory Belgian work with scalloped edges. "I wore it at my wedding, and my mother wore it at hers. I thought maybe you could fasten it to your tiara, or to a wreath of flowers. But perhaps it is not smart enough . . ."

Emma slid off the bed and went to take the veil in her hands. It was soft with age, lightly scented with the lavender it had been packed away in. It was elegant and perfect. "I adore it," she said. "I would be honored to wear it, Lady Osborn."

She bent to kiss Lady Osborn's cheek. She could scarcely believe that this pale creature had brought forth a being of such vividness as Jack, but Emma loved her already. She loved her for bringing this veil and for gifting Emma with her son.

Lady Osborn smiled and touched Emma's cheek with her gloved hand, tiny as a child's. "I always wanted a daughter, my dear," she whispered. "Now I shall have one. And you must call me Jane."

Lydia came over to examine the veil. "It is indeed a beautiful piece of work. You will be the most lovely bride, Emma."

Emma stared down at the veil and blinked her eyes hard, fearing she might start weeping. She was so surrounded by love and approval, like being wrapped up in a soft blanket. She had spent so much time in her life in dreams, in solitude, that for a moment so many good wishes were almost too much. She thought she might fall onto the floor and sob in a frenzy of emotion.

Even Madame Ana peered at her with misty approval from behind her spectacles.

Aunt Lydia squeezed her arm. "Are you quite all right, Emma dear?"

"Yes. Yes, I am fine. It is just—just that the veil is so nice."

Lady Osborn smiled shyly. "Then it is yours, Lady Emma. Perhaps one day you will want to give it to your own daughter."

Her own daughter? Emma had an image of a girl flash in her mind, a girl with the veil on her smooth fall of dark hair, with vivid blue eyes and a crooked smile. Her own daughter, a woman who did not yet exist but one day would, because of her. And because of Jack.

Oh, dear, she *was* getting sentimental! Sentimental and silly. What was it about weddings that brought such things out in people?

Lady Osborn dabbed at her own eyes with an embroidered handkerchief. "Oh, now I am crying! And I have made you cry, Lady Emma. I must go now, before we all become watering pots." She closed her reticule and straightened her bonnet and shawl. "Will you still join us for supper this evening at Howard House?"

"Of course, Lady Osborn—Jane," said Emma. "I am looking forward to it."

"Wonderful! I know that my husband is eager to get to know you better." Lady Osborn leaned closer and whispered, "He is a great deal of bluster, my dear, but really he is quite harmless."

Emma laughed. Lady Osborn, blushing as if she had said something enormously daring, kissed her cheek in farewell and hurried away.

Madame Ana followed, saying, "I will see you out, Lady Osborn."

Aunt Lydia sat down on Lady Osborn's abandoned chair. "Natasha, you may go now. We will ring for you when Lady Emma needs to change for supper."

"Of course, Countess." Natasha bobbed a curtsy and left the room, the blue wedding gown draped over her arm to be taken away for pressing.

The door closed behind her, and suddenly the chamber was silent, quiet and still after all the bustle of those feminine fussings. Aunt Lydia seemed as if she was intent on telling Emma something, something perhaps not entirely pleasant.

Emma wished she did not have to hear it, whatever it was. She wanted nothing to spoil this golden afternoon.

"Emma, dear," Lydia said, and patted the seat of the chair next to hers. "Sit down here for a moment. We need to have a quiet coze, just the two of us, and I do not think we will have another opportunity."

"Of course, Aunt Lydia." Emma slowly sat down on the chair next to her aunt's, smoothing her skirt across her lap.

Lydia nodded but still looked as if she was not sure how to begin what she wanted to say. Emma wondered, with a little pang of misgiving, what it could be. Were they going to forbid her to marry Jack, even after all these preparations? And what would she do if they changed their minds?

Now that she had made up her mind to have Jack for her husband, she thought she might just shrivel up and blow away if he was denied her.

That, apparently, was not what Aunt Lydia was going to say, though. She reached out to gently touch Emma's hand.

"Dear," she said. "I know I have been strict with you at times, and our lives have not always been easy. But I have loved you as my own daughter; you have been a blessing to me, and to Nicholas. We have always tried to do our best for you, as I know my sister, your mother, would have wanted."

"Oh, you have!" Emma cried. "You and Uncle Nicholas have been the best of parents to me, always."

Lydia smiled at her warmly. "I am glad you have been happy with us. I always knew this day would come, the day we would have to part from you, and I admit I have dreaded it. You seem to have found a fine young man who cares about you, though, and I could have asked for nothing more."

Emma nodded, wondering where her aunt's words were heading. What she had to tell her.

Lydia took a deep breath. "And now, in your mother's place, I want to talk to you about something. Marriage, as you know, entails many duties. You have been well taught to run a household, to take your place in Society. But there is one duty you may not know a great deal about." Lydia's stoic face looked as if it were made of marble.

Emma felt her own cheeks burn. Why, her aunt was talking of—of *the deed*. The act she had read about in books, though she had never been quite sure what it entailed. Oh, she knew the mechanics of it, vaguely but not exactly the *how*. It was something terribly secret and unimaginable, something that happened between men and women in the marriage bed. Something that surely had to do with the rush of excitement that curled her very toes whenever Jack kissed her.

She looked down at her hands, folded in her lap. "Do you mean *the deed,* Aunt Lydia?"

"The deed?" The marble of Lydia's face cracked just a bit in a tiny smile. "Well, yes. I suppose you could call it that. You know what I am talking about, then?"

"Yes. I have read about it." Emma did not add that she had her doubts about the entire procedure.

Lydia nodded. "When our mother told Lizzie and me about the—the deed before our marriages, she said that we would find it unpleasant, but that it was necessary to beget children. She said we should close our eyes and think of fat, beautiful babies, and it would all be over soon. And we should never, under any circumstances, allow our husbands to completely remove our nightdresses."

Emma was completely appalled. Stoic forbearance had nothing to do with the feelings Jack inspired in her with his kisses, his touch! Thoughts of babies and never removing her nightdress sounded dull in the extreme.

But then Aunt Lydia laughed. "My mother, though a very virtuous woman and wise in many ways, was wrong about this. It can be—most pleasant, once the first, uncomfortable time is past. Just remember that it is *not* wrong in the least. And if you ever have any questions at all, you need only write to me. Or ask Madame Ana. She is a widow, you know."

Madame Ana? Emma, jerked from curious thoughts of *the deed,* looked at her aunt. "Madame Ana? How can I ask her anything?"

"She and Natasha will stay with you, of course. You will need a great deal of help in setting up your new household."

Emma almost groaned. She had been looking forward to her new free life. Now Madame Ana was going to be watching her through those spectacles, no doubt insisting they make out lists every day and writing to her aunt of everything Emma did. "Oh, Aunt Lydia, that is so very— generous of you. But do you not need Madame Ana back in St. Petersburg?"

Aunt Lydia gave her a serene smile. "I can spare her for a few months. She is so efficient and will be a huge help to you. You will see." She stood up and kissed Emma on the cheek with the satisfied air of someone who has dispatched an irksome errand. "Now I will go and send Natasha up to you. You should be getting ready for your supper at Howard House. Remember, if you have any other questions, you need only ask."

She swept out of the chamber, leaving Emma alone in the clutter of their wedding preparations.

Questions! Truly, she was full of them. But they were nothing she could ask her aunt, and certainly not Madame Ana.

Jack stood on the doorstep of Howard House, dressed in his fine supper clothes, peering through the crowds that hurried around the square and looking for the carriage that would deliver Emma to him. He should be waiting politely, properly, in the drawing room with his parents. They would sip port and tea and talk of wedding plans and marriage settlements until the butler ushered Emma in to join them. He could not seem to sit still, though, to listen to his father's pontifications on how good it was that Jack was "mending his ways," taking his proper place in Society, marrying a true lady. So he had come outside to wait for Emma. To wait for the only thing that seemed to make sense in this strange new world of "respectability," after months of convincing people he was less than respectable, less than interested in his duty.

Emma. Soon she would be here, within his reach. He could breathe her lilac perfume, convince himself that she was indeed real, that she existed, that she was not a dream.

That they would be together, and that their new marriage would prosper despite everything.

It all seemed possible, but only when she was with him.

A carriage stopped at the foot of the stone doorstep, and a footman leaped down to open the door and lower the steps. A pink satin slipper appeared, a white silk hem embroidered with pink rosebuds, a pink velvet cloak; then she was there. Emma smiled up at him and rushed up the steps to hold her hands out to him.

"What a grand welcome!" she said, standing up on tiptoe so he could kiss her cheek. "Did you just arrive here, too?"

He drew her against him. "No, I have been here for a while. I just wanted to wait for you." They really should go in; his parents were waiting. But this moment felt so good, he wanted to hold onto it for just a bit longer. "Did you have a good day today?"

"Oh, yes, lovely. Your mother came to the hotel and helped us with wedding preparations. She is truly a lovely woman." Emma leaned closer and whispered. "She says your father is a great deal of bluster but is really harmless."

Jack threw back his head and laughed. "Did she, indeed? Well, I daresay she is right. I am glad you liked my mother. I hope you will be good friends."

"I am sure we will. And how was your own day?"

Jack thought of his meeting with Mr. Thompson, of the papers that now rested beneath the floorboards of his sitting room. Of the man's guarded congratulations on Jack's marriage, his thoughts on how useful it could be to have such a connection to the unpredictable Russians—his warnings that Emma must never know what was truly happening. Warnings Jack had repeated to himself dozens of times.

"My day was fine," he said. "Bertie and I went to Tattersall's, and then lunched at the club."

"Tattersall's?"

"A horse showroom of sorts."

"Indeed? Well, I must say my own day was a great deal more fun than looking at smelly horses! But I hope you found what you were looking for."

"Oh, I did." Jack drew her closer and pressed a kiss to her fragrant hair. "I most certainly did."

Chapter Nineteen

*I*t was her wedding day.

Emma stood by her bedchamber window and stared down at the street. Even at this relatively early hour, there were people gathered there. Vendors of warm gingerbread and roasted almonds were setting up shop. It was not as crowded as it would be later in the day, but it was quite enough to be interesting.

Could it have been only a very few days ago that she had first stood just here, peering down on this same scene, and thought that her life would never change? That it would go on in the same stifling, etiquette-bound manner as before. That even when she married, it would be the same existence under a different name.

Now here she was, on the very edge of a new, unknown life, one she could never have imagined when she slipped out of the hotel disguised as a maid. She could never have imagined a man like Jack waited for her.

A man like Jack. What exactly *was* a man like Jack? And what could their life together hold?

Emma tapped her fingertips on the windowsill, still looking at the people on the street, yet not truly seeing them. Instead, she saw the supper of the previous night, a supper that had all the appearance of so many other suppers in her life. She liked Lady Osborn, and she even rather liked funny, pompous old Lord Osborn, but their conversation was quiet and full of politeness and careful questions.

But then Jack had given her a secret glance across

the table, waggling his eyebrows comically at some stuffy anecdote his father was telling. She had been nearly overcome by a fit of giggles and had to cover her mouth with her napkin to hide it.

Life with Jack would surely never be dull, never be totally what was expected even as they fulfilled their duties in Society. She was happy about this wedding, about this match, truly she was.

Why, then, did a tiny, niggling doubt still worry at the back of her mind?

Emma remembered the tiny flicker in Jack's eyes before he had told her he spent the day at Tattersall's with Bertie, the way he glanced away for the tiniest second. He was always so very jovial, so lighthearted.

Too lighthearted?

She stepped back away from the window with a self-conscious laugh. Why was she thinking this now? It was her wedding day! She was meant to be joyful, not conjuring up doubtful ideas out of sheer air. Perhaps it was only the fabled bridal nerves.

Jack could only be what he appeared, what he said he was. Even though he *had* lied to her the day they met and had never explained what he was doing wearing rough clothes . . .

No! She would not think of this any longer. There was too much to do. She liked Jack, he liked her and they were to be married. That was that.

She sat down at the dressing table and reached for her hairbrush.

There was a knock at the door. Thinking it was Natasha, she called, "Come in!"

But it was not Natasha; it was Madame Ana who came in, bearing a tray of chocolate and toast. She was clad in her usual black silk and spectacles, but there were no lists in sight and her lips were set in what looked like—could it be uncertainty?

It could not be. Madame Ana had never displayed the tiniest hint of uncertainty since the day she came into Aunt Lydia's employ years ago.

"Good morning, Lady Emma," she said. "Natasha is assisting the florists belowstairs, so I brought your breakfast. Is there anything I can help you with?" Madame Ana put the tray down on a table and brushed her hands together, folding them at her waist. Without her notebook and gold pencil, she seemed awkward.

For the first time, Emma was not scared of her. Not a great deal, anyway.

"Thank you, Madame Ana," she answered. "I should dress, I suppose. There are so many things to do this morning."

Madame Ana's shoulders straightened. She was once again in her element. "Countess Suvarova is already with the dressmaker, discussing last-minute alterations. As I said, Natasha is helping the florists, and the Grand Duchess of Oldenburg herself is conferring about the arrangements of the drawing room for the ceremony. More chairs will have to be brought in. The count has spoken with the vicar. All is in readiness for this afternoon."

All was in readiness? Then, what was there left for her, the bride, to do? She pulled the brush through a knot in her hair. "Oh. Well. That is splendid."

"Here, let me do that, Lady Emma." Madame Ana took the brush and neatly separated Emma's hair into sections, smoothing it carefully. "And Countess Lieven is downstairs in the small salon. Since Countess Suvarova is so busy, perhaps you could go see her when your toilette is complete?"

"Countess Lieven? Oh, yes. Certainly."

The countess waited in the luxuriously appointed small salon where Emma had met Jack two days ago, with a tea tray and a newspaper to occupy her. She was beautifully attired, as always, wearing a morning costume of topaz-colored silk and a tall-crowned hat trimmed with dark yellow and gold-green feathers. Two days ago, Emma might have felt pale and prissy in her white muslin dress and blue Indian shawl beside Countess Lieven, but not today. Today was her wedding day.

"Good morning, Countess Lieven," she greeted the lady, coming into the salon to sit down across from her guest. "What a pleasure to see you!"

Countess Lieven smiled and tucked the paper into her reticule. "I hope I am not calling too early, Lady Emma. I know it is not at all the hour for calls, but I thought perhaps I could be of some assistance with the arrangements."

"That is so very kind of you! But I believe everything is taken care of."

"Of course. Countess Suvarova's great style and efficiency are known even here in London! I am sure it will be a lovely affair." The countess laughed. "It is already being talked of as the wedding of the Season, despite its diminutive size—or perhaps because of it. People who were not invited are quite eaten up with envy."

Emma had realized that people would be interested, but not *that* interested. After all, she had been in England only for a few days and knew almost no one. "Indeed?"

"Oh, yes. No one thought Lord St. Albans would *ever* be caught in parson's mousetrap. Every young miss has set her cap for him, with no success. Yet, here you have snatched him from beneath all the young ladies' noses, after so brief a time. You must tell me what your secret is."

Emma could definitely understand that the ladies would find Jack attractive. She did, after all. But she was not so sure she liked the suggestive arch of the countess's brow. It hinted of sophisticated suggestions that Emma could not even begin to comprehend. "I have no secret, Countess Lieven. Lord St. Albans and I are simply fond of each other and think we will do well together."

The countess took a small sip of her tea. "Yes, certainly. Well, you are a fortunate young lady. I am certain that you will be more than able to settle the 'Firebrand Viscount' down. He will not be an easy one to tame."

To tame? Whatever was the woman talking about? Jack was not some unbroken colt. "I am sure."

Countess Lieven gave a silvery little laugh. "You will not know what I am talking of, of course, being so new to Society in London. But the viscount has been so very—amusing since he returned from the Peninsula. It has been in all the scandal sheets." She took up the publication she had been reading from her reticule and laid it on the table, giving it a little pat. "So, of course, everyone is agog that he is to wed."

Emma stared down at the paper, almost as if it could reach out and bite her. "Of course."

"Well, my dear Lady Emma, since there is nothing I can do here, I will be off on my errands. I will see you at the ceremony!"

"Good morning, Countess Lieven. Thank you so much for coming," Emma said, with automatic politeness.

After the countess left in a cloud of exotic scent, Emma poured herself a cup of tea and reached for the paper. She riffled past the fashion plates to the page of *on-dits* in the back. Lady R. seen dancing five times with Lord T. at the Duchess of M.'s ball. Miss A. turned down seven suitors last Season, only to wed some poor nobody of a vicar.

Lord St. A., better known as "Firebrand," after breaking the hearts of all the young misses and many of the demi-mondes, as well as racing his curricle to Brighton and fighting with Lord S. at White's, has succumbed to the charms of Lady E. W., fresh from the frozen north. Much to the great surprise of everyone at Lady H.'s ball, where the announcement took place.

Hm. So Jack was a rake. And a heartbreaker.

Emma stared down at the paper for a moment longer, then tossed it onto a table floor and left the salon.

She would not think of that now. Those words had nothing to do with the Jack she knew. She would be happy. She *would*. By Jove, it was her wedding day!

Her wedding to a rake. She laughed aloud, surprising a maid dusting in the corridor. This was all really too much like some novel.

*   *   *

" 'Firebrand Viscount!' How utterly ridiculous." Jack snorted in derision as he tossed the paper to the table next to his coffee cup. It jarred the porcelain, causing a splash of ebony liquid to fall across the paper and obliterate the article with a great stain.

Exactly what the rag deserved.

They had all been speculating about his romantic life ever since he returned from Spain, as if they had nothing better to think about. And while the bits about the race and the fight were true enough, the "heartbreaking" certainly was not.

He just hoped Emma did not read such silly stuff. He should not be reading it himself.

Emma! He was to see his bride, to join their familes, in only two hours. His heart, which had felt still and closed for so long, gave a little leap at the thought.

He pictured her face, imagined the way her small, soft hands felt in his. Soon she would be his wife, and he could see her, be with her, all the time.

And Jack, who had once dreaded the very mention of the word *marriage,* found that he did not truly mind the thought of that one little bit.

Chapter Twenty

"*You* look beautiful, my lady! Just like a princess in a story. Like Vassilissa," Natasha said, attaching the last of the pins that held Lady Osborn's veil to Emma's pearl and diamond tiara.

Emma fidgeted with impatience. She was not allowed to look in the mirror until her toilette was complete, and the suspense was terrible. "Oh, can't I see now, please?"

Aunt Lydia laughed and handed her a pair of long white silk gloves. "Put your gloves on, my dear, and then you may see."

Emma tugged on the close fitting gloves, helped by Madame Ana, and smoothed them over her elbows. The scalloped hems almost touched the blue silk cap sleeves of her wedding gown. "There. Now?"

"Now." Aunt Lydia turned her toward the full-length mirror.

For a moment, Emma thought she was peering at another person, a stranger who had come silently into her chamber. Then she realized that the stranger was *herself*, a prettier, taller, more grand self than she could ever have imagined.

Her dark hair was drawn back sleekly, crowned with the tiara and iced with the elaborate pattern of the veil. The edges of the lace fluttered over her shoulders and the pleated bodice of her gown. Her mother's pearls gleamed at her throat and ears.

Emma reached up to touch her cheek, which had been

carefully powdered by Natasha and glistened like another pearl. She was a grand creation, indeed. Yet she almost wished for her gray maid's dress again, so that she could recognize herself as the girl who had danced with Jack in the light of the illuminations. So that Jack would recognize her as that girl, too. As his Tonya.

Lydia hugged Emma carefully so as not to muss her gown or her own violet satin creation. "You are so lovely, my dear. Just like your mother."

"Really?" Emma turned to her aunt, clutching at her sleeve. "Do I truly look like her?"

"You are Elizabeth's very image." Lydia smiled, almost sadly, and adjusted the fall of Emma's veil. "She was the truest Diamond London had ever seen, and all the swains wanted to marry her. But she would have none but your father."

"Just as you would have none but Uncle Nicholas?"

Lydia laughed. "Exactly! And as you would have none but Lord St. Albans. Your mother would be so proud to see you today."

"Would she?"

"She loved you more than anything. I know I have not spoken of her enough to you. It has pained me so much sometimes to think of her. We were as close as two sisters could ever be. Now, though, perhaps you can come to know her better, once you are settled at Weston Manor."

"Weston Manor?" Emma felt as if she was behaving like a trained parrot, asking such dull questions, but everything was moving so very quickly. A marriage and her old home, too? Her head was spinning.

"Of course. Did Lord St. Albans not tell you?" Lydia giggled like a girl. "Well, I am sure you two have had other things to speak of! You are going to Weston Manor for your wedding trip. It is all arranged."

Much to Emma's shock, she started to cry. Little hiccoughing sobs that could be of sudden joy or sudden trepidation, she did not know.

"Emma, Emma! What is amiss? Do not cry, you will

muss yourself." Lydia pulled a handkerchief from her beaded reticule and used it to dab at Emma's tears. "Tell me what is wrong. Do you not want to go to Weston Manor?"

"I *do* want to go there! I do not know why I am crying. I am just so—so happy." Emma blew her nose inelegantly as Natasha rushed forward with a powder puff. "And I will miss you so much. You and Uncle Nicholas. And Russia, too, that wonderful old freezing place."

"As we will certainly miss you. We will see each other again, though, and we will write all the time. Now that this terrible war is over, your uncle will be more settled at home." She leaned forward and whispered, "And we will be expecting grandchildren very soon!"

Emma gave a choked, embarrassed little laugh.

"There, now, that is better." Lydia patted her cheek. "Only smiles are allowed at weddings."

Natasha handed Emma her flowers, a neat little nosegay of white roses and blue forget-me-nots. Emma clutched her hand around its silver holder as if it were a lifeline holding her up in this sea of unfamiliarity, unknowability.

"Are you ready to go downstairs now?" her aunt asked, turning to face the mirror and adjust her own attire. "Your uncle will be waiting to escort you down the aisle."

Emma took a deep breath. "Yes. I am ready."

The crème de la crème of the *ton* was gathered in the large drawing room of the Pulteney Hotel. Baskets and vases of fragrant white roses and orchids were banked along the silk-papered walls, creating a country bower, a garden enclave in the middle of the city. A string quartet played quiet strains behind a large potted palm, and candles cast a glow on the elegant satins and velvets of the guests as they made their way to their places on the gold and white chairs. The Tsar and his sister, Prinny and young Princess Charlotte, all sat in their own small box slightly above the fray.

Jack stood with his back to the elaborate marble fireplace, decorated for today as a makeshift altar, dressed once again in the heavy red wool of his uniform. He accepted the congratulations of the guests, the last-minute, Polonius-like silly advice from his father, with a careless grin and a laughing joke. Inside, though, he was reeling.

This was his wedding. His *wedding*. Any moment now, those doors would open and his bride would appear. His bride, his Emma.

Up until this moment, during the two dizzy days of their engagement, it had not seemed exactly real. Oh, it had seemed *real* that he and Emma were together, that they would be wed. But now he saw that he would be responsible for her for the rest of their years together. What if he disappointed her, what if she was made unhappy by the fate they had been dealt?

Battles, swordplay, guns, he knew. Marriage—he was lost.

There was no time to panic, though. Bertie, his supporter, drew him to his place before the vicar, and the drawing room doors opened.

Emma stood there with her uncle, looking as stunningly lovely as she had at the reception where he had first seen her. And as much like the ice princess, her posture straight and perfect, her pale blue gown and white lace veil the color of a winter morning in Russia.

Then she smiled, and she was *Emma* again. She was his Tonya.

And he knew that all would be well for them. Somehow.

Emma's hand tightened on her uncle's arm as the doors opened and she was faced with the gathering of what seemed to be all Society. The Tsar was there, and the English Prince Regent, and Countess Lieven, and Sir

Jeremy Ashbey, who watched her with perfect impassivity on his handsome face. Suddenly, Emma could not breathe. Her light stays, her silk bodice, seemed designed to suffocate her.

"Are you all right, my darling?" her uncle murmured. "If you have changed your mind . . ."

Her gaze swept over the room, over all the splendidly dressed people, and landed on Jack. It was undoubtedly Jack, with his brilliant eyes, his crooked smile, even though he seemed so awfully grand in the white pantaloons and red wool tunic of his dress uniform. One of his gloved hands rested on the hilt of his dress sword. The other he held out to her in a tiny but unmistakable gesture of welcome.

"No, Uncle Nicholas," she whispered. "I have not changed my mind."

"Well, then. We should get on with it."

"Oh, yes. We absolutely should."

The music changed to a more gentle, stranger sort of march waltz, and Emma moved forward to Jack's side. She did not see any of the people, did not notice them staring at her. She just saw Jack and felt his hand take hers as her uncle handed it to him. Even through their gloves, his clasp was warm and strong, a clasp that could surely hold her up through all the years to come.

Surely *not* the clasp of a rake, as that silly newspaper had suggested.

Together, they turned to face the vicar.

"Dearly beloved, we are gathered together here in the sight of God, and in the face of this congregation, to join together this Man and this Woman in holy matrimony . . ."

Chapter Twenty-One

*T*he hotel's kitchens had prepared a sumptuous repast for the wedding guests, a vast buffet of mushroom tarts, lobster patties, medallions of lamb with mint sauce and fruit pastries. There was also a beautiful white cake decorated with ribbons and roses of pink marzipan, a champagne fountain and great silver samovars of three kinds of tea.

Emma nibbled at a strawberry tart, but she did not really taste its sour sweetness. She listened to the rise and fall of conversation around her, the echoes of laughter and the clink of crystal and china, but she did not really hear a thing. She nodded and smiled at what seemed like appropriate moments. All she could think, over and over, was that she was married.

Married!

The man who stood beside her, so handsome and noble in his uniform, had been a stranger only a very few days before, yet he was now her husband.

She looked at him as he laughed at something Bertie Stonewich told him and marveled that this could all be real. Jack was dashing and bright, like a flash of lightning, the roil of a blue sea, and as she saw the way the young women in the crowd watched him, she knew he could truly have had any woman he wanted, just as that silly newspaper had said. Yet he had chosen her, short, dark, daydreamy her.

Not that the circumstances of their betrothal had been

ideal. He had been forced to offer for her, after all. But when she offered him a way out of this mess, he had refused. He had insisted on going through with this wedding. That meant he must have some sort of feelings for her, did it not?

Just then, he turned to her, caught her staring at him. She must have had some odd expression on her face, for the grin faded from his lips and he leaned toward her, looking concerned. "Are you well, Emma? You look pale."

She smiled at him. "I am very well. Just a bit tired. It has been a very busy few days."

"Busy indeed." He took her empty plate from her hand and gave it to a passing footman. "I am sure this does not have to go on very much longer. We can cut the cake, perhaps have a dance; then we can be off."

Off on their wedding trip, where they would do the—the deed. Somehow she could not think of it yet by any other word. Emma felt her face grow uncomfortably warm again, and she wished she had a fan to hide behind.

"I will just fetch you a cup of tea, while you sit here and catch your breath," Jack said, escorting her to one of the small satin chairs near an open window.

As Jack set off across the room toward the buffet table, pausing here and there to accept good wishes, nodding and smiling, Bertie Stonewich appeared beside her. He sat down in the chair next to hers, without even being invited, and said, "It was a lovely wedding, Lady St. Albans."

Emma tilted her head to peer up at him. He was quite different from the affable, slightly drunken man she had met the night of the illuminations. Today he wore his dress uniform, shining with gold braid and brass buttons, his golden cap of hair brushed to a bright luster. She was not too sure about Bertie. He seemed all surface, all jokes and brainlessness, yet she sensed that that was not all there was to him. She was not sure she liked him, though there must be something to him if he was friends with Jack.

And since he *was* Jack's friend, and therefore sure to be a part of their lives in the future, she would always be polite to him. She nodded and said, "Thank you. It is too bad Lottie could not come."

He had the good grace to appear a bit abashed, his cheeks turning a faint pink, and he looked away with an embarrassed little laugh. "Indeed. I am sure she would want to send her good wishes. But you may rely on my discretion about that day entirely."

"Did you know who I was all along?"

"I had my suspicions. But I had confidence that Jack must know what he was doing. He always does. *Almost* always."

"Have you known each other very long, then?"

Bertie nodded slowly. "For many years. Jack saved my life in Spain, more than once."

"As you saved mine," Jack said, coming upon them in time to hear this. "If either of us owed the other any favors, they were more than repaid. Many times over." He gave them a grin, as if he had not just spoken such serious words.

Bertie gave him an answering smile and stood up to shake the hand Jack held out to him as he balanced a teacup in his other hand. "It is to be hoped there will be no need for such favors in the future."

"Not until after the wedding trip, anyway. I am sure you will both be very happy."

"I am sure we will," Jack answered. Bertie moved away from them, joining a beautiful redhead and blending into the crowd with her.

Jack sat down in Bertie's abandoned chair and handed Emma the cup of tea he bore. She sipped at the smoky brew, grateful for its bracing strength. It helped to clear the champagne and sugar and giddiness from her mind. "Your friend is a very—interesting man," she said.

"Bertie? He is harmless, really. I think what he really needs is a wife of his own."

Emma laughed. "Do you think so? Any candidates in mind, Monsieur Matchmaker?"

"Oh, lud, no. I am horrible at matchmaking. I am just beginning to have the suspicion that *everyone* should be married."

"I agree. So far, anyway, I am finding marriage to be a great success," Emma said lightly.

Jack took her hand and kissed it, his lips lingering on the silk covering her knuckles. Then he turned it over and kissed her wrist, in the tiny bit of bare skin that showed between the pearl buttons.

Emma's breath caught in her throat.

"I would agree," he murmured, pressing her palm to his cheek. "Marriage assuredly has its advantages."

It was as if they were all alone in that crowded drawing room, their own small island of two in the midst of the waves of celebration. The doubts she had had seemed silly and vastly insignificant now that they were together. All that was important was that, by some great miracle, they had found one another.

Jack seemed to feel the same. He groaned low in his throat, and it vibrated against her skin, deep inside of her. "We must still be dutiful for a while longer," he said. "But soon we can be alone."

"What a touching scene!" Emma's aunt's voice said. Emma reluctantly turned her attention from Jack to Aunt Lydia and Uncle Nicholas, who stood before them arm in arm. Now that all was settled and done, the marriage and all its attendant settlements concluded, they looked more relaxed, happy even.

"You are truly a handsome couple," Lydia said, and leaned down to kiss Emma's cheek. She smelled comfortingly of violet scent, satin and champagne. "And I know you would rather be quiet together, but perhaps you should cut the cake now? The Prince Regent has already devoured all the lobster patties and profiteroles and will be looking for marzipan."

Emma laughed at the vision of the pudgy little man with the immensely high collar points stuffing his mouth with the cake's exquisite candy ribbons. "Of course, Aunt Lydia. We will be there directly."

She rose and followed her aunt to the small table where the cake waited in solitary splendor.

Jack started to follow her but was stopped by her uncle, who said something quietly in his ear.

Emma wondered what it could be.

"I wish you happy, Lord St. Albans," Count Suvarov muttered through his smile. "Just always remember, Russia may seem a very great distance from London, but no expanse will protect you if you mistreat my niece. We will always protect her, even from you, if need be."

Jack regarded him solemnly and saw the fierce protectiveness of true fatherhood in his expression. Jack could not help but feel a flush of resentment at the implication that he might mistreat Emma, but he understood. He imagined that he himself would one day feel just the same about his own daughter.

"You need never fear such mistreatment of me, Count Suvarov," he answered. "I will always treat Emma with every consideration and affection."

The count nodded. "That is all very well. But remember that the English are not the only ones with spies— as you well know."

Jack had nothing to answer that with, so he remained silent. Count Suvarov nodded and went to join his wife, taking her arm as she arranged the cake knives. She turned to him with a radiant smile, and they both turned beaming glances onto Emma. They were the very picture of proud parents.

Emma glanced up at Jack with a quizzical half-smile, a questioning quirk of her raven brow. He nodded to her, and came to take her hand in his. His wife's hand.

They folded their fingers together on the etched silver handle of the knife and cut into the rich, white icing of their wedding cake.

"It was a beautiful ceremony," Lydia said, watching as Natasha fastened the jeweled buttons at the back of

Emma's garnet-colored carriage gown. Nearby, Madame Ana, already dressed in her cloak and bonnet, carefully folded the wedding gown into a box. "Especially considering how quickly we had to plan it!"

Emma smiled and shrugged into her matching pelisse. "It was indeed beautiful. I did not expect anything less from an event *you* arranged, Aunt Lydia! I will always remember it."

"I'm glad, my dear." Lydia kissed her and held her in a gentle hug for a long moment. "I will always remember it, too, because of how you glowed with happiness."

Emma thought she might start to cry. She had known she would have to part with her aunt and uncle, of course, but somehow it had not seemed exactly real in the excitement of the wedding. Now it *was* real. She would go downstairs and get into the carriage with her new husband, and Lydia and Nicholas would go back to Russia without her. She would not see them again for a very long while.

Suddenly, she felt almost shockingly alone.

Lydia drew back, smiling, and tapped Emma gently on the chin. "Oh, now I have made you sad, Emma dear! Do not feel sad. You have a whole new life before you."

"I know. But I will miss you and Uncle Nicholas so much."

"As we will miss you. But we will always be with you." She kissed Emma one more time and let her go. "Now, your husband will be waiting."

Emma nodded and picked up her reticule and a small bandbox. All the trunks and cases had already been loaded onto the carriage Natasha and Madame Ana would travel in. All was in readiness. Letting her sadness float away as if on a bubble, Emma decided that she had to be ready, too.

She went down the stairs to where Jack waited, changed from the splendor of his uniform into traveling clothes. He took her hand, and they rushed through the foyer in a shower of rose petals and good wishes.

It seemed to Emma in that moment that nothing could go wrong for them, that their lives would always exist in this same enchanted plane.

This perfect, perfect place.

Chapter Twenty-Two

*T*he carriage jolting to a halt jerked Emma awake when she did not even know she had fallen asleep. The last thing she remembered was talking quietly with Jack as they raced along in the dying light of day, leaving the streets of London behind and moving into the quiet of the countryside. They had spoken of the wedding, she remembered, of the people who had been there, the decorations, nothing very deep or profound. The darkness that crept into the carriage, wrapping around them like black velvet, the champagne she had drunk, must have conspired to put her to sleep.

Now the carriage was stopping, a beam of light arcing across her face. Emma blinked and slowly sat up. A weight fell from her shoulder, and she realized that Jack's arm was around her, that she had fallen asleep against his shoulder. She was half-sprawled against his side, her pelisse collar unbuttoned, and she could feel the strands of loose hair against her neck like tickling feathers.

Emma gave an embarrassed little laugh and tried to push the hair back into its pins. She suddenly felt uncomfortable with Jack, uncomfortable in her disarray. All evening they had talked and laughed together so easily, and she had no idea why she should so worry about such things now, but she did.

"I am sorry," she said. "I did not mean to fall asleep." She glanced back over her shoulder at Jack. He still lounged against the leather squabs, completely at ease even though the dark waves of his hair were tousled and she had pulled the capes of his greatcoat askew. He smiled at her and reached up to tuck a strand of her hair behind her ear.

"It is of no matter," he said. "It has been a very long day, a very long several days. You probably have had very little rest ever since you came to London."

That was very true; she had not even really been able to rest since she left St. Petersburg. It was strange that her deepest sleep had come in this swaying, lumpy carriage. His casualness made her feel better, but she still could not quite meet his eyes.

The light outside the carriage window moved, and she could hear the blur of voices. "Where are we?"

"An inn. I made arrangements for us to stop here on the way to Weston Manor. I thought you might be too tired to drive all the way through."

"Oh. Yes, of course. How thoughtful." She touched her hair again, unsure of what to do now. What she should do at an inn with a *husband*.

Jack's smile widened. "Would you like to get out now, Emma?"

"All right. Yes."

As if at some invisible command, a footman opened the carriage door and held out a hand to help her down onto the gravel of the inn's courtyard. Emma tipped back her head to look at the building, working the kinks out of her neck. The inn appeared to be a solid, respectable sort of establishment, a Tudor half-timber with welcoming golden lamplight spilling from the mullioned windows. The door opened, and a woman, round and solid to match the house, appeared there, wiping her hands on her apron.

"My lord, my lady?" she called. "Welcome to the Dog and Duck! Your servants have already arrived, and all is in readiness. We have prepared a supper and our finest chamber for you."

"Excellent! Thank you." Jack offered Emma his arm.

He had pulled his coat straight and run his hand through his hair, and now he looked perfect. It was really so unfair, the minimal preparations men could make.

Emma herself still felt like a ragamuffin. But the landlady was smiling eagerly, and the inn looked welcoming and warm, a quiet haven after a busy day. She slid her hand onto Jack's arm and let him lead her out of the night.

The landlady led them to a private parlor where a fire crackled in the grate and supper was laid out on a table before it. The meal was a simple collation of cold ham, cheese, bread and wine, but to Emma it looked like a feast set before her in a palace. Their first meal alone as husband and wife.

She took off her pelisse and laid it with her gloves and reticule on a bench just inside the door before seating herself at the table.

Jack dismissed the landlady, telling her they would serve themselves, and came to sit across from Emma. He poured some of the ruby red wine into their glasses and said, "It is just plain fare, I fear."

Emma shook her head. "It is perfect. The food at the wedding was wonderful, but I scarcely had time to eat any of it!"

He smiled at her and lifted his glass in a salute. "Here's—to the future."

"To the future." To *their* future? Emma touched his glass with hers and sipped at the sweet, rich liquid. She looked forward to that future, to seeing what it would bring.

Most of all, she wondered what their *immediate* future, this very night, would bring.

She still felt a bit strange, a bit flustered, with Jack, a bit unsure of what to say. What did a proper wife, a true wife, do? What did he expect? But the wine and the warm fire did their slow work, and she relaxed back into her chair, giggling at some silly story Jack was telling her. She slid her feet out of her slippers and popped a morsel of cheese into her mouth.

It was beginning to feel like Jack and Tonya having a quick meal at the public house again.

As the level of the wine in the bottle diminished and the food disappeared, the conversation slowed and stilled, lapsing into silence, but it still felt natural and comfortable to just sit there together.

Emma rested her chin in her hand, a little drowsy, a little tipsy, and just looked across at her husband. He also appeared sleepy, his hair falling forward over his brow again, his cravat loosened. He nudged aside his plate and glass and leaned his forearms on the table, so close to her that she could see the traces of green in his ocean blue eyes. "I dreamed of a scene just like this," he said softly.

She smiled lazily and reached out with her finger to nudge the wave of his hair back. "A scene like this?"

"A fire, a good meal, a beautiful lady. Most assuredly the stuff of dreams."

Emma laughed. "You are certainly easy to please!"

"Who could ask for more than this?"

"Some people dream of riches, gold, jewels, exotic lands."

"Do you dream of those things?"

"I've always dreamed of doing just what I wanted, of not having to dance with some elderly man with hair in his ears because he was a duke. Of being able to sit in my dressing gown and read all day if that's what I want. Of eating as much as I want." She put the last bit of bread into her mouth and chewed happily.

Jack shook his head with a grin. "*You* are the one who is easy to please. I can tell that our life together will be very successful."

Emma certainly hoped so. "When did you have dreams of a place like this, Jack?"

His grin faded. "In Spain."

"During the war?"

He nodded and sat back in his chair. "People who have never experienced war think it is all glorious adventure, but it is not. It is dirty and hot and very, very dull.

Sometimes at night when I could not sleep, I would lie under the sky and look at the stars and imagine that it was all over. That I was at home again, in England where it is cool and green and quiet. That I had a wife, a lady with soft hands and a sweet scent, who waited to welcome me in our home."

Emma's eyes itched with tears at the images his words conjured, at the heartbreaking thought that he had been lonely and sad. Just as she had.

She wanted to put her arms around him, to hold him, to be that sweet-scented wife. She contented herself with reaching across the table and taking his hands in hers, folding his long, callused fingers inside of her own.

He raised her hand up and kissed it. "So, this is what I thought of. And now it is mine. Ours."

"Yes." Emma could say nothing else past the lump in her throat. Just that one word.

He gave her a regretful little smile. "I am sorry, my dear. This is meant to be our wedding trip, and I have cast a cloud over it with my own maudlin thoughts. You must be so tired."

She was, a bit. Her head felt thick with wine and exhaustion, but she still did not want to let this evening go. She wanted to hear more about his time in Spain, his hopes for the future. She wanted to tell him of her own wartime in the lonely, cold Russian countryside. But perhaps this was not the time. Perhaps this evening was complete in itself, and of course they would have many others.

She nodded. "I *am* tired. As you said, it has been a long day. I am sure Natasha is waiting to help me undress."

Oh! She had not meant to say *undress* in front of Jack. It seemed wrong, silly somehow. She pressed her fingers to her lips to hold in a drunken giggle.

But Jack did not seem to notice her little indiscretion. He just nodded and let go of her hands to lean back in his chair. "I will see you later."

Emma stood up the leave the room. At the door, she

glanced back at Jack once more, but he was not watching her. His gaze was on the dying fire, his hands flat on the table. He did not seem to be there anymore. He was somewhere far away.

Emma thought perhaps she should go back to him, kneel beside him, hold him close. She was loath to interrupt his perfect quiet, though, to disturb the invisible bubble that surrounded him. Instead, she shut the door quietly behind her and followed one of the inn's maids upstairs to the bedchamber that waited.

Natasha dozed in an armchair there. The large, high bed was ready, the bedclothes turned down, her new nightdress, a frothy affair of handkerchief linen and pink satin ribbons, laid out. Her traveling valise sat on a stand, next to Jack's brown leather case.

Emma frowned in puzzlement. Were they meant to share this room, then? That seemed a bit odd to her, but then she had never been a bride on her wedding night before. Perhaps it was just how things were done. Perhaps it had something to do with *the deed*.

She was just too tired to puzzle it all out right now. The excitement, the tension of the past few days drained out of her very muscles and bones as she looked at that white, inviting bed. Whatever had been keeping her upright flooded away, and she sagged against the door, as weighty as a bag of rocks.

Natasha awoke, startled, sitting up straight in her chair. "Oh, my lady!" she cried, and jumped to her feet. "I did not mean to fall asleep. I was waiting for you . . ."

Emma waved away Natasha's words with a feeble gesture of her hand. "It is no matter, Natasha. It has been a very long day, and we are all tired. Has Madame Ana already retired?"

"Yes, my lady." Natasha unfastened the buttons at the back of Emma's carriage gown and began unlacing her light stays. "We have the room right above this one, very comfortable. The landlady apologized for having to put you and Lord St. Albans in the same chamber, but it was the last large one still available."

Ah, so *that* was the explanation. A mere happenstance of practicality. "It is quite all right. We *are* married, after all."

Natasha giggled. "So you are, my lady! I keep forgetting."

"I confess I find it a difficult fact to hold in my mind, as well," Emma murmured. She leaned against the back of a chair as Natasha reached down to take off Emma's shoes.

Natasha paused. "My lady?"

"Hm?"

"Where are your shoes?"

"My shoes?" Emma looked down to see the strange sight of her stocking-clad feet. The white silk was smeared with dust, a tiny run just starting over the arch of her foot. She remembered slipping them off under the table, to ease the ache of her toes. She must have forgotten to put them back on.

How very odd, she thought. How truly improper to go walking around a public inn in her bare feet. This must really be the beginning of her new life.

She laughed at the silliness, the sheer exhaustion of it all. "I must have left them downstairs in the dining parlor."

"The dining parlor, my lady?"

"Don't worry, Natasha. We can fetch them in the morning."

Natasha gave her a doubtful glance, clearly wondering what exactly Emma had been *doing* downstairs, but she said nothing. She just reached for Emma's nightdress and dropped it over her head in a drift of cloudy, perfumed white.

As Emma tied the pink satin ribbons at the neck and wrists, Natasha released her hair from its pins and brushed it out. Thus arrayed, Emma climbed up into the bed and sank gratefully into its feather softness.

Natasha tucked the bedclothes around her. "Good night, my lady," she whispered, a note of some avid reluctance in her voice. "Will you—will you tell me about it in the morning?"

Emma peered up at her drowsily. "It?"

"Yes. *It*."

"Oh. It. Yes, of course." Emma was really only distantly aware of what *it* might be at this time, but she was so tired she would have said anything to be alone. "Good night, Natasha."

The maid left her then, with a soft click of the door to mark her passing. One candle still burned, casting its soft goldenness over the room. The curtains at the window were closed, but a small opening where the damask did not quite meet showed a sliver of the night sky.

Emma stared at that bit of starlit darkness and thought that really she ought to stay awake and wait for Jack. It seemed somehow important that she do so. But the tiredness that weighted her mind and eyelids was stronger, and her eyes drifted shut.

Jack waited what seemed a decent interval for his bride to do whatever it was brides did, waited until the clock on the wall chimed the hour. He had never actually possessed a bride before so was not sure of the exact protocol.

He had never had this precise blend of emotions before, either, a bizarre concoction of eagerness, need, desire, reluctance, uncertainty. He wasn't sure he liked it. He *knew* he did not like the uncertainty. He was a man accustomed to certitude, yet with Emma, with his *wife*, he always seemed on the very knife's edge of suspense, always wondering what she might do next. Run away dressed as a maid? Row a boat across a pond like the veriest midshipman? Fall over a blasted potted plant and tear her skirt?

With Emma, one never knew, and that was part of her great attraction for Jack. But it also meant that he had no idea how she would react to having a husband—a greatly aroused husband—climb into her bed.

Jack shifted in his chair, staring at the last dying embers of the fire. The ensuing scene could really be almost anything. Just as he had never had a wife before, Jack had never bedded a virgin, either (at least not *knowingly*). He did not want to frighten her, didn't want to overwhelm her with the desire that came over him like an inexorable tide whenever he saw her. This was the beginning of what would, he hoped, be many years together, and he wanted to make it right. He wanted to make it perfect.

Jack laughed at himself, at his ridiculous, circuitous thoughts. He could never make it perfect by sitting here alone while his bride waited in their nuptial chamber, perhaps growing more and more uncertain as she waited for him. He swallowed the last of his wine and left the dining parlor with a falsely confident step. The inn was quiet now, everyone abed except for a yawning footman who waited to clear away the supper remains and direct Jack to his chamber. In the thick silence, the creak of the stairs beneath Jack's boots seemed to him like thunder.

He reached for the doorknob, half-fancying that it might be locked, but it turned easily in his hand. He slipped inside, closed the door behind him—and paused.

One candle, set on the dresser, lit the room, casting flickering shadows into the corners and over the figure of the woman who reposed on the bed. She was not waiting for him, nervous or otherwise. She was fast asleep.

Jack grinned at himself for working himself into such a state, imagining Emma worried and nervous and scared. She did nothing in the usual way—she would not have the usual bridal nerves. She appeared to have no nerves at all. He was the one who had been truly frightened, scared that his ardor for her, for his night-and-snow princess, would consume them both if unleashed.

At the sight of her there, peaceful against the pillows, he knew that his ardor burned no less bright but not so urgent now. He could touch her and not be consumed in the flames. Not at once, anyway.

He tossed his coat over a chair and unfastened his waistcoat, unwound his cravat. He pulled off his boots and moved forward in his stockinged feet to sit carefully on the edge of the bed.

Emma stirred a bit and wrinkled her nose in her sleep but did not wake. Her hands curled in the bedclothes, and she sighed. Jack reached out to gently disentangle a strand of her black hair from the pink ribbons at her neck. He kept his hand there—resting on the soft white material that covered her shoulder, feeling the gentle rise of her breathing—and just looked at her.

He should not have been so maudlin about his time in Spain, he thought. It was their wedding trip; things should be light and bright, not full of war and sadness. Yet there, in that quiet parlor with her, he had felt he *could* speak of it for the first time since he returned to England. It seemed safe and so far away. Her presence made all that horror, that ugliness, seem the distant unreal dream, and this time the only reality.

As he looked at her now, sleeping so peacefully, looking so beautiful and so breathtakingly young, he knew very clearly what he had faced those horrors for. It was not for some abstract concept of "England." It was for women like her, so they could be safe and live their happy lives with no dark threat over them. It was for *her*, his wife, who lay so trustingly on her feather pillows, so that one day, just maybe, he could leave that ugliness behind him and curl up inside her lilac sweetness and be at peace.

He threw his cravat and waistcoat onto the floor and crawled beneath the warm bedclothes next to her. She murmured and rolled toward him, curling into his arms as if she had been doing it for years. For forever.

Jack drew her close and buried his face in the satin spread of her hair. He listened to her soft breathing, to the sounds of the night outside their window, and fell asleep to its lullaby.

Chapter Twenty-Three

$\mathcal{A}$ bright beam of light arced into Emma's eyes, cutting her sweet dream in half. She had been dreaming she was in a warm summer meadow, lying in soft, scented grass. She groaned and turned her head into the pillow, but it was too late. She was awake, and the dream was gone.

She flopped onto her back and opened her eyes onto a strange room, a new day. It took her a moment to remember that she was at an inn, that she was on her wedding trip. It was the second day of her marriage.

Emma turned her head to look at the sunshine coming through the gap in the heavy window curtains. It was too bright to be very early in the morning. The last thing she remembered was coming upstairs after supper, climbing into bed, trying to stay awake and wait for Jack. Apparently, she had not succeeded, because here it was morning, and she was all alone in the middle of the large bed.

Emma pushed back the blankets and sat up against the bank of pillows. She saw some of Jack's clothes piled up on a chair, a waistcoat, a shirt, a rumpled cravat. His leather case was open, shaving kit laid out beside a basin of water on the dresser. Obviously, Jack had been here at some time, but he was gone now.

Had they, could they, have done *the deed*, without her even knowing it? Emma lifted the bedclothes and peered down at herself. Her nightdress, still neatly tied at the neck and wrists, lay pristinely over her legs. She did not feel at all different. Nothing had happened. But the pillow next to her still bore an indentation, a strand of waving dark brown hair caught in the white linen case.

Emma frowned as she glanced from that hair back to her own legs. Why had he not woken her up?

Still behind the shield of her upheld sheet, she heard the chamber door open, the tune of a soft whistle.

She peeked over the edge of the sheet. Jack stood there, dressed in a fresh blue coat and simply tied ivory-colored cravat, an overloaded breakfast tray in his hands. He grinned when he looked up and saw her peeking at him, interrupting the whistled tune.

Emma dropped the sheet and smiled at him tentatively. She did not say anything. She wanted to see what would happen next.

Jack came to the bedside and balanced the tray on one hip while he smoothed the covers over her legs so he could place the tray there. "Good morning, Lady St. Albans! I told Natasha I would bring your breakfast to you. There is tea and toast, some fruit—I hope that is fine?"

"It is perfect." Emma watched him as he poured out the tea for her. He seemed quite cheerful this morning, smiling, happy, perfectly at ease. Not like the man who had spoken of Spain in such a quiet, pained voice. Not like a man who had been deprived of—*something*. She wondered what exactly had happened when he came to this room last night.

Jack kissed her cheek and sat down in the armchair, lounging back against the cushions. He hooked his leg over its arm, swinging his booted foot. "Well, eat up!" he urged. "We can leave when you are ready, but there is no hurry. Weston Manor is an easy half-day's drive from here. Perhaps we could stop for meat pies and ale at luncheon."

Emma laughed at the reminder of the simple fare she had enjoyed with such gusto on the day they met. She reached for her tea cup, feeling a bit more at ease. This was *Jack*. She was silly to be so nervous around him. But nervous she was. She wished she knew what was expected of her. She wished she had one of Madame Ana's lists for married life.

When she had eaten a piece of toast and drunk all the tea, she pushed the tray away and looked over at Jack. He had left the chair and was packing away the shaving kit, the rumpled cravat.

"Why did you not wake me last night?" she asked quietly.

He put the last item into his case and turned to face her, his half-smile fading. "You were so tired after supper and were sleeping so very peacefully. I did not want to disturb you."

Unable to meet his gaze any longer, Emma looked down at her hands on the sheet. It would be so very easy to leave it at that, to agree that she had been tired and go on with their day. But something was left undone, something vital. She knew that their sudden marriage must have been as disruptive to Jack's life as it had been to hers, even more so, and she did not want him to have regrets. *Any* regrets.

She would do her duty. But how to go about expressing that to him? She was not sure she even knew the right words.

"My aunt said . . ." she began, then swallowed hard and tried again. "My aunt said there would be—expectations about my wedding night."

Jack's smile returned, yet now it had a rueful quality, a mockery that could be either for himself or for her. She could not tell which.

"Oh, Emma," he said. "I can only begin to imagine what else your aunt might have said to you." He came and sat down on the edge of the bed and took one of her hands in his. He cradled it on his palm as if it were some fragile and precious piece of porcelain, looking down at it. "Close your eyes and think of England, perhaps?"

That was so close to what Lydia's own mother had told *her* that Emma had to laugh. Her laughter seemed to ease something in Jack. His fingers closed over hers, and his shoulders relaxed. "Or of fat, pink babies," Emma said.

"Yes, well, that, too." He looked right at her, then, serious and steadfast. "Emma, I truly did not want to wake you last night because you were so very tired, and I was, too. It has been a very strange few days, for both of us. But I was glad of the time, because I was able to think."

Emma wasn't sure she liked where this conversation was going. She felt an ominous cold tingling in her toes, at the back of her neck. But Jack still held her hand, and she could not look away from him. "To think?"

"Yes. We have not known each other for very long at all, and the last thing I would ever want to do is frighten you in any way. We will be married for the rest of our lives, and I want us to be as happy as possible. I want us to begin properly."

Emma frowned in utter confusion. "Properly? What do you mean?"

"I mean, that I want you to know that I respect you. That I am willing to wait a few days, a few weeks, until we know you are comfortable. I will do whatever you wish."

She *wished* he would talk to her like Jack again, not like some tiresome storybook knight to his fair damsel. Those words, that voice, did not seem to belong to her Jack at all. He was treating her like some delicate doll, and she did not like it.

What did he mean, anyway? That he did not want to do the deed with her? That he wanted to *wait*? What man would do that?

Oh. Her confusion slipped slowly sideways into suspicion. A man who did not truly desire his wife would do that, that was who.

When she was Tonya, she had thought he might desire her. The way he gazed at her, the way he kissed her, had seemed to express the same feelings she held in *her* heart. But, very often, she had seen the husbands of her married acquaintances place their wives on some distant pedestals. Wives were meant to be admired, perhaps, but not desired. That was for other women, bolder women.

Lord St. A., the heartbreaker.

Emma remembered the words in that scandal sheet with a sharp pang. She would never have thought such a thing of Jack! She wanted to scream at him, to wail, "Why don't you think I'm *pretty*!" She even had the insane notion of tearing open her nightdress to see what he would do then.

But she did not, because that would be undignified, and right now, above all, Emma wanted to keep her dignity. She would not show Jack her confused desire.

Not until she had time to think. To figure out what she should do.

She gently removed her hands from Jack's and said quietly, "Very well. If that is what you wish, we shall wait."

He gave her a smile, half-tentative, half-relieved. "Very well." He kissed her gently, briefly, on the lips, and stood up to go. "I will send Natasha to you, and we will be off as soon as you are ready."

Emma nodded and turned to stare at the window until she heard the door close behind him. She was still looking at, though not really seeing, the expanse of blue sky, when the door reopened to admit Natasha, who carried a basin of fresh warm water for Emma to wash in. Emma slowly turned back to the room to watch her maid put down the basin and pick up Emma's pink satin dressing gown.

"Well, my lady?" Natasha said, with a hopeful, teasing note in her voice. "How was your evening?"

Much to Emma's everlasting shame, she burst into tears at Natasha's question and flung herself back down into the pillows.

"Oh, my lady!" Natasha cried in obvious horror. "It was *that* bad?"

* * *

You are a damned fool, Jack thought over and over, as he paced the inn's courtyard next to their waiting carriage. *A noble, ridiculous fool.*

What had he been thinking, when he told Emma they could wait to consummate their marriage? He had seen the confusion on her face, before she hid it behind her ice-princess mask. He felt the stirrings, the protests of his own body. *It* had wanted to make love to her right there in the morning light, but *he* had said no. *He* was a complete fool, a simpleton.

But, really, he knew what he had been thinking. He had been so caught up in the romance of the night before, in the thrill of knowing that he could *feel* again, that he could leave the war behind him and enjoy the beauties of this world. Chief among them, of course, being Emma.

He had wanted to do all he could not to frighten her away, to make their marriage work. This had seemed to be the best way to do that, to tell her that there was no hurry, that they had time to wait. Truth to tell, it had given him the satisfying feeling of being a noble, self-sacrificing gentleman, a knight of old.

For about a minute and a half. Then he had seen Emma's puzzlement, her coolness, and had the unmistakable sensation of having made a mistake. Only he was not exactly sure what the mistake had been or how to fix it.

Perhaps he should go back into the inn and make love to his wife right now, this very minute.

He half-turned toward the door, but Emma was already coming out. She wore a pristine, ladylike traveling costume of rose-colored wool and a tall-crowned bonnet of off-white, with a frill of rose silk framing her face like a flower. She handed her maid a neatly tied bandbox and smiled and nodded at something Natasha said. The earlier coolness had vanished, and she seemed like his sunny, happy Emma again.

Surely he had been right in his decision after all. When

he and Emma made love, it would be wonderful—all the more wonderful for the heightened anticipation waiting would bring.

If it did not kill him first.

Chapter Twenty-Four

$\mathscr{E}$mma had not seen Weston Manor since she was six years old, and her memories were the hazy, vague ones of childhood. She remembered that there was a garden, with twisting pathways of roses where she would walk with her mother or her nurse. There was a wide, winding staircase, perfect for hiding and peeping down at grown-up parties below. The rooms were large and sunny with tall windows. Her mother would sit in the light that fell from those windows, her head bent over embroidery or a book, the sun gleaming on her black hair.

Emma had few memories of her father. She remembered that he was tall, that the bristles of his whiskers tickled her when he picked her up and kissed her at the end of the day. He smelled of some citrus soap, and he laughed a great deal.

She remembered more of her mother. That light on her hair, the scent of her perfume, the gentle way she smiled at her daughter. She would hum a lilting tune as she cut flowers from the garden. She loved parties and people.

That was all, really. Emma wondered if she would remember more of them once she was back in their house. If she would find anything there at all. She was so full of excitement and anticipation at seeing it again that she almost forgot her strange morning with Jack. Almost.

She peered out of the carriage window, twisting her

head around to try to glimpse the house, even though she knew it was too early to be able to see it. She wanted to find something familiar in the passing scenery, but she did not. It appeared like any piece of summertime countryside, green, bounded by hedgerows, trees shading the road.

"We will be there soon," Jack said, squeezing her hand reassuringly.

Emma looked at him and smiled. Here in this carriage, with both of them fully dressed, he was her friend again. Her partner in this great adventure, this new life. "How soon?"

He laughed. "Soon enough."

They passed through a small village, shops, cottages, a lovely stone church beside a matching vicarage, where a man in a black coat, obviously the vicar, tended a small garden. As they drove past, he straightened and peered at the carriage, waving in a most friendly manner. Other people, sweeping the doorsteps of shops, hurrying along on errands, waved.

Almost as if they knew her. Remembered her. As if she could almost belong here.

Impulsively, she turned to Jack and kissed his cheek. "Thank you," she whispered.

Jack laughed, and kissed her back. "For what?"

"For bringing me here, of course. And for—for just being you."

The house was not exactly as Emma recalled from the depths of her memory. It was smaller, the gardens and floral borders not as lush. But the mellow pale pink of the bricks, the tall windows, were the same. Several of the windows were open to the warm day, with draperies fluttering there. Neatly trimmed topiaries, much like the one Emma had fallen over on Lady Hertford's terrace, lined the front steps.

It *was* familiar, yet new and strange at the same time. It had been her home such a long time ago; it would be the first home she would share with her new husband.

She wondered what its rooms and corridors would hold for them, what she would find there.

A sudden nervousness seized her, clutching at her stomach. She reached up to make sure her bonnet was straight, her hair still dressed in neat curls at her temples.

"You look beautiful," Jack said.

Then why don't you desire me? she thought, the words popping unwillingly into her mind. But she only had time to give him a glance before the carriage stopped at the foot of the steps. She couldn't think of that now or of anything else. She was home.

As they stepped down onto the driveway, the front door opened and a tall woman in a neat gray dress and white cap came out. She was followed by some house-maids, footmen and a man in a black butler's coat.

"Lord and Lady St. Albans?" the woman said. "I am Mrs. Hemmings, housekeeper here at Weston Manor. Welcome home."

"Thank you," Emma answered. Still in a dreamlike state, she acknowledged the introductions to the butler and the other servants and presented Natasha and Madame Ana. She followed Mrs. Hemmings on a quick tour through the main rooms of the house, the small beeswax-and polish-scented library, the sunny morning room, the grand dining room. She nodded, made all the correct responses, asked all the correct questions, placed her hand correctly on Jack's arm. But she was glad her aunt had trained her so well in all the niceties of running a household; otherwise she was not sure she could do all these things. All she really wanted to do was sit down on a marble step of that remembered staircase and stare and stare.

"And this is the drawing room." Mrs. Hemmings opened tall double doors and led them into a long, elegant room. The walls were painted a pale blue, edged in mouldings of purest white. Inviting groupings of chairs and settees, gilded and upholstered in blue striped satin, were clustered around small tables covered with dainty figurines and tiny jeweled boxes.

Hanging over the marble fireplace was a portrait of a beautiful woman in a white muslin gown, sashed in blue silk. Her black hair fell in glossy waves over her shoulders and down her back. She was seated under a towering oak tree, and in the background was a view of Weston Manor. And the woman smiled down at the black-haired toddler in her lap.

Emma. That was Emma, her baby self. She moved across the room toward it, drawn to the bright scene.

Behind her, Mrs. Hemmings said, "I will send tea in to you, Lady St. Albans, and make sure your maid is sent to your rooms. Is there anything else you require?"

Emma looked back at her. "No, thank you, Mrs. Hemmings."

The housekeeper gave her a smile. "I was a parlormaid here when your parents were in residence, my lady. May I say welcome back?"

Emma was truly touched. "Thank you, Mrs. Hemmings."

When she had left, closing the drawing room door behind her, Emma returned to the portrait.

Jack came to join her, also staring up at the painting. "Is that your mother?"

"Yes. And me, though of course I have no remembrance of that scene!"

"She is beautiful. You look so much like her."

Overcome by all the emotions of the house, of her marriage, of everything, Emma threw her arms around Jack and held him close, burying her face in the warm curve of his shoulder.

His own arms closed around her, encompassing them in their own small world. "What is it, Emma? Is something amiss? Do you not like the house after all?"

"I adore the house."

"Then, what is it?"

Emma tilted her head back to look at him. "I am just so very glad we are here. I think we will be happy."

He smiled, the bewilderment vanishing in relief and

his familiar charm. "I think so, too. I most definitely think so, too."

Sir Jeremy Ashbey strode down the great hall of his family home. There were no servants about, and the ancient gray stones held so deep a chill that not even the summer's day could warm them. His travel boots struck the wooden floor with a hollow thud at every step.

He did not know why he had left London to come back here, leaving his promising career. Especially since Lady Emma would be just on the neighboring estate, reminding him at every moment of what he had lost. No, what had been *taken* from him. Because of that—that blackguard, she no longer belonged to him Yet, she was always in his mind, her pretty face, the sound of her voice, tormenting him at every turn.

No, he had no desire to be here. But his sister's letter had sounded so urgent, frantic. She had threatened to run away, to send their mother to Bedlam, if she received no help.

That Jeremy would not stand for. If the nature of his mother's illness, now just a rumor, became known for certain, if she was taken to a public place like Bedlam, their family would be a laughingstock. If needs be, he would lock both his mother and his sister up here forever before he would tolerate being laughed at.

He stopped at the heavy door to his mother's chamber and knocked shortly. It was several silent moments before there was the scrape of a key in the lock, and his sister swung the door open.

Maria Ashbey was three years younger than her brother, but she looked ten years older. Her face was pale and tinged gray with tiredness, her blond hair scraped back beneath a plain white cap. She was thin, almost emaciated, beneath her plain dark blue dress, and her lips were locked in a pinch.

Jeremy expelled an impatient breath. Maria was the sister of a baronet, yet she always dressed like the veriest kitchen maid. She could at least *try* to make an effort to appear befitting her status.

He pushed past her into the room, and she closed and locked the door behind him. "So you are here at last, brother," she said, in her quiet, colorless voice, a voice that was utterly different from her hysterical letter.

"I came when I received your letter, Maria," he answered shortly. "It came at a very inconvenient time, with the allied monarchs in Town. It does no good for my career for me to be here. And you know that I *must* have a career of some sort, for the money."

Maria shrugged. "It is inconvenient *here,* as well. Mother's nurse has left, and I cannot manage on my own any longer. You must do something."

Jeremy could have shouted at the frustration, the maddening selfishness of it all. "What can I possibly . . ."

The words were scarcely out of his mouth when a shout from the corner cut him off. A figure launched itself out of the shadows at him, nearly knocking him from his feet. He fell back against the door, clutching at his mother.

She caught his coat with her clawlike hands and stared up at him through the veil of her gray-blond hair. Ursula, Lady Ashbey, had once been the loveliest woman in the neighborhood next to Elizabeth Weston. Now she was a thin, twisted old woman with a lined face, rheumy eyes and tangled hair.

"Edward!" she screamed, calling Jeremy by his dead father's name. "You bastard, I knew you would come back from hell to get me!"

"Mother!" Jeremy cried, trying to peel her off him. She just clung harder, the strength of her thin hands inhuman.

"It is time for her medicine," Maria said, still in that toneless voice. She poured out a glass of milky, sticky liquid, diluted with some wine. "You must hold her still for me to administer it to her."

As Jeremy wrestled his screaming mother's hands behind her back, he thought of the elegant life he had planned with Lady Emma and how he had lost it all. This, *this,* was all that was left for him.

Or perhaps—perhaps there *was* something he could do to gain back all that was lost.

Chapter Twenty-Five

"Look at all these, Jack! We have been in the neighborhood only two days, and yet we are invited everywhere." Emma sifted through the stack of cards and letters placed beside her plate at the breakfast table. There was an invitation to tea at the vicarage, supper at someplace called Watley Hall from an old friend of her mother's, Lady Watley, even a dance at the assembly rooms in the village.

Jack smiled at her over his coffee cup. "Such a social whirl! We might as well have stayed in London," he said teasingly.

Emma laughed. "Well, perhaps it is not quite *that* much of a whirl! But it still seems a great deal. I thought the country was a quiet place."

Jack shrugged. He already seemed the casual country squire in his tweed coat and plain waistcoat, his hair a wind-tossed mass of waves. He had spent all yesterday and the day before, and even this morning before breakfast, out riding. Galloping down rustic lanes and through wooded groves, no doubt, Emma thought. As well as who knew what else.

Emma wished she knew the secret of his ease. She also wished she knew the secret that would open the door connecting their two bedchambers, but it quite eluded her. Was she meant to say something when she felt the time was right? Would *he* say something to *her*?

Or perhaps she should just knock on the door. Would that be terribly brazen?

Sometimes it was just inconvenient to be so—so inexperienced. She half-wished she had some sophisticated friend to ask. She did not, of course. There was only Natasha, who knew no more than she did, and Madame Ana. Though Madame Ana was a widow, there was just no way Emma could ask her such a thing, she was so perfect and proper. Even if Emma wanted to, she probably could not catch Madame Ana, the way she dashed about the house after Mrs. Hemmings, asking how things were run in an "English household." She seemed far more concerned with the domestic arrangements than Emma, who also spent a great deal of time studying the house.

Emma sighed. At least Madame Ana would be happy with the invitations. It would give her something else to organize.

And, truly, aside from the bedroom door issue, married life was fine. Better than fine. She loved living in her parents' home, walking the garden paths her mother had trod, playing her mother's pianoforte (though perhaps not as well as her mother had!), and moving slowly into the life of the house, making it her own.

In the evenings, she and Jack would dine at one end of the grand table in the dining room and talk over their days, their plans. Afterwards they would play cards or read together in the drawing room. Last night, they had taken a stroll through the moonlit garden, hand in hand, talking quietly.

It was all very well. It was everything she had imagined married life could be. Almost.

Jack put his coffee cup down, the soft clatter of the china pulling Emma from her musings. "Country life can be just as quiet as you like," he told her. "We do not *have* to accept those invitations, you know, Emma. We can just burrow in here like two little mice and no one will bother us."

"Oh, no, we cannot do that!" she said, with another little laugh. "The dance especially sounds quite jolly, and Lady Watley was a friend of my mother's. We really should meet some more of the neighbors. I do not think two or three evenings out will disturb our pastoral idyll."

"Are we having an idyll?" Jack asked, idly folding up the newspaper he had been reading.

Were they? "Aren't wedding trips supposed to be idyllic? And we are having ours in the country. A pastoral idyll." To cover her silliness, Emma gathered her empty plate and went to deposit it on the sideboard. As she came back, Jack caught her arm and pulled her down onto his lap.

" 'Come live with me and be my love, / And we will all the pleasures prove,' " he quoted, and kissed the side of her neck.

Emma giggled and put her arms around his shoulders. " 'That valleys, groves, hills, and fields, / Woods or steepy mountain yields!' "

"What is a steepy mountain?" he said, his voice muffled against her skin.

It tickled, making her giggle even more. "I do not know! You are the one who started spouting poetry."

"Just because I know the words, that doesn't necessarily mean I know what they *mean*. Besides, it is not my poem—it is Christopher Marlowe's."

"Oh, so you are an educated man, are you?"

"Yes, and here you thought me just a poor buffoon who could not even row a boat across a pond. Now I am dazzling you with my knowledge of great literature." His arms tightened around her and he leaned back in his chair, pulling her even closer. " 'And we will sit upon the rocks, / Seeing the shepherds feed their flocks, / By shallow rivers to whose falls . . .' "

Emma finished with him in rising chorus, " 'Melodious birds sing madrigals!' "

They dissolved into laughter, and the force of their hilarity sent them tumbling from the chair into a heap on the floor. Emma's hair, loosely tied up with a ribbon, fell over her face and shoulders, enclosing them in a shining black curtain.

She pushed it back and sat up, looking down at Jack, who still lay sprawled on the carpet. "Oh, indeed, sirrah, that is most impressive!" she said. "But I fear you must use poetry on all the ladies, 'Firebrand Viscount.' "

Oh, now, *why* had she said that! She had never wanted to think of that silly piece of gossip again, and here she was, spouting it out, using it to tease her husband.

But Jack just laughed and reached up to finger the ends of her hair, wrapping the silk of it around her hand. "So, you read that scurrilous rag, did you?"

"I did. But it was terribly unthorough. It made no mention that you can quote Marlowe."

"Shakespeare, too. But they did not mention it because I was saving it for a very special lady indeed." His expression turned more serious, and his hand tightened on her hair to draw her closer to him. "You should not believe everything they print in such rags, Emma."

"I do not." She placed her hand flat on his chest, felt the rise and fall of his breath. "So, you were not truly a, er, firebrand?"

He laughed reluctantly. "Perhaps I was, every once in a while. But not to the extent some people say, and not for the reasons they thought."

"No?"

"No. I was just looking, searching."

"Searching for what?" Emma whispered.

"For this, of course." He drew her across the last few inches that separated them and took her lips with his.

Emma leaned both hands against his chest and moved deeper into the kiss, sighing at the very deliciousness of it. *This* was what married life had been missing for the last few days. This heat and sweetness.

Jack groaned deep in his chest and dragged her atop him. She went most willingly, sliding her hands up into his hair, holding him still for her.

Unfortunately, she went with a little too much alacrity and not enough grace. Her foot, clad in a sturdy half boot for after-breakfast walking rather than a dainty slipper, caught on the edge of the table and pulled off the cloth. The linen, along with the dishes and silverware, came tumbling off in a great heap, showering them with cold coffee and toast crumbs.

"Blast!" Emma cursed, rolling off Jack in shock.

Her husband muttered something far more rude and reached up to peel a bit of melon from his cheek.

Emma stared at him in absolute mortification. Why, oh why, was she so terribly clumsy? Why did such perils always fall on them? The fall into the pond, her tumble over a topiary and now this. Was she destined never to know the full force of passion?

The breakfast room door flew open and Madame Ana appeared there, for once not entirely prepared. Her lace collar was unbuttoned, her spectacles pushed atop her head. "My lady, what happened? There was such a crash . . ."

She broke off and stared agog at the scene before her. Behind her appeared Natasha, Mrs. Hemmings and two of the footmen, who also looked about with expressions of almost comical astonishment.

At least, it would have been comical if *she* was not the one with toast in her hair, Emma thought.

Jack quickly regained his aplomb. He stood up and drew Emma to her feet, half-pulling her since it seemed her legs had suddenly turned to water. "I am sorry we disturbed you," he said. "As you can see, there was a slight mishap. Madame Ana, would you be so good as to see Lady St. Albans to her chamber and send for some hot water for her?"

Madame Ana stared. "Of—of course, my lord."

"Thank you." Then, quite as if he was *not* stained with coffee, he nodded to the servants, bowed to Emma and strolled elegantly out of the room.

Emma had a slightly more difficult time, due to the fact that she felt like an utter fool, but with Madame Ana on one side and Natasha on the other she managed to go up the stairs and into her bedchamber.

Oh, dear heaven above, but she was doomed! Doomed by her clumsiness to a life of chastity.

Jack waited until his bedchamber door was closed solidly behind him before he collapsed into whoops of laughter.

He laughed until his sides ached, until his cheeks hurt and his voice grew hoarse, and still he could not cease. When the laughter would begin to taper off, he would recall how Emma looked with toast crusts in her hair, her face the very picture of chagrin, and he would be off again.

Finally, he collapsed in the nearest chair, leaned his head back against the cushions and closed his eyes. He found that the complete hilarity of the scene did not quite erase the profound frustration he felt at having their kiss interrupted.

For once in his life, Jack had dug himself into a hole he could not find his way out of. He had made the offer to wait to consummate their marriage in a fit of romance and sentimentality after their sweet wedding night supper, and now he was not exactly sure where to go next. Did he wait for his bride to say something? Did he ask her straight out if she was ready? That did not seem right. For all her boldness and mischief, Emma was a lady. She might not even have the words to talk about their situation.

Jack was not accustomed to being unsure of what to do with a female. He did not like the feeling one bit, and it just added to his sense of turning into a buffoonish fool in front of his wife.

His wife that was not yet *entirely* his wife. Not even the long rides and walks he went out on during the day, wending his way through the greenness and mud of the English summer countryside, helped very much.

Something would have to change—and soon. And, of course, it was up to him to make that change.

Chapter Twenty-Six

*E*mma appeared to be brushing her hair calmly, preparing for an evening out—a supper party at Watley Hall—like any normal young wife. But inside, she was taking deep breaths and gathering her courage.

She put the brush down and turned to face Madame Ana, who was writing in a new little notebook while Natasha arranged Emma's gown for the evening. "Madame Ana," she said. "My aunt told me that you are a widow."

Madame Ana looked up, blinking behind her spectacles. That was her only outward show of surprise. Through everything—arrival at a new household, food on the breakfast room floor—she had always been cool and composed. She had never betrayed any feelings at all about leaving Russia to live in a country manor with her employer's young, silly niece.

She did not even say anything now. She just lowered the notebook to her silk-covered lap and said, "Yes, Lady St. Albans. My husband was killed in battle, before I came to work for Countess Suvarova."

Emma stared at Madame Ana, bewildered. She had had no idea that the cool Madame Ana had suffered such a tragedy. What a selfish, selfish creature she was! What else did she not know? Was Natasha a princess from the Caucasus in disguise? Was Mrs. Hemmings a French spy?

She felt so terrible, she almost could not ask her question. But Madame Ana watched her with eyebrows raised inquiringly. "My aunt said I could ask for your, er, assistance, if ever I needed it."

"Of course." Madame Ana clutched the notebook against her and smiled happily. Emma had obviously spoken the magic word—assistance. "That is what I am here for, Lady St. Albans. To help you in any way I can. Would you like to arrange a soiree?"

"Perhaps one day soon. Right now, I need your help on a more—personal matter."

Madame Ana leaned forward, and Natasha slowed in mending the lace trim on Emma's gown to listen. "You may rely on my discretion, Lady St. Albans," Madame Ana said.

"Then, as a widow," Emma began, then paused to damp her dry lips with the tip of her tongue. "As a widow, perhaps you could advise me on how a woman can go about attracting a man."

Madame Ana's brows flicked just a bit as she stared at Emma, expressionless. Natasha gave a startled giggle and pressed the lace she was arranging to her mouth.

"There is a man you wish to—attract?" Madame Ana asked slowly.

Emma had the terrible sense she was making a mess of this conversation, just as she had made a mess of most things of late. She had to press forward, though. She had to *know,* and Madame Ana was the only one she could think of to ask. "Yes," she said.

"And—did you meet him here? Recently?"

Madame Ana's tone was delicate—too delicate. Emma suddenly realized that they must think she was already planning to take a lover. And since they had met no one new here in the country, they probably thought it was a gardener or a footman.

Emma giggled like Natasha and suddenly didn't feel so very unsure anymore. She still felt silly, but that did not matter so much. "Well, yes, I did meet him recently. He is my husband."

"Oh!" Madame Ana laughed aloud in her surprise. It

was the first time Emma had seen her laugh, and it made her seem younger, more approachable. "You want to attract Lord St. Albans? But, if you will forgive me saying so, you are already married to him."

"Yes, of course. But I want him to, er, look at me in a different way. If you see what I mean."

Natasha stared at her, all agog. "Is that why you were crying the morning after your wedding, my lady?"

Madame Ana's eyes widened with sympathy. "Oh, Lady St. Albans! Was it so awful? My own wedding night was not as—comfortable as it might have been. But his lordship seems like such a gentleman . . ."

"No, it was not awful," Emma said. She sensed she was making a hash of things again. "It was—well, it was nothing. We have not done anything yet."

Natasha gasped.

"You mean—even after that scene in the breakfast room this morning?" Madame Ana asked.

Emma shrugged. "He said he wanted to wait until it was *right* for me."

"Ah. So then, he is not, um, incapable?"

Incapable? Emma had to think about this for a moment, to figure out what Madame Ana meant, but—"No. I do not think that is it at all."

"No. I would imagine not." Madame Ana tapped her chin with one finger thoughtfully, her eyes glowing with the light of a challenge. "Well, the first thing I would suggest is perhaps Natasha could make a few small alterations to that gown you are wearing this evening?"

Natasha held up the gown, a fashionable but modest creation of raspberry-colored silk and white lace. "Oh, yes! I could do that."

"And perhaps you have some *interesting* underpinnings?" Madame Ana continued. She reopened her notebook and scribbled furiously in it with her gold pencil. "Perhaps you could . . ."

She went on with her ideas, and Emma listened with

great fascination. She had had no idea that Madame Ana had such hidden depths!

She just hoped she had some of the same depths in herself.

They were probably going to be late to supper at Watley Hall, Jack thought carelessly as he looked at the clock on the drawing room mantel. Not that it particularly mattered to him. He had been enjoying the quiet of their time in the country and did not miss the rush of the social calendar. He would prefer an evening at home with Emma, a simple meal, perhaps a card game or a walk in the garden.

He particularly liked those walks in the garden, with the moon shimmering down on the trees and the flowers, Emma's hand in his.

Jack laughed and swallowed the last of his brandy. He was becoming a terrible romantic in his old age, he thought, a besotted country squire who wanted nothing but to stroll in the garden with his wife! How his friends would ridicule him if they could see it; how Mr. Thompson would fear he was "turning soft." But Jack could not seem to care.

The door opened behind him, and he said, "So, here you are! I was wondering what was keeping you . . ." He turned and his words trailed away.

Emma stood there, drawing on her long gloves and wearing the most extraordinary gown. It was of a dark pink silk, with the rich sheen of summer fruit falling ripe from the tree. Thick white lace fell from the hem, and framed the low—*very* low—square neckline. The tiny puffed sleeves skimmed the very edges of her shoulders, baring the clean line of her collarbone, the swan-like turn of her white neck. Her necklace was a chain of diamonds, with one large, pear-shaped stone seeming to point the way to her exquisite décolletage. More diamonds dangled from her ears. Her hair was simply dressed in a knot low on her neck, with curls falling free against her skin.

Jack put his brandy glass down on the nearest table, his fingers suddenly nerveless. She gave him a slow, sweet smile and moved toward him, her shimmering skirts swaying.

"I am sorry I'm late," she said, in a low voice. When she reached him, she slid her hands over his shoulders and went up on tiptoe to press her lips to his. They moved in a slow, sensuous glide, light and beckoning.

Jack reached out and pulled her closer, but she slid out of his hands with a mysterious little laugh.

"Tardiness can be excused, if this is the result," he said, and wished fervently that his voice was not so ridiculously breathless. "You look beautiful."

"Thank you, Jack dear. Better than I did this morning, with toast and coffee all over me?" She turned in a slow circle, peering back over her shoulder as if to be sure that no food clung to her backside.

Her dainty, delectable backside.

Jack wondered if there was any brandy left or perhaps something even stronger. "You look beautiful no matter what you wear, Emma."

"You *are* full of compliments tonight," she answered, with a small toss of her head. The diamonds danced in a multicolored sparkle.

Jack leaned forward and kissed the spot of skin just where her neck touched her shoulder. Her lilac perfume filled his senses until there was room for nothing else.

Emma tilted her head, giving him room for his kiss, but only for the merest moment before she backed away. "We should be going," she murmured.

He grinned at her. "I was hoping perhaps we could stay home for a quiet supper, maybe a walk in the garden."

She shook her head, with what he hoped was a regretful air. "No, I accepted the invitation for the supper party. Lady Watley was a friend of my mother. She would be so disappointed if we did not appear."

"*I* would be disappointed if we did not have our walk in the garden," Jack protested.

Emma laid one finger lightly against his cheek, drawing the butter-soft kid of her glove along his skin. "Perhaps we could have that walk—later. For now, the carriage is waiting." She gave him another of those small, mysterious smiles and sashayed out of the drawing room.

Jack followed. Really, he could do nothing else. He would be fortunate if he could survive the long, night-dark ride in the close confines of the carriage, since his wife had decided to behave so strangely.

Chapter Twenty-Seven

*E*mma hoped she was just doing this right and didn't look like a complete simpleton. She was trying to follow the advice of Madame Ana and Natasha, but really their advice had been a bit—inconvenient. More a jumble of guesses and wild suggestions than a sensible plan. Madame Ana may have been married before, but her marriage could not have been a very passionate union, judging from her blushes and vague conjectures, mixed with suprisingly clear advice. And Natasha only knew about romance from novels, much as Emma herself did. But, still, they were all Emma had, and their advice had to be better than nothing.

Didn't it?

So she took a deep breath and slid closer to Jack in the warm darkness of the carriage. She eased her lace shawl back from the altered neckline of her gown, resisting the urge to tug the silk and lace higher, and laid her hand lightly on Jack's leg.

He glanced down at her quizzically. She gave him a smile, but it felt more like a simper, so she turned away instead, staring into the night in what she hoped was a mysterious manner.

Oh, how she wished he would just kiss her and get this all over with! With his lips on hers, his arms holding her close, she never worried or felt awkward at all. It was the trying to *get* him to kiss her that was so awful. If only she could have skipped over some of the lessons

in deportment and music and etiquette and learned about
how to be married instead.

But she had not, and now she was groping about in
the dark. Literally.

She must have made some low, involuntary moan of
misery, because Jack said, in a concerned tone, "Are you
quite all right, Emma?"

"Oh, yes," she squeaked. "Yes. I just wish the—the
party was not so far away."

He put his arm about her shoulders and gave her a
reassuring squeeze. "I am sure the coachman is going as
fast as he can. I am sure we will not be set upon by
highwaymen or wild wolves here!"

"That is not what I am afraid of," Emma muttered in
acute frustration.

"What did you say, m'dear? I am afraid I could not
quite hear you."

"I said—oh, *blast*!" Emma could no longer contain
herself. She feared she was simply terrible at playing the
coquette. No one was watching her now, judging her on
her social impropriety; the direct way was surely best.

She reached her arms around Jack's neck and pulled
him to her, drawing him down to meet her kiss. She put
everything she had learned from him into that kiss, every
bit of the passion she was feeling.

For an instant, Jack's shoulders stiffened with surprise,
but then he quickly moved into the spirit of things. His
own arms came around her waist, pulling her across his
lap, bending her head back against his shoulder.

The carriage hit a rut in the road, jolting them apart
just as things were truly becoming interesting. Jack lifted
his head from hers and stared down at her, his breath
coming fast. The only light was a beam of chalky gray-
white moonlight, and it cast an unearthly glow over his
sharpened features. He stared at her almost as if he had
never seen her before, as if she were some elfin creature
just landed in his arms.

"By God, Emma, I do not know what has gotten into
you," he whispered hoarsely. "But I like it."

Emma laughed and dropped her head back to rest against the carriage cushions. Relief flowed through her like a cool wash of rain, and she felt like herself again. Like she and Jack were *themselves,* and everything would be all right. Everything would work out as it should, whether she swayed her hips and wore low-cut gowns or not.

"Oh, Jack," she said. "I do not know what has gotten into me, either. It must be your pernicious influence. You are very bad for me."

He chuckled and bent his head to kiss her shoulder, the first gentle swell of her breast. Emma shivered and closed her eyes in complete delight.

"I think you are the one who is bad for *me,*" he said against her skin.

Vague snatches of Madame Ana's advice floated through Emma's fog-shrouded mind, and she followed them as if mesmerized, kicking aside her skirt to run her leg up and along the length of Jack's. Her silk stocking caught on the fine wool of his trousers in a delicate friction. Jack groaned, and Emma smiled. So, some of that advice *was* good, after all.

But the delicious moment was cut all too short, when the carriage turned and slowed as it made its way to the front doors of Watley Hall.

Jack sat back and helped Emma pull herself upright. She reached up to smooth her hair and arranged her gown to rights, straightening her necklace and disentangling her earrings from her curls. Jack performed his own hurried toilette, his breathing ragged in the shadows.

Emma drew her shawl closer around her shoulders and watched out the window as the doors to the house opened and their own footmen jumped down to help them alight from the carriage.

"I am sorry," Emma said. "I picked a very poor time to, er, express my feelings."

Jack laughed and drew her closer for one last quick kiss. "My dear, please feel free to 'express your feelings' any time you like. Except perhaps when we are at church or some such. I *do* have my reputation to maintain, you know. I would not like you to besmirch it."

Emma choked on her own laughter and smacked at his shoulder.

He caught her hand in his. "And you *may* want to restrain your lustful impulses at supper tonight. I know it will be hard to resist my handsome face . . ."

Emma slapped at him again. Jack just laughed, and jumped down from the open carriage door. He reached back to help her out, holding her against him for just a moment longer than was strictly proper before lowering her feet to the ground.

He offered her his arm politely, as if they had been doing nothing more in the carriage than discussing the weather. "Shall we go in, Lady St. Albans?"

"Oh, my dear Lady Emma! How glorious to see you again. You are every bit as lovely as you promised to be when you were a child." Lady Watley, a tall, imperiously beautiful matron in a dark green satin gown and towering green and gold striped turban, swooped through the guests in her drawing room to kiss Emma on both cheeks. "Oh, but I cannot call you Lady Emma any longer, can I? It is Lady St. Albans now."

Emma smiled, drawing on every bit of her social training to be properly polite in the midst of this whirlwind. It was quite bewildering to be taken from the intense feelings in the dark carriage to this crowded gathering, this effusive welcome.

"Lady Watley," she said, returning the woman's greeting kiss. "I am very glad to see you again as well."

"You must call me Aunt Amelia, as you did when you were a child. But you do not remember that, of course; you were so small when we lost your dear parents. You are the very image of your mother!" Lady Watley reached out with a tiny, casual movement that flicked the lace ruffle at Emma's neckline back into place.

Emma had not even realized it was still in disarray. "And this must be your handsome° new husband! At least I *hope* that it is."

"Yes, of course." Emma, hoping fervently that the rest of her clothes were straight, drew Jack forward. "This *is* my husband, Viscount St. Albans. Jack, Lady Watley was a great friend of my mother's."

"We were bosom bows." Lady Watley held her hand out for Jack to bow over and gave an almost girlish giggle when he flashed her a flirtatious smile. "And *you*, Lord St. Albans, are famous even here in the country! I will be a renowned hostess for securing you for my little supper. It was so dear of you both to interrupt your newly-wed idyll to come here."

Emma hoped Jack would not launch into Marlowe at the mention of the word "idyll."

He did not. "It is our pleasure, Lady Watley," Jack answered. "We are hoping to spend as much time as possible at Weston Manor in the future, and we wish to know more of our neighbors."

"Then you have come to the right place. Everyone who is anyone is here this evening, and most of them knew your family, Emma." Lady Watley tucked Emma's arm through hers and drew her forward into the gathering. "Come, let me introduce you. Or should I say reintroduce you?"

Emma, conscious of Jack always beside her on her other side, followed in Lady Watley's wake. It was like being drawn forward by a green satin tidal wave. They met the vicar they had seen tending his garden on the day they arrived, his wife, a local baronet and his wife and four daughters, an earl and countess newly returned from Town, their dandyish son—and an elderly viscount who wanted to tell them all about the philosophical treatise he was writing. It was dizzying and confusing, but also delightful—they all offered reminiscences of her parents, memories of her as a young child.

She just hoped she could remember all their names later.

"And now, my dears, I would like you to meet your

own neighbor! He surprised us by arriving from Town just a few days ago. This is Sir Jeremy Ashbey. His family's estate lies right next to Weston Manor." Lady Watley reached out to catch a gentleman's blue velvet-clad arm and draw him to her side. "All of the local young ladies have tried for years to catch his eye, to no avail! But now that you are here, Emma, perhaps you can help me in a spot of matchmaking for him."

Emma stared in shock at Sir Jeremy's familiar features and pale hair, features she had hoped were left behind in London. She could feel her smile slipping sideways, and struggled to hold onto it, to maintain her polite expression and not show her bewilderment. She felt Jack's protective clasp on her arm, felt him move up next to her.

Lady Watley chattered on, not even noticing the sudden tension in the air of her drawing room.

"We have already met Sir Jeremy," Emma managed to say. "In London."

Sir Jeremy's stare did not move from her, but Emma could not meet that unwavering look. She stared past his shoulder at a painting on the wall—a still life of sliced fruit and a dead duck.

"I had the great honor of attending Lord and Lady St. Albans's wedding," Sir Jeremy said. "Their very *sudden* wedding."

"Oh, of course!" Lady Watley cried. "I should have known you would meet in Town. So many exciting things going on there now. You must tell us all about it." A bell chimed, interrupting the stream of her words. "Time for supper! I do hope you care for lamb. My chef is quite the wizard with mint sauce. Mr. Smithson, would you escort me in?"

Emma took Jack's arm and moved automatically toward the dining room, following the trail of Lady Watley's green and gold train. She still smiled, still held her head up as if she was having a marvelous time. But some of the luster was gone from this homecoming, this beginning of public life as a couple with her husband.

What was Sir Jeremy doing here? Why did she have to see him again? Had he followed her? He was meant to be in London, at the embassy.

As Jack helped her into her seat at the table, he leaned down and whispered in her ear, "Do not worry, my dear. He won't bother you. He cannot ruin this evening in any way."

She smiled at him and reached up to touch his cheek. He sat down beside her, a solid, reassuring presence next to her. He was right. This was *their* evening, and no one, especially no spurned suitors, could touch it. She took a sip of her wine and laughed at a joke the vicar was telling. This was a perfectly ordinary supper party, and she would treat it as such. She would completely ignore the looks Sir Jeremy Ashbey was sending her down the table.

What the devil was that man doing here?

Jack drank his wine, ate the courses that were set before him, talked and laughed just as he was expected to, but all the time he was aware of Sir Jeremy Ashbey just down the table from them. He wanted to move closer to Emma, to put his arm around her. She also talked, sipped at her wine and smiled, yet Jack could see the careful stiffness of her slim shoulders, the pointed way she did not look in Sir Jeremy's direction.

But *he* looked at *her,* and Jack did not like it at all. He wasn't exactly sure why the man so unsettled him. A woman as lovely as Emma was certain to have had other admirers. Most men, though, once they lost the object of their interest to another, would bow out with good grace and turn their attention to a different lady. They would not follow her on her wedding trip.

And surely that was what Ashbey were doing, family house in the neighborhood or no. Following Emma—watching her.

Her hand trembled just a bit as she placed her wine glass back on the table, though her smile remained beautifully in place. Jack reached out to touch her fingers, briefly, reassuringly. She gave him a grateful glance.

Jack wished this blasted supper was over, that they were alone in their own home.

"It is so very nice to see a young newlywed couple so *fond* of each other," the vicar's pretty, round little wife said, with a romantic sigh.

Emma laughed and blushed the palest of sunset pinks. Jack wasn't sure what to say.

"Indeed it is, my dear!" the vicar agreed. "And we are all very glad you have decided to settle in our fair county. Such welcome additions!"

"I am really not sure where we are going to settle permanently," Emma said. "Though I do hope we will spend much time at Weston Manor. I had not realized how homesick I was until I returned there!"

"Of course, of course," said the vicar. "And I hope you will join us for services on Sunday."

"We are looking forward to it," Emma assured him.

"Reverend Mr. Smithson has been an excellent shepherd to our flock," said Lady Watley. "His homilies are always so inspirational."

The vicar laughed. "You are too kind, Lady Watley. I merely do my best."

"You are far too modest!" Lady Watley admonished, and gestured to the servants to bring out the dessert. "We are all proud to be part of your congregation. Though we have not seen Sir Jeremy's mother or sister at services for quite some time."

Everyone who heard her words turned to look at Sir Jeremy Ashbey. Forced to move his gaze from Emma and stare out at the company, he turned a bit pale.

"Yes," he finally said. "I fear my mother has not been entirely well of late, and Maria has been taking care of her."

"Oh, I *am* sorry to hear that!" Lady Watley exclaimed. "Perhaps I should come visit her and give Miss Ashbey a bit of a rest?"

"No!" Sir Jeremy said, too loudly. He seemed to notice the surprised glances of the other diners, for he went on in a quieter voice, "You are very kind, Lady Watley, but I fear my mother is not quite well enough for callers. I am sure Maria would like to visit you here, though."

"I would enjoy that very much," said Lady Watley; then the talk turned to other topics as everyone finished their lemon trifle.

Perhaps that was all there was to it, then, Jack thought. Sir Jeremy had just come back to take care of his family. Jack doubted it, though. He doubted it very much.

Emma was very glad when Lady Watley rose and led the ladies back to the drawing room for tea, leaving the gentlemen to their port. An evening she had been looking forward to, a time to become reacquainted with old friends, had become a strain due to Sir Jeremy's unexpected appearance. She still did not care for the way he watched her from his pale green eyes, as if expecting her to do or say something.

She was sorry to hear of his family's troubles, of course, but that did not mean he had to watch her so. She shivered despite the summer warmth of the breeze from the open windows.

"Are you cold, my dear Emma?" Lady Watley asked, sitting down next to her on the satin settee to hand her a cup of tea.

"No, not at all. It is perfectly comfortable in here." Emma sipped at the strong brew. "A lovely evening altogether, Aunt Amelia. Thank you so much for inviting us."

"Oh, pish! I was very glad to hear you had returned. It somehow seems to make our little circle complete again." Lady Watley sipped at her own tea and gave a little sigh. "We are quite close-knit here, as you can see. So I was very sorry to hear Sir Jeremy speak of his mother's illness."

"Hm," Emma murmured softly. "Indeed. Are you very good friends with Lady Ashbey?"

"Friends? I am not sure one *can* be friends with Lady Ashbey. She has kept rather to herself, ever since her husband died several years ago. But she is a part of the neighborhood, and Maria is a sweet girl, if very quiet." Lady Watley gave Emma a smile. "Lady Ashbey did always seem to like your mother, though, and always attended her gatherings. And her son seemed so fond of you when you were children, always following you about, fetching you sweetmeats and such. Do you not remember him from those years?"

Emma shook her head. She really did not want to talk about Sir Jeremy or any affection he may have held for her. "No, I fear not."

"Ah, well, you were so small then. Things here must seem so strange to you, after living in Russia for so long! Are there really bears and wolves roaming the streets there? And snow all year around?"

Emma laughed, glad of the change of topic to one she was comfortable with—her *other* home. They talked of Russia, of her aunt and uncle, until the men came to rejoin the ladies.

"Well, we are glad you have come back to England," Lady Watley said, rising as Jack came to stand beside his wife. "And with such a handsome husband in tow! We must persuade Mrs. Smithson to play the pianoforte for some country dances, so I may partner with Lord St. Albans."

Jack gave her his charming smile. "It would be my honor, Lady Watley."

"Handsome *and* accommodating!" Lady Watley twittered, then moved off in her green satin cloud.

Jack sat beside Emma and took her hand in his. "Are you quite all right, my dear?" he whispered. "Would you like to go home?"

Emma *was* all right, now that he was with her. Even the presence of Sir Jeremy, talking with the earl's dandyish son over by the fireplace, did not matter one whit. She smiled and said, "And miss the dancing? Certainly not!"

Nothing was going to mar the rest of their evening, she determined. Nothing.

Chapter Twenty-Eight

*T*he house was quiet when they arrived back from the supper party, without even the butler or a footman to greet them. Since they had not been out in the evening before, there was no formal routine set, but Emma did not mind what her aunt would have decried as slackness. She was just happy to be back in their own safe, warm haven.

In the darkness of the foyer, lit only with one small lamp set on the table, Emma turned to Jack and moved into his arms. She buried her nose in his shirtfront, inhaling his clean scent of starch, soap and brandy. She dropped her shawl, letting it tangle at their feet.

He held her, too, rocking her gently and pressing kisses to her hair, her temples, her cheek. "You looked lovely tonight," he said, his voice enticingly low. "Not that you don't look lovely at all other times, as well . . ."

Emma laughed. "Thank you, Jack. And so did you. Look lovely, that is."

"I'm sorry Sir Jeremy Ashbey appeared there. What could the man have been thinking? I will have to have a conversation with him."

A *conversation*? "No, dear, don't do that. We shall just ignore him as if he did not exist. And he doesn't, not here." She tilted her head back to stare up at him. The flickering light of the lamp cast shadows across his sharp cheekbones, his eyes, the lock of hair that fell over his forehead. He was so unbearably beautiful to her that it made her very heart ache. It made her want to cry, but it also made her happier than she could ever have imagined being. "No one exists here but you and me."

"Just you and me. My beautiful wife." He lowered his head to kiss her, and she practically glowed with anticipation, her lips tingling with the need to feel his on hers.

Their lips had just barely brushed, her hand tangling in his loosened cravat, when a door banged open and the light from another lamp flooded across the marble floor of the foyer. Emma could have ignored those things, thought them a figment of the glorious dream state that came over her when Jack kissed her, but she could not ignore the sharp cough that sounded. And the tap of a foot.

Emma drew back from Jack and blinked away the haze from her eyes. Madame Ana stood outside the drawing room door, which she had obviously just shut. She held up a lamp, which showed that she still wore her black silk gown and a black shawl around her shoulders, but her spectacles were gone and her hair slightly loosened. For Madame Ana, this was deepest dishabille.

Emma feared she herself was even more awry. She stepped back and picked up her shawl, glad that it was dim so her pink face could not be seen.

"Madame Ana," she said. "Were you waiting for us? I know we are late . . ."

Madame Ana shook her head. "There is a visitor, my lady. In the drawing room." With that, she turned and marched off up the stairs, taking her light with her.

Emma glanced up at Jack, who appeared as puzzled as she felt. "A visitor? So late?" she said. "Who could it . . ." A horrible idea struck her. "Sir Jeremy Ashbey would not have come here, would he?"

"Surely not. Even lunatics have *some* manners," he muttered.

"Then, who could it be?"

"There is really only one way to find out, my dear." Jack took her arm and led her into the drawing room.

A small fire was lit in the grate, and seated before it

was Bertie Stonewich. They had seen him last at their wedding, handsome in his dress uniform, flirting with all the young lady guests and making them giggle. Tonight, he appeared a bit the worse for wear in dusty travel buckskins and boots, his golden hair rumpled. It was obvious he had ridden hard, but his smile was wide and happy. Probably due to the decanter of port that sat, half empty, on the table next to his chair.

Emma stared at him. He seemed an apparition, swept up from London from Jack's wild past, and dropped into this new country life.

"Hallo, Jack, Lady St. Albans!" he said cheerfully, saluting them with his glass. "Nice to see you again."

"And nice to see you, too, Bertie," Jack said, in a harsh voice that belied the words. "But, what the, the—blazes are you doing here?"

"Oh, just enjoying your very fine port," Bertie answered. "And trying to talk to that pretty maid of yours, but I must say she is not very friendly."

Emma frowned at him, remembering Madame Ana's abruptness in the foyer. "Madame Ana is not my maid; she is my secretary. I will thank you not to annoy her, Mr. Stonewich."

Bertie's golden brows arched. "Oh, I say . . ."

Jack took Emma's arm, turned her to face him. "My dear, you must be tired. Why don't you go up to your chamber? I will see to our—guest."

Emma nodded. She *was* tired, and her planned romantic evening did not appear that it would happen, thanks to this midnight arrival. The best she could hope for now was her bed and perhaps a warm milk to drink.

"Good night, Jack," she said, and kissed his cheek, softly, lingeringly. "Good night, Mr. Stonewich."

"Good night, Lady St. Albans," he replied happily. As Emma left the drawing room, she heard him say "Join me in a port, Jack?"

She shook her head ruefully and went up the stairs, following the same path Madame Ana had taken earlier. Natasha waited for her in her chamber to unfasten her altered pink gown and help her into her nightdress. She even had the warm milk, liberally laced with brandy, waiting.

"Ah, Natasha, you are a marvel," Emma said, crawling beneath the bedclothes with her drink. "What would I do without you?" Suddenly, she realized what a long evening it had been.

"Oh, I'm sure you would be just fine, my lady," Natasha said with a laugh. She shook out Emma's gown and hung it up in the wardrobe. "Madame Ana said a guest from London was here."

"Yes. One of his lordship's friends."

"Madame Ana did not seem very happy to meet him."

"I'll speak to her in the morning." Emma leaned back on her pillows, letting the warm lassitude of the brandy wash over her. "I do wonder what he's doing here, though."

She also wondered if Bertie had come to try to lure Jack back to the wildness of Town life before their married life had even started. And she wondered what Jack would do if he had.

Jack closed the drawing room door behind Emma and leaned back on it, watching Bertie impassively. "What are you doing here?"

Bertie put his glass down and stood up, the tipsy n'er-do-well falling away. "Bad timing, I know. You are no doubt enjoying your wedding trip with the delectable Lady Emma, but it cannot be helped. There is to be a meeting in London, day after tomorrow, and your presence is required."

A meeting? Jack said nothing, just folded his arms across his chest, but his mind raced. What meeting could be so urgent that he was *required* to be there? They were in peacetime now. Mr. Thompson had assured him that it was a perfectly convenient time for him to be away from London. What could have happened in the few days he had been here?

And how could he leave his "delectable" wife now?

They were just beginning to come together. And Sir Jeremy Ashbey's presence was bothersome. Jack was almost certain the man would not try anything, but he made Emma uncomfortable. He should not leave her alone.

For the first time, two duties warred for preeminence in his heart. Two loyalties, equally strong, pulled at him.

Bertie watched him closely. "Is something amiss here?"

Jack shrugged. "Not amiss, exactly. But it is something I cannot like. Sir Jeremy Ashbey, who had hopes of marrying Emma himself, has come into the neighborhood. He was at the supper party this evening and watched her in such a way that it made her uncomfortable."

Bertie nodded thoughtfully. "Do you think the man will—try something? Try to hurt Lady Emma, take some revenge on her for spurning him?"

"I do not know what he might do. I *do* know that Emma will not feel at ease about being alone now." Jack frowned. "Did they say what the meeting was about?"

"You will have to discover that for yourself, I fear. Perhaps I can help you, though, Jack my friend."

"You, Bertie? How?"

"You should only be gone for a few days. In the meantime, I could stay here and keep an eye on the situation for you. I already have *my* orders."

Jack laughed, but it sounded dry and humorless even to his own ears. "So I should leave you here to harass my wife's staff?"

Bertie shrugged. "How was I to know the woman was a secretary? And all I did was give her the tiniest pat on the bottom as she walked past. The way she screeched and shouted Russian curses at me, you would have thought I tore that hideous black dress off of her!"

"Madame Ana is very proper. If I leave you here . . ."

Bertie held up his hand in a gesture of surrender. "I will be the very picture of gentlemanly rectitude, I vow! And this Ashbey fellow will not dare to come near Weston Manor. I promise you that."

Jack nodded, reluctantly, but what else could he do?

He was needed in London. And at least with Bertie here he would know Emma was protected. It was not much; it was not the same as being here himself. But it would have to do, for now.

"Very well," he said. "I will be counting on you."

"You saved my life in Spain," Bertie answered, very seriously. "I will protect your wife with my own, if need be."

"You had better. Now, is there any of that port left? Or did you drink it all in your usual greedy way?"

Chapter Twenty-Nine

*E*mma awoke, startled by some noise. She slowly sat up against her pillows and looked out the window. The gleaming half-moon was low in the sky, which meant she had been asleep for some time. Her head still felt thick and misty with dreams and brandied milk.

What was the sound that woke her? Her gaze darted around the chamber, yet she saw nothing amiss. There was another noise, a sort of shuffling, and she realized it came from the room next to hers. Jack's room.

He must have come up from the drawing room, but that meant he had been there with Bertie Stonewich all this time. What could they have been talking about?

She would just have to go in there and ask.

She must still be tipsy, she thought, as she pushed back the blankets and climbed out of bed, crossing the room to the door connecting her to Jack. Either that or she was dreaming and none of this was actually happening. Whichever, she somehow did not care.

She reached up to rap on the wood but changed her mind and tested the knob instead. It turned under her touch. She slipped into the room and closed the door behind her.

A candle burned on Jack's bedside table, showing Emma the plain, dark furniture deemed suitable for a lord's chamber, so different from her own gilt and satin. At first she did not see Jack, but his coat, waistcoat and cravat were tossed over the back of an armchair.

His evening pumps and stockings were piled on the carpet.

As her eyes adjusted to the light, she saw him. The shuffling noise she had heard must have been the draperies opening, for he stood by the window, peering out, one hand holding the velvet fabric. He stood as still as marble, as quiet, as—alone. He stared out at the moon and the stars like some solitary, eternal god, pondering all the weight of humanity that had been placed on his shoulders. As if he were not part of this world, *her* world, at all. As if he was beyond her touch.

His very stillness made her hesitate and glance back at the door she had just shut. Maybe it was a mistake for her to be here at all. He obviously had something weighty on his mind, and she was not sure why she had come anyway.

But it was too late for turning back. "Emma?" he said softly, without moving.

"Er, yes. It is I." She left the wall and moved to his side, joining him by the window. The evening light fell across his face in a pale gold wash. He was still her handsome Jack, but he seemed tired. No, not just tired, *weary*. He gave her a small smile and held his hand out to her. His skin was cool, and she held it tightly between her two palms, trying to warm it.

"I thought you would be asleep," he said. "It is very late, and we had a long evening."

"A long evening? A supper party?" She gave a little laugh, trying to make his smile widen. "La, I could have danced until dawn, I could have sung and marched . . ."

"All right, so my merry-making wife is not tired!" he said, and took his hand from hers to put his arm around her waist, drawing her close to his side. "But it *is* late."

"You are up late as well," Emma pointed out. "What did Mr. Stonewich want? It was obvious that he came here upon some errand, despite his silly behavior."

"My dear, you are too right. But let us not talk of Bertie tonight. Let us just enjoy the moon. It will fade away all too soon."

Emma leaned against Jack and looked out at the sky. It was deepest black, sprinkled with a few diamond stars and full of moonglow. The edges were growing faintest blue, though, heralding the distant dawn.

"Fading or not, it is lovely." For some reason, the night scene made her think of Russia. Her bedroom in their country home had possessed a cushioned window seat, and many an evening she had sat there, looking out at the scene. It had sometimes been thick and soft, with nuts dropping from the trees and water rippling off the pond where she liked to row. More often, it was covered with thick, smooth snow, purest white, with icicles glistening from the trees. Yet always, always there had been the moon, watching her, waiting, unchanging.

It watched her still.

"When you spoke to me of your time in Spain, Jack, of how you would watch the sky and dream of a better future, I understood what you meant," she said, still looking at the moon but sensing that he was listening to her, paying close attention to her words. "I often felt the same, though my war was cold, not hot, like Spain. So very cold."

"Where did you spend the war, Emma?" he asked.

"When it looked dangerous, as if Bonaparte might be coming closer, my aunt and uncle sent me to their country estate for safety. It was safe enough, off the path of the terrible invasion, but we were sometimes hungry even there, unable to bring in supplies at all. There was the household to feed, and Natasha and I did our best, yet the Russian winter was hard. Particularly that year, which was colder than what anyone could recall in living memory, and we often had no news. We did not know where anyone was. My aunt and uncle were with the Tsar, but I could never be sure of their safety." Emma did not like to think of those bleak, dark days. When the memories were locked away silently in her heart, she could almost persuade herself that they had not happened at all.

Tonight, though, they seemed closer to her. Maybe it

was the contrast of that lonely, cold time to this warm, soft happiness, these days of peace. It made her new life, her marriage, her home, even this dear moon all the more precious.

Jack's arm tightened. "You were hungry?" he said, his voice appalled.

"Only sometimes. Natasha and I would go out to find food, and I learned to make bread from the most amazing ingredients!" She tried to laugh, as if digging in the snow for forgotten roots and stretching flour with straw was a lark. Here, with her feet warm and her stomach full, it almost seemed it *was*. "You would not have imagined it of your spoiled little wife, would you, Jack?"

He turned her in his arms, staring down at her as if he had never seen her before. "I had no idea, Emma."

"I do not like to speak of that time. It is all very long ago."

"You are truly the bravest person I have ever met."

Emma stared up at him, astonished. Her, brave? She had faced only what everyone in Russia had. Her own life then had been positively easeful compared with the people on the front lines. Compared with Jack himself, battling on the sun-baked Spanish ground. "I only did what I had to. I was not as brave as you. You fought; you faced death every day. You volunteered to protect your country."

"I volunteered to annoy my father."

"What do you mean?"

"I am his heir. No one expects or even wants firstborn young peers to be risking life and limb in battle, but I did it anyway. I took pleasure in his blustering chagrin, and I admit I had dreams of glory, too. Of course, I found precious little of that, but I was very young and foolish. I could not know what I would really find."

Emma felt like crying, like stopping up her ears so she could hear nothing of this. She could not. All she could do was whisper "What did you find?"

"What must have been found in Russia, too. Starving people, a land torn apart by a war not of their own making. Young men full of foolish ideas. Young women forced to forage for food. But I found one other thing, as well."

"Did you?"

"I found myself. Not the selfish young pup I had been, but my true self. And do you know what I found of myself, there under the hot sun?"

Emma shook her head wordlessly.

"That I was not so very bad after all. Yet not nearly as courageous as those foraging girls." His hands slid up to hold her face between them, cradling her, cherishing her. "Not as brave as you, making your way alone in the winter."

She put her hands over his, holding him to her. With his support, she *was* brave. But that winter she had been scared to death. She wanted to forget it, to forget it all and make Jack forget, too. "Kiss me," she commanded, standing on tiptoe and tilting her head so he could reach her easier. "Jack, please, just kiss me."

He smiled at her crookedly. "I am always happy to oblige a lady."

This kiss was as sweet as the others they had shared, but there was something else beneath—something urgent, desperate even. As if this was the one embrace that could save them. Save them from what, she could not say, and yet they clung to each other, moving closer and closer until there was not a beam of moonlight between them.

Jack's mouth slanted over hers. He tasted of port and of something deeper and darker, almost like a bitter chocolate but not exactly. It was just something that was Jack himself. It was rich and intoxicating and perfect. For a moment, Emma was sharply aware that she herself was a mess, rumpled and smelling of sleep. She wished she could run back to her room, tidy herself and start all over again, but that wish was quickly lost when Jack's hand slid along her ribcage to gently, ever so gently, touch her breast.

"Oh!" she gasped, surprised by the sensations that

simple touch evoked. It tingled and burned like—like stars bursting in the night sky.

His hand moved back to her waist. "Sorry," he muttered hoarsely, kissing the side of her neck, the soft spot just beneath her ear.

"No, no. I like it." She took his hand and placed his strong fingers back where they had been. "Please, Jack. Do that again."

He raised his head to look at her, dazedly, questioningly. "Are you sure?"

"Yes." She had never been more sure of anything. "Oh, yes."

He kissed her again, with a wild desire that stole the very breath from her. When his lips broke from hers, it was only so he could bend and catch her behind the knees, sweeping her up into his arms.

They fell back onto his high, velvet-draped bed together, a tangle of limbs and cloth and sighs and exclamations. Emma never even noticed when the moon vanished from the sky, and only blue-black darkness was left.

Chapter Thirty

E mma stirred when she heard the housemaids walking by in the corridor outside the bedchamber, their
ash buckets clinking as they went about the work of
cleaning grates. She hoped they would leave her chamber
for last, as they usually did, so she could sleep until the
palest pink light at the windows turned yellow and bright.
She was so tired, deeply tired. Sleep was still pulling her
back down when she heard a mutter beside her, felt the
gentle dip of the mattress as the person who muttered
rolled closer.

Her eyes flew open, the last hazy chains of slumber
vanished, and she remembered. She remembered *everything*. She was not in her own room. She was in her
husband's, and he was asleep beside her.

He was also naked, as naked as she was herself. She
giggled and pushed herself back against the pillows to
peer down at him. He lay on his back, one arm flung
towards her, one draped down by the side of the bed.
His hair fell in tousled waves over his brow, and his face
in sleep was smooth as a young boy's.

Emma thought he was achingly beautiful. She reached
out to smooth back that hair. He stirred but did not
waken.

She leaned down and pressed a soft kiss to his cheek.
As she inhaled his distinctive scent, she recalled everything about the night before. Every beautiful second.

It had been even more splendid than she could have

imagined. More splendid than anyone could have said! And she wanted to do it all again. Yes, she would wake him, and then . . .

But as she straightened up against the bank of pillows, her muscles screamed in aching protest. Perhaps she could not do it again just *yet*. Besides, Jack looked so very peaceful. She did not want to wake him.

There was another clatter in the corridor outside, reminding Emma sharply that there was a world outside this enchanted chamber. A household, part of which would soon be coming in here to clean the grates. Goodness, whatever would they think, if they found her here like this? Suddenly, she sat up and climbed down from the bed.

It seemed ridiculously priggish to worry about what the servants would think, she thought with a giggle. After all, she and Jack were married!

But she knew that married couples generally slept in their own chambers, with only discreet visits in between. She knew little of married life, so perhaps it would be best if she followed at least the appearance of that convention. For now, anyway, while things were so very new and delicate between them.

Though she truly loathed leaving her husband, she found her nightdress in a rumpled ball by the bed and pulled it over her head. As she pushed back her tangle of hair to tie the ribbon at the neck, Jack sighed and rolled over.

On a whim, Emma decided to leave him a small memento of their night. She pulled the blue satin ribbon from its loops and placed it in the indentation of her abandoned pillow.

"Good morning, Jack darling," she whispered, and kissed him gently on the cheek. Then, before she could change her mind, she slipped back through the connecting door to her own chamber.

"Emma!" Jack muttered, and his own voice pulled him out of sleep. He blinked against the remnants of sleep, opening his eyes to see that pale morning light already streamed from the windows.

He rubbed at his face. He had been having the oddest, sweetest dream . . .

He rolled over—and saw the sky-blue ribbon on the pillow next to his. A smile tugged at his lips. It had not been a dream after all. It had been reality, but more wonderful than reality had ever been before.

Jack's smile grew, and he reached for the ribbon, pressing the thin satin to his lips. It still held a trace of her lilac perfume. The sweet scent made him remember everything—her kisses, the way she felt in his arms, so soft and yielding, how very desperate he had been for her. Perhaps it had been the long wait or the talk of war and the past that made every moment of life precious, but he had needed her in a way he had never needed anything or anyone before. He had been wild to see her, to embrace every inch of her, to inhale her springtime lilac scent and hold her inside him forever.

And miracle of miracles, she had wanted him, too. Her arms had encircled him, holding him fast. Her words, tumbled and incoherent, urged him closer. It had been wild and crazed and sweet and—perfect. A night he never wanted to end.

But it had to, of course, as everything did. He had not heard her leave, yet he knew why she had as he listened to the servants going about their business. They would have to wake and dress and go about their ordinary lives. He would have to tell her of Bertie's message, that he had to return to London, when all he really wanted to do was run into her room and lift her into his arms again.

Somehow, this all seemed like exceedingly poor timing. Yet he would not have traded their night for anything. They were truly married now. She was truly his.

As he was hers. And he could not wait to see her again, to hold her.

But she was probably sleeping now, and he would be

a complete rudesby to wake her! He would get up and go for a ride before breakfast. That was the only way he could think of to work off some of his new energy, so he would not frighten Emma with his ardor when next they met.

When Emma next awoke, the sun was high in the sky, a bright yellow brilliance in a perfect summer-blue sky. She tried to keep her eyes closed against its dazzle, to hold onto her dream for as long as possible. And what a wonderful, *perfect* dream it had been!

She shifted and stretched—and suddenly froze, surprised at the unexpected stiffness in her limbs. She cautiously opened her eyes and peered down at herself. Her nightdress was wrinkled, her hair falling over her shoulders in disarray.

It had been no dream. It had been reality—wonderful, amazing reality! In truth, nothing anyone could have said would have prepared her for it. It was like moving into some exotic new land with no maps, no guide. It was strange but unbearably beautiful. A place a person could happily visit again and again.

She lay back and closed her eyes, remembering every step of that voyage. Every step she could *remember*—much of it was a tangle of impressions, of sensations and feelings. She had thought it quite perfect, but then she had nothing to compare it to. She wondered what Jack had thought of it. Had thought of her.

She was still contemplating this when the door clicked. Emma opened her eyes to see Natasha carrying the breakfast tray in just as she did every morning. It seemed so odd, so incongruous, that today should begin just like every other day. There should be music, fireworks!

Instead, there was toast and a pot of chocolate. Ah, well, Emma thought, as she looked down at the little jar of marmalade, the tiny pats of butter. There *was* something to be said for toast and chocolate, especially when one was completely ravenous. She spread the marmalade on one of the golden squares of bread and popped it in her mouth.

"Good morning, Natasha!" she sang out, when she had swallowed that first delectable bite.

"Good morning, my lady," Natasha answered, going about her daily business of pouring out water for washing and laying out a morning dress and all its accessories. "You sound very cheerful today!"

"Oh, I am, Natasha. I am." Later, she would surely tell Natasha, and Madame Ana, too, of what had happened. They deserved it, after all their advice. For now, though, she wanted to hold it close, keep it as her very own secret.

She just hoped Natasha would not notice the disgraceful state of her nightdress.

"You know, Natasha, I have been thinking. We should have some sort of gathering here at Weston Manor," she said, as she stirred her cup of chocolate.

"A gathering? Like a ball?" Natasha paused in fussing with the ruffled cuff of the morning dress, her face lighting up with interest.

"Perhaps nothing so grand as a ball. Not in the middle of summer." Truth to tell, the idea of a soiree had only just occurred to Emma, and she had no idea as to the particulars. She liked the thought, though. She liked the idea of her and Jack entertaining as a real couple. A real family. "Maybe a picnic? Or a garden party. My mother used to have those here, I think."

"Yes, Mrs. Hemmings has spoken of it. Everyone enjoyed them so much! Madame Ana would love to help you plan a gathering, my lady. I think she has been a bit bored with no social calendar to arrange!"

"Has she? Well, we cannot have that. She will help me plan the picnic. I will have to talk to Ja—Lord St. Albans about it. Did he come down to breakfast, Natasha?" Emma asked, trying to stay casual and nonchalant, not to show her enormous eagerness, her delight in just saying his name.

"Oh, yes, my lady. He and that Mr. Stonewich took breakfast early and then went out riding. I do not think they have returned yet."

"Indeed? Out riding?" Emma took a sip of her chocolate to cover her disappointment. It was ridiculous to be disappointed, of course; she could hardly have run through the house to him now, in her dishabille. But she was. "Hm. Well, after I am bathed and dressed, I will go back over the menus for luncheon and supper. I want to be sure there is enough, now that we have a guest."

Only as she finished her food did she notice the note tucked neatly beneath her plate. A note with her name written on it in her husband's strong, sprawling hand.

She read it and smiled, pressing the paper to her heart. " 'Come live with me and be my love . . .' " she whispered.

It was almost time for luncheon when Emma, closeted with Madame Ana in the small sitting room at the top of the stairs she used for an office, heard Jack come back to the house. She listened to him and Bertie enter the foyer downstairs, laughing loudly.

Apparently, he had been off having a grand time while she thought back over last night, wondered what would happen when they met again. Well, really, who could blame him? She felt like running and laughing herself.

She glanced at Madame Ana across the desk, over the lists of guests and supplies for their picnic. Madame Ana still wrote in her notebook, not looking up, and Emma remembered that she needed to ask Bertie Stonewich to curb his licentious tendencies around her.

"Perhaps another dozen of those small lemon cakes from the confectioner in the village, Lady St. Albans?" Madame Ana asked, jotting down a note. "And some sparkling cider?"

"Yes, I think so. That, added to what we already listed, should be enough food for the guests, don't you think? I do not want anyone to be hungry."

Madame Ana gave a small smile. "Oh, I doubt anyone will be hungry."

"Except for us, right now! It is almost time for luncheon. Will you join us?"

"For luncheon?" Madame Ana's gaze shifted uncertainly behind her spectacles. She stared down at her notebook as if the answer might be written there.

"Yes, for luncheon," Emma said. "If you are concerned about Mr. Stonewich . . ."

"Why should I be concerned about Mr. Stonewich? Forgive me, Lady St. Albans, for I know he is friends with your husband, but last night he showed himself a drunken lout. I have dealt with such men before, and I have no fear I can do so again."

A drunken lout. Emma knew that Bertie went to great lengths to give just such an impression. She remembered watching him stagger down a crowded street with Lottie. But she also remembered the shrewd, serious glances he would give her when he thought she did not notice. There was more to Bertie Stonewich, she was sure—just as there was more to Jack.

That did not give him the right to harass Madame Ana, or anyone else, though.

"You will not have to 'deal with it,' " Emma said. "He will not bother you any further. And I would truly appreciate it if you would join us for luncheon. We needn't be formal here at our own home."

Madame Ana considered this and finally nodded. "Very well. I will just go and tidy myself first."

After Madame Ana left, Emma straightened her own hair at the small mirror on the wall and fluffed up the lace ruffle of her chemisette. She *looked* the same as she had before. How strange that was, she thought. Shouldn't she have changed in some marked, outward fashion after last night?

She laughed at her own silliness and caught up her shawl to go downstairs to the drawing room.

Jack was alone there, his dark hair damp and brushed back, obviously fresh from a washing after his ride. He had changed from his outdoor tweeds and buckskins into a neat blue coat and fresh cravat.

He stood beside one of the tall windows that looked out onto the back gardens, its green expanse sloping away into the distance. He seemed to be deep in thought, and not a truly pleasant thought at that. A tiny frown creased his face between his eyes, and the grooves that ran alongside his beautiful mouth were deeper than usual.

Emma had an irresistible urge to kiss those lines away, to make a smile appear on his lips. She went to his side and slid her arm around his waist.

He glanced down at her, and that smile appeared. He put his arms about her and kissed her forehead. "There you are, my dear!" he exclaimed, as if he had not seen her face for days even though it had truly only been hours. "How was your morning?"

"Not as fine as my *night*," she teased, surprising even herself with her boldness.

Jack laughed and pulled her closer. "Nor was mine, I daresay! I took Bertie about to see the estate. It was terribly dusty, but we met some new people."

"Did you? You must tell me about them. Madame Ana and I have been planning a picnic to be held in the garden next week. I could invite them."

His smile dimmed a bit. "A picnic? Next week?"

Emma leaned back to look up at him, a tiny misgiving forming as she watched his gaze slide away from hers. "Yes. I thought we should begin to entertain, to meet all our neighbors. Do you think a picnic would not be a good idea?"

"I think it is a fine idea," he said. He smiled again, but it was not quite the same. It was too hearty and reassuring. "It is just that I must go to London, and I do not know if I can return by then."

"London!" Emma cried, and stepped back from him. "This is our wedding trip. Is there some emergency? Is— is someone ill?"

"No, no, nothing like that," he said, hastening to reassure her. He took her hand, holding it in his, forcing her to stay connected to him. "I just need to go on business. That is why Bertie came here, to bring the message. I will not be gone long."

"But what about the picnic?" she asked wistfully, trying not to let her voice slide into a pathetic whine—even if she felt like whining.

"I will be sorry to miss it, but you should go ahead with it. It will be good to get to know our neighbors, just as you said. Perhaps when I return, we could have a card party or a supper."

"But . . ." Emma scarcely knew what she was going to say, what her protests were. She only knew that she did not want him to go, not now, not when things were suddenly so very right between them.

She half feared that if he went away, the distance between London and Weston Manor might break that fragile new cord connecting them.

"I will not be gone for long," he said again. "And you need not fear that anyone will—annoy you while I am away."

She had no idea what he was talking of. Someone might annoy her? She could barely process the idea that he was leaving. "Annoy me?"

"Such as Sir Jeremy Ashbey."

"Oh. Yes." She had forgotten he was even in the neighborhood. Surely that should just be another reason for Jack to stay at Weston Manor?

"Bertie will stay here and keep a watch for me. If anything happens, you need only write to me. But . . ."

"But you will not be gone for long," Emma finished for him, smiling to keep from dissolving into childish tears.

He smiled, too, and leaned down to kiss her. "Correct! A few days at the most. I may even be back in time for your picnic."

She kissed him back, leaning into him, holding onto him for as long as she could. She only moved away when she heard the drawing room door open.

Emma wiped quickly at her eyes with the back of her hand and turned to smile at Bertie and Madame Ana, who stood there watching them. "Well!" she said brightly. "I do hope you are all hungry. Cook has promised us her famous salmon croquettes!"

Chapter Thirty-One

*E*ven with all the allied monarchs and their entourages gone, London was still busier than ever, Jack thought. He stepped out of his lodgings onto a street crowded with people laughing, shouting, hurrying to who-knew-where. He moved out into the flow, knowing *exactly* where he was going—to a meeting with Mr. Thompson. But in the meantime he could enjoy the journey. And decide what he would do after the meeting.

He had no desire to go to his club, to get foxed with his old cronies. He did not want to go to his parents' house to hear any more talk of his supposed "reform."

He only wanted to see his wife. To talk to her, laugh with her. Make love to her again.

That above all.

He paused on the corner of the street, watching the life of the city move past him. None of his old pastimes appealed to him at all. Even the work, as necessary as it still was, did not hold the same thrill.

He had to laugh at himself, even as he reached inside his coat to touch Emma's blue nightdress ribbon there. Jack Howard was certainly a bachelor no longer.

"I am glad you could join us in Town, Lord St. Albans," Mr. Thompson said, cool and expressionless as always, as he poured out a brandy for Jack. "I know it must be difficult for you to tear yourself away from your lovely wife so soon after the wedding."

"Indeed," Jack answered shortly, and sipped at the warm liquid. He wondered where the colonel was, or some of the other men. Why was he alone with Thompson this evening?

The man seemed in no hurry to explain, however. He placed his own glass on the table and steepled his fingers together, regarding Jack over their tips.

Finally, he said, "And since I know how eager you are to get back to your bucolic pleasures, I will be brief. We need you to travel to Vienna, to attend the congress planned there. Perhaps your wife would care to join you? She will no doubt be happy to see her relatives again."

"Of course. I would be honored to go to Vienna," Jack answered. And Emma would be glad to visit her aunt and uncle there. But this could have been written in a letter. He did not have to come to London to hear it.

Thompson seemed to have the same opinion, for he nodded shortly and continued, "There is one other matter. I believe you are currently neighbors with a certain Sir Jeremy Ashbey?"

Ashbey? Jack's fingers tightened on his glass, and he sat up straighter. "Yes, we are."

"We have been watching him for a while now. He is, shall we say, a suspicious character."

Jack knew that very well—he had been suspicious of the man ever since he had seen him escorting Emma at the reception. But there must be something more to all this if a man like Thompson concerned himself with it. "Suspicious in what way, sir?"

"For one thing, suspicious in how eager he was to gain the position with the Russian embassy. His family has no history of diplomatic service—indeed, his father was a terrible wastrel, and his mother a very odd woman from a very odd family. And he spoke little Russian, though he progressed remarkably well in learning the language. He was told by the Foreign Service that there was no place available, and there was not. Until a certain Lord Travers passed away."

Jack remembered vaguely hearing of this. A young

though already distinguished diplomat had died in his
sleep of a sudden illness and been replaced by—Ashbey?

Thompson went on. "Yes, you are thinking that many
people die in their sleep, even young people. Yet Travers
was perfectly healthy, an active young man. The only
thing our people could find was that Travers had taken
supper at his club the night before—with Ashbey."

Jack stared at him in mounting horror, stared as
Thompson pulled out a thick sheaf of papers from under
the table. Ashbey a murderer? And he was right next
door to Jack's own wife.

"Shocking, I know," Thompson said. "I would not
have called you here if I had not known that young Stonewich would stay at your home for these few days and
keep an eye on things. But I felt you should see these
papers. Seeing that you are the man's neighbor and all."

Still cold with fear and anger, Jack pulled the documents toward him and began reading. What he saw there
was not comforting at all.

He had to go home.

The day of Emma's picnic dawned bright and warm,
ideal for alfresco dining, with a blue, blue sky and a
sweet freshness in the air. The footmen, under the careful
direction of Madame Ana, hurried around the garden,
setting up tables and chairs and adjusting canopies for
shade. The housemaids followed behind, spreading the
tables with freshly pressed cloths in soft tints of pink and
blue. Later, they would bring out the china, silver and
crystal, but not until just before the guests arrived.

Rich, enticing aromas drifted up from the kitchens as
the cook plied her art, delighted to finally have an audience to enjoy her creations.

It would have been perfect, Emma thought, as she
watched all the activity from the terrace. Perfect—if it
hadn't been more than a week since Jack left.

She had received one note from him, saying he had
arrived safely in Town and would be staying at his old

lodgings if she had need of him. That was it. Nothing since.

She had busied herself in that week, and the days had gone quickly. She had supper at Watley Hall twice, and attended her first Altar Society meeting at the vicarage. She planned to attend the dance in the village assembly rooms on Saturday, and arrangements for her "simple" picnic took more time than she had thought they would. She took supper each evening with Bertie and Madame Ana in the dining room, just the three of them at the long table.

Bertie, once he left behind his Town dandy trappings and settled into country life, was an entertaining companion. He told amusing stories and kept them laughing. He went into the village with them when they needed to shop and did not seem to care how long they spent poring over ribbons and hats. He played cards with them in the evening and once even played the pianoforte, at which he was surprisingly adept.

Even Madame Ana seemed to be softening toward him, just a tiny bit. She allowed him to help her sort her embroidery silks and even condescended to smile at one or two of his jokes.

Despite the fact that he had proved to be more amiable company than Emma would have supposed, though, he was irritatingly closemouthed about Jack. Oh, he was free enough with tales of their boyish pranks together and some of their exploits in Spain, but whenever Emma tried to draw him out about Jack's sudden London "business," he would adroitly change the topic.

It was maddening! If only she would receive a message from him, or hear *something*. Things had been going well here—*very* well, she thought. It was disconcerting, to say the least, to have her husband suddenly vanish.

Emma sighed and peered down at the guest list propped on the table beside her glass of lemonade. Almost everyone she had invited had accepted and been checked off the list. Including Sir Jeremy and Miss Maria

Ashbey—the one other thing that kept the day from complete perfection.

It was a minor matter, of course, especially compared to Jack's absence, but one that was disquieting still. She simply could not be comfortable in the presence of Sir Jeremy. She could not forget the strange, heated way he had stared at her on their drive in the park or the way he watched her from a distance whenever they had met since.

Fortunately, they had only met twice since Jack left, once at Watley Hall and once by accident in the village. Bertie had been present both times and had neatly kept Sir Jeremy at a distance from her. It had been so neat as to be unnoticeable that that was what he was doing, but Emma had been very grateful. It was as if he guessed at her discomfort and did what he could to help.

There was nothing she could do to avoid asking Sir Jeremy and his never seen sister to the picnic, though. It was a very small community, and they were a part of it. She hoped all would go well, though. It had to.

Emma laid aside the guest list and looked at her to-do list. It was quite short, thanks to the formidable efficiency of Madame Ana. The tables and canopies were set up, the wine fetched up from the cellars, musicians hired to serenade the guests as they feasted on pâté and spinach tarts. Really, all she had to do was change her gown and wait to be the gracious hostess, greeting her guests.

She drank the last of her lemonade and smiled as she wondered if her mother was looking down on her now, happy to see her beloved home coming to life again.

It was a comforting thought, and one that distracted her from Jack and Sir Jeremy. She was even further distracted when Natasha came out onto the terrace, holding the morning's post on a tray.

"Letters for you, my lady," she said, putting the tray down on the table. She wandered over to the balustrade to watch the flurry of activity in the garden. "It does look lovely, doesn't it? Like something in a storybook."

"Yes. It is all coming together very well," Emma answered, shuffling through the post. "Ah, a letter from Aunt Lydia! I did wonder when we would hear from her." She put the neatly penned, pale blue letter aside to read slowly and savor later. There were notes and invitations from her new local friends, and at the very bottom of the stack, the thing she had been waiting for. A missive addressed to her in Jack's strong, black scrawl.

There was no waiting for this one. She broke the wax seal and read it right away.

"News from Lord St. Albans?" Natasha asked.

Emma smiled at Natasha's teasing tone. "Perhaps."

"It must be, my lady, for you to seem so pleased! It is good news, then?"

Emma scanned the short message again, then folded it up carefully. She smiled at the sweet words there. "Good enough. He says his business is soon to be concluded, and he will be arriving back here at Weston Manor on Friday evening. So he will be able to attend the assembly on Saturday!"

"Oh, that *is* good news, indeed! Is that all his lordship says?"

Emma could feel herself blushing at the thought of the short, but intimate, postscript. "Yes. That is all. Now, I really must go upstairs and dress! The guests will be arriving soon." She gathered up her letters and hurried back into the house, Natasha following.

In the foyer, just as she put her foot on the staircase, a footman rushed up to her.

"Oh, my lady!" he said breathlessly. "Cook says you must come to the kitchen at once. There is a dire emergency with the strawberry trifle."

"A trifle emergency, is it? Well, we cannot have that! Of course I will come at once." Emma turned to Natasha and said, "Natasha, can you just lay out my blue muslin, and I will change into it as soon as everything is set in the kitchen."

"Of course, my lady." Natasha ran up the stairs, as Emma turned toward the door that led to the kitchens.

She put her letters down on one of the tables in the foyer, intending to fetch them as she went to her chamber.

But after the kitchen dilemma was solved, there was a question about the wine and a problem with some of the tablecloths. By the time she was able to attend to her attire, she had quite forgotten the letters and did not fetch them until much later, after the picnic was already over and done.

Despite the last minute flurry of small difficulties, the picnic seemed to come off beautifully. Talk and laughter, the clink of heavy silver against delicate china, the strains of the string quartet's Mozart divertimento, mingled in the warm summer air. There was an atmosphere of great conviviality and gaiety, becoming even more so as the afternoon moved on and more and more wine was consumed. Tiered china trays filled with beautifully decorated cakes and pastries, slices of glistening fruit and wedges of plump, pale cheeses were brought out and passed around to many exclamations.

Lady Watley took two tiny cream cakes, then a lemon one decorated with a sugared violet. "Oh, my dear Emma, I should *not* be so greedy, but I cannot seem to help myself! These cakes are an utter delight."

Emma laughed and helped herself to a cake topped with slivered almonds. "No, Aunt Amelia, you must take as many as you like! It is a party, after all."

"And a most enjoyable one," Lady Watley said. "I must say it is wonderful to see Weston Manor looking so very full of life again."

"I hope you are enjoying your stay here, Lady St. Albans," the vicar said.

"Oh, yes, very much," answered Emma. "My husband and I hope to spend a great deal of time here in the future."

The vicar's wife nodded. "Such additions you have been to the neighborhood! It is just too bad that Lord St. Albans had to miss this lovely day."

Emma opened her mouth to explain yet again the reason why Jack missed this picnic, when someone behind her said, "Indeed it *is* a pity Lord St. Albans is not here. So derelict of him to leave his lovely bride."

Emma peered over her shoulder, startled to see Sir Jeremy there. She had been so enjoying her day that she had not even noticed him leaving his own table and crossing the garden to hers. She darted a glance over there and saw that his pale, quiet sister still sat there. She also saw Bertie Stonewich leaving his companions and edging closer.

Emma gazed at Sir Jeremy, who stared back at her with that odd, intent stare he always seemed to wear. He stood closer than he should have, and his hand moved slightly, as if to touch her. Though Emma found this all to be most disconcerting, she had no fear, as she might have before. Not here in the bright sunlight, with all these people around her. Not with the knowledge that Jack was coming home soon.

Sir Jeremy could do nothing but stare at her, really. He could not *hurt* her.

She stood up and reached for her parasol, which was furled and leaning against the table. Despite the absence of fear, she still liked the solid feeling of its heavy, carved ivory handle in her grip. "Lord St. Albans had urgent business to attend to, or else he never would have missed this picnic. He will be back very soon, though."

"Indeed?" Sir Jeremy said.

"Indeed," Emma answered emphatically. "Now, if everyone here will excuse me, I would so much like to speak with your sister, Sir Jeremy. I have not had the chance to converse with her since you arrived."

"Of course, Lady St. Albans. Maria would be delighted. Shall I escort you to her?" Sir Jeremy offered her his arm.

Emma hesitated, but finally placed her hand on his green wool sleeve. It would be too odd to refuse him here at her own home, and the last thing she wanted to do was cause a scene with him. The man seemed so tightly wired, as if any small thing would be likely to set him off into—something. Like the way the muscles in his arm clenched when she touched him.

She walked off with him along the rose-bordered path toward where his sister sat. Emma tried to smile and chatter as if this was a perfectly ordinary situation. "Such a very fine day! I am so glad it did not rain and spoil things."

"A fine day," he agreed. "Just like that day when we were children. It was so—perfect then."

That blighted day again. Emma wished her mother had never thought of having a picnic then, so she would not have to talk about it now. "I do not remember that day," she said, as gently as she could.

Sir Jeremy stopped walking, pulling her to a halt on the pathway. "I am sure you *could* remember, if you just looked about! It was just like today, except now you are even more beautiful. I dreamed we would come back here, have our own picnics, watch our own children walk here . . ."

"Sir Jeremy!" Emma stepped away from him, clutching at her parasol. "You must not speak to me like this. I am a married woman."

He turned his back to her, his shoulders heaving with the force of his deep breaths. "You were meant to be married to me," he muttered, but Emma was not entirely sure she heard him correctly, his voice was so muffled.

"Lady St. Albans!" she heard Bertie call, and she turned to him gratefully as he came hurrying down the path to her side. "I am sorry to tear you away, but I fear Madame Ana has a question for you that cannot wait."

Emma could have hugged the man in her joy at not being alone with Sir Jeremy any longer. Ashbey was really the outside of enough, and she could not stand his creeping behavior a moment longer. It was too strange. No one stayed obsessed with a girl he had met as a child, for heaven's sake. No sane man. "Of course, Mr. Stonewich, I will come immediately." She glanced once more at Sir Jeremy's back before she turned away. "Sir Jeremy can have nothing more to say to me."

Sir Jeremy slipped into the house once Emma had been carried away by that damnable Stonewich man. He did not want to see anyone at the moment, did not want to speak to anyone, especially Maria with her silent, questioning glances. The fire of anger, of fury, was in his blood, and it had to come out or burn him alive from the inside! He feared that if his sister came too close, he would take out his fury at Emma on her and strangle her with his very hands.

He had been a fool. He saw that now. A fool who had carried the dream of love in his heart for so long that he had not been able to see that the sweet and tender girl child he loved had grown into a cold, scheming harpy.

She said she did not remember that long-ago picnic, but he knew that she must. No one could have forgotten its sweet perfection. She just did not care. She had the chance to marry a great title, and she had abandoned their love, the love that had been growing for so long, without a second thought. Just to become a viscountess!

Jeremy stared up at the portrait above the fireplace, of a dark-haired woman and the very child he had loved. Innocence and joy shone from those painted eyes, not the avarice they held now.

He whirled around and ran from that portrait, out into the foyer. It was so far from the party that no sound penetrated there. There was no one to look at him, to laugh at him. There was only a table there, decorated with a large vase of garden roses.

Even *they* seemed to mock him, with their pink and white beauty. With a furious cry, he dashed it to the marble floor, shattering the crystal vase into a thousand pieces. Flowers, water and shimmering shards scattered everywhere.

He also knocked a pile of letters to the floor, and one landed on his boot. He bent and picked it up, and even read it when he saw that it was from *him*, from the demon who had stolen away Jeremy's lovely girl.

The tender postscript written there was like another sliver of crystal driven into his wounded heart. But there was more there than his lying love words. Much more.

He dropped the letter and ran out the front door, forgetting that his sister waited for him, forgetting everything but a new plan that was forming in his mind. A plan to help him retrieve everything that had been stolen from him.

Everything.

Chapter Thirty-Two

*H*er husband was coming home this evening!

Perhaps. Her shoulders slumped at that thought. *Perhaps* wasn't good enough. She wanted him beside her now.

Emma stood by her bedroom window and watched the rain that poured down outside, steady, silvery sheets of it. Evening was coming, and the only way she could tell was that the thick clouds overhead were slowly changing from gray to black.

"The roads will be muddy," Madame Ana observed, from the small table where she was going over household accounts. "I hope his lordship doesn't become stuck somewhere in the mud."

"Stuck," Emma murmured, and sighed. That was the one thing she had not yet worried about. She had thought he might have to shelter at an inn or perhaps had not even left London. But it was true that if he was traveling in a carriage there was every likelihood that he could get caught in the mud. It would probably be tomorrow before he arrived. And after they had planned a special supper to welcome him home, and Emma had asked Natasha to press her loveliest evening gown!

Oh, well, she thought. The weather could not be helped, and the supper would still be delicious. She tried to push the disappointment away, but it still sat there, cold and hard, in her stomach.

Emma pushed away from the window and went back

to sit at the table with Madame Ana. She was supposed to be going over the accounts with her, not sighing at the window like some silly girl in a romantic play!

"The rain appears to be easing a bit," Madame Ana said. "I am sure Lord St. Albans will be home tomorrow, if not this evening."

Emma smiled at her. "I am sure you are right. Now, how much should we allot for new draperies in the drawing room? I do like that blue brocade . . ."

Oh, the things a man will do for his wife! Jack thought with a grim smile, as another rush of water poured down from his hat into his eyes. The hat, and indeed his coat, did nothing to keep the rain away. He had been a fool to eschew the carriage, leaving it behind at an inn and going forward alone on horseback. He could be sitting beside the inn's fireplace right now, enjoying a glass of warm wine!

But he had known that the carriage could not go on along the rain-washed roads and that Emma was expecting him this evening. So he pressed on, hoping that she had missed him as much as he missed her. Or even half as much, for he had missed her a great deal indeed.

And feared for her, too.

The week preceding his final meeting with Thompson had been filled with long meetings and circuitous discussions, plans fueled by brandy and cigar smoke, concerns over the security of Napoleon's person on Elba and about the cohesiveness of the allied monarchs that grew greater now that they had all departed from London. Once something of a resolution had been reached, he wanted nothing more than to hold his wife in his arms, smell her perfume and kiss her until they were both breathless.

After he had kissed her, and kissed her again, there could be a warm bath and a warm meal, a glass of brandy. And he could surprise her with his news—that they would be joining her aunt and uncle in Vienna soon for the congress. Surely she would be happy to see them again.

Jack urged the horse into a faster gallop and ducked to avoid a low-hanging tree branch. When the explosion cracked above him, he thought it was just a particularly loud clap of thunder—until the second one sounded, and a voice shouted "Stand and deliver!" above the rush of the rain.

An ambush! By a highwayman? What sort of a foolish highwayman would be out on a night like this? Jack had no time to ponder this; another shot rang out, this one taking off the tree branch above his head.

Jack's horse, frightened by the branch striking against his flank, gave a terrified whinny and bucked up, into the stormy sky. Jack scrambled to clutch at the reins, shouting, "Hold! Hold!" His battle instincts obviously needed hardening, though, because it was too late. He went flying off the horse, landing in the muddy road with a sickening thud. Vaguely, through a haze of pain, he heard the blasted horse go running off, and he was alone in the sudden water-rushing silence.

Or almost alone. At first, he thought perhaps the highwayman had run off as well, the night was so quiet around him. His head hummed from the effort of listening, of being alert for any tiny sound. Then he heard it, the crackle of branches from the trees on the opposite side of the road, the fall of a footstep.

Jack's left ankle shot sharp, hot pains along his leg as he rolled to his side, but the rush of adrenaline, so familiar from those old battles, was stronger. He climbed to his feet and ducked behind a tree, to the surprised shout of the villain and the scrabbling sounds of reloading. Whoever the thief was, he was obviously not terribly well prepared. There also seemed to be no accomplice, only the one man.

Damnably, Jack's own pistol was in the saddlebag of the fleeing horse. But he did have his dagger tucked into his boot. He drew the blade and waited. Waited for the

man to come to him, so he could cut him to ribbons for
daring to delay Jack's arrival on his wife's doorstep.

He did not have long to wait. He heard a footstep
near his hiding place and with a great shout came out
swinging his dagger.

The highwayman cursed and backed away, bringing his
pistol up to fire. There was only a faint clicking noise,
and the thief, his face covered with a kerchief and his
body with a long black coat, gave it an astonished look.

Jack saw that instant of opportunity and attacked,
lunging forward with his dagger. The thief, after that
moment's hesitation, pulled out a long dagger himself
and fought back with a fierceness that surprised Jack. He
had usually found men of this ilk to be cowards underneath, hunting only easy prey. He had expected him to
flee at the first sight of a knife, but it only seemed to
inflame the villain.

Something that sounded like "You *will* pay!" was
shouted into the night, muffled behind the man's kerchief. He fought like a man possessed, but that very passion was his undoing. As he lunged at Jack, his boots
slipped in the mud and he fell heavily.

Jack leaned in, pressing his blade to the man's chest.
He reached down and yanked off the kerchief.

He had thought once that nothing in battle could ever
surprise him again, that he had witnessed every bloody,
grotesque, bizarre thing one man could do to another.

He had been wrong, for he was shocked to his very
marrow now, despite the documents he had read in
Thompson's sitting room "Ashbey!"

Sir Jeremy Ashbey lay in the mud, his breathing la-
bored, his pale eyes shining up at Jack with a malevolent
light visible even in the darkness. He said nothing, just
stared, but that look spoke volumes.

It spoke of a hatred so deep, so long nurtured, that it
led him out on this unholy night to destroy Jack—but
perhaps it was not really about Jack, or even about
Emma, but about something terrible and twisted deep
inside himself.

Jack felt cold, a deep cold that owed nothing to the rain, as he stood there with his dagger poised above Ashbey's chest, and he was very disturbed. He had thought Sir Jeremy relatively harmless, though with a ridiculous obsession for Emma, someone who just bore keeping a faintly amused eye on. Not someone who could be driven to a murderous rage. And Jack had left his wife, his home!

What would he find at Weston Manor? A burned out house? A murdered wife? The glowing eyes of the man under his dagger said he was capable of all that.

"You have to pay," Ashbey said, his voice unnaturally calm and even reasonable. "I never lose, you see. I *never* lose. She has belonged to me since we were children."

Fast, so fast Jack could not even sense any warning movement of eye or muscle, Sir Jeremy drove forward with his dagger. Its blade just nicked Jack's thigh, but Jack, pulled by the forward momentum, saw his own dagger drive deep into Ashbey's chest.

The man gave a surprised, horrifying gurgling noise. His eyes widened, and he fell back heavily into the mud. He lay there, perfectly still.

He would never move again.

An unutterable weariness flooded through Jack's very veins, flushing away the last vestiges of the adrenaline that had driven him. For the first time, he was aware of the pain in his leg. It buckled beneath him, and he sat down clumsily, letting go of the dagger hilt and watching it drop.

He tipped his head back to the pouring rain, but not even that cold baptism could wash away the sickness of this night.

Chapter Thirty-Three

The loud pounding at the front door startled Emma from her after-supper lassitude. She, Madame Ana and Bertie were gathered by the drawing room fire, sipping tea and chatting lazily. It was time to be thinking of retiring, not time for guests. Especially guests who were so insensitive.

The knocking continued as the three of them trailed out of the drawing room into the foyer. The butler was there already, shrugging into his black coat as he opened the door.

There were five men in the doorway, including Emma's own coachman and groom. Between them they bore a makeshift stretcher, a blanket attached to long poles. At first confused glance, Emma just saw a tangle of mud and water and dirty cloth. Then bright blue eyes blinked open, and a voice croaked, "Emma, my love. I am home."

She screamed and clapped her hand to her mouth as she ran to his side, falling onto her knees on the cold floor. "Jack! Jack, what happened to you? Why were you trying to get home in such weather?" She groped for his hand, clutching at it desperately in her horror at the sight of him hurt. She screamed out again when she realized that there was dried blood, deep burgundy, mixed with the mud on it.

Jack twisted his fingers with hers, even as he whispered, "I am a mess; I will get your pretty dress dirty."

"Oh, who cares about that! Tell me what has happened."

"We found him on the road, my lady. We knew when his horse came back to the inn without him that he was in trouble. And, begging your pardon, my lady," the coachman interrupted, "but should we carry his lordship to the library and put him down there? It can't be good to jostle him about so."

"Of course, of course! Just put him on the settee there, and build up the fire in the grate." Emma moved out of their way as they carried Jack away, and then she turned to Madame Ana and Bertie. Her mind was whirling, a jumble, a mess, but one thought *did* come through clearly enough. "We should send for the physician."

"I will go," Bertie said, already striding away, calling for his coat and a horse.

"And I will fetch hot water and towels, so we can get Lord St. Albans cleaned up," said Madame Ana, still efficient despite the sudden white pallor of her cheeks. She dashed off in the direction of the kitchen.

"You may also want to consider fetching the magistrate, my lady," the butler suggested quietly.

Emma, who had turned to follow the men into the library, turned back. "The magistrate?"

"I fear so, my lady. That wound on his lordship's leg was not from anything natural. It was a stab wound."

A stab wound? Emma whirled about and ran into the library. The men had put Jack down on the leather settee by the fireplace before silently filing out again. His eyes were closed, his face tight with pain, white under the dirt. Emma grabbed the decanter of brandy and a glass from the desk and knelt down beside him. She looked at his leg; the cloth of his trousers was torn over his left thigh in a jagged rent, crusted with blood.

She shivered and tore her gaze away from the ugly wound. "Jack?" she said gently, brushing the matted hair back from his brow. "Can you hear me?"

His eyes did not open, but he nodded. "I can hear you. Your voice sounds like angels' wings."

Emma choked on a laugh. "You *must* be in pain, to be hallucinating so! Can you drink some brandy?"

He nodded, and she poured a generous measure into the glass and held it to his lips. He drank of it deeply, taking it from her hand into his own muddy fingers.

"Better?" she asked, dampening her handkerchief with more brandy.

"Always better, when I am with you."

"Good. Then perhaps this will not hurt so very much." She pressed the cloth to his leg, wincing when he gasped. To distract him from the sting, she said, "The physician will be here very soon, and Madame Ana is bringing some water. Jack, dearest, what happened to you? How were you wounded? Was it some sort of—accident?"

He gripped at her hand and was silent for a long while, so long she began to think he had fallen asleep again. But finally he nodded again and said, "I fear I was wounded quite deliberately. I was foolish; I should have waited out the storm at the inn, but I was eager to be home. I hadn't gone far when I was ambushed by a highwayman."

Emma gasped in shock. "A highwayman! Jack, how can that be?"

"Ah, my dear, it was not just any highwayman. It was Jeremy Ashbey."

At first, Emma thought she must not have heard him correctly, that the terrible shock of the night had made him delusional. "Jeremy Ashbey?"

Jack opened his eyes and stared up at her with great sadness and understanding. "I fear so, my dear. I knew he was unpredictable, not one to be trusted. That was why I left Bertie with you. I never should have left you. I should have realized . . ."

"No!" Emma cried out, clutching at his hand. She pressed it to her lips, feeling the reassuring warmth, the *life* in it. "No, it was my fault. I was unkind to him at the picnic. But I never could have imagined he would do something so insane!" She paused, tightening her fingers on his as a new realization occurred to her. It must have been Ashbey who destroyed the vase in the foyer the day of the picnic.

"Insane is exactly the right word." Jack's voice was growing fainter, his grip on her hand loosening weakly. "And that is why we, neither of us, should blame ourselves for what happened this night."

"But what if . . ."

"No, Emma. Listen to me. I am getting very tired, and soon we will be inundated with doctors and servants. I have to tell you something. I rode here tonight just to say it."

Emma leaned closer to him, puzzled. "What could it possibly be, Jack darling? What could be so dire?"

He laughed weakly. "Nothing dire at all. Just this. I love you."

Emma could say nothing. All she could do was stare at him, blinking. She glanced down at his leg, carefully covered with her brandy-soaked handkerchief, to see if he was losing any blood. It seemed clean, or at least as clean as it had been before. Perhaps it was not the loss of blood; it was the loss of his mind.

Or maybe *she* was losing *hers,* for it sounded as if he said he had ridden through the rain to say he loved her.

Loved her!

At last, what he had said truly sank into her consciousness. Her lower lip trembled, and she felt the wet prickle of tears at her eyes. She did not, *could* not, let go of his hand to brush them away.

"Oh, Jack," she choked, laughing and crying all at the same time. "You beautiful, ridiculous man. I love you, too."

He smiled faintly and raised her hand to his lips. They could say nothing more, for the door opened and Madame Ana and Natasha rushed in, their arms full of basins and towels. Truly, though, they did not need to say anything else, for those few words had spoken volumes.

Chapter Thirty-Four

Some small noise woke Emma suddenly, jerking her from her fitful sleep. She sat up slowly, gasping at the sharp crick in her neck. She rubbed at it, leaning back in her chair.

She had fallen asleep in the chair next to Jack's bed, slumped across the edge of the mattress, and her bones and muscles hated her for it now. She could not be sorry, though. She would have sat here for a thousand nights and more to be sure he was well.

Was it Jack stirring that had woken her up? She looked down at him, but he was still, his face as smooth and relaxed as a boy's in healing sleep. She laid the back of her hand gently against his brow. Only the tiniest bit warm, thankfully. The physician's medicines seemed to be working.

Emma tucked the bedclothes closer about him and stood up to stretch her aching and stiff back. She went to the window and pulled the draperies back, so that Jack could see the starlight of deepest night when he awoke. It was so lovely and still, as if the earlier storm had never been at all.

The gardens were quiet and dreaming, no movement at all except the trickle of water from the overflowing fountain reflecting the moon. Emma leaned her forehead wearily on the cool glass, twisting her hand in the velvet of the drapery. How very much of her life she had spent staring out of windows, she thought. Usually pining for whatever was on the other side! Tonight, though, she wanted to be no place but exactly where she was.

With a husband who had miraculously survived tonight's attack. A husband who loved her and had ridden, quite literally, through fire and rain to tell her so.

Emma smiled, despite her weariness. Despite the terrible events of this night and everything that might wait in the clear light of day, she was happy. A bone-deep, soft contentment that had never been hers before. She knew she would never have to disguise herself again, for she was truly home now.

And she hoped Jack felt the same. That he knew the feeling that, in each other, they had all they could have asked for.

She heard a rustle from the bed behind her. "Emma?" Jack called, an edge of panic in his voice. "Emma?"

"Here I am." She left the window and went to perch on the edge of the mattress next to him. For a second, he looked feverish again, but his expression cleared when he saw her, and he gave her a tired smile. His arm came out and wrapped around her waist, drawing her closer to him.

"Be careful!" she admonished, leaning carefully over him. "You will hurt yourself again, and after Madame Ana was so careful in changing your bandages."

"Don't worry, I will not tear the bandages. I was just afraid you had left me."

"Of course not. I just went to open the curtains so you could see the stars when you awoke. Is it not a beautiful night? The rain has ceased completely."

"The most beautiful of nights," he said, tightening his arm around her. "I feared for a moment, when Ashbey fired that gun at me, that I might never see the stars again. Or you. That I would never be able to say I loved you."

Emma laid her hand tenderly against his cheek. "I had fears, too. Fears of—of so many things. But they are nothing compared to the fact that, thanks to God, you are here with me. You are safe, and we are together. I love you, too. So very much."

"There are other things I must speak of as well. Such as the reason I went to London in the first place . . ."

"Shh." She laid her finger over his lips. "Not now. You must sleep and heal. There will be time for everything tomorrow, when you are feeling better."

He frowned and opened his mouth as if to argue. Apparently he thought better of it and nodded. Instead, he reached up to move her finger, held that hand tightly in his, and said, "Very well. I will rest, but only if you stay here beside me."

Emma smiled at him. That sounded like something she could happily do. She stretched out beside him, carefully not jarring his bandaged leg, and laid her head on the pillow next to his. "I am beside you, Jack, my love. Always."

"Always," he answered, and it sounded like the deepest vow ever made.

And, together, their hands entwined, they slept, as the stars smiled down on them.

A Loving Spirit

by Amanda McCabe

England is a cold, forbidding place for Miss Cassie
Richards, who has spent most of her life in Jamaica.
Fortunately, she's found warmth in the care of her aunt
who's enjoying introducing her niece in high society
circles. Their latest visit is to Royce Castle, reputed to be
haunted by the family's ancestors. Cassie is intrigued not
only by the possibility of glimpsing a specter or two—
but by the enigmatic lord of the manor.

Phillip, Earl of Royce, has no interest in his mother's
frivolities among members of the ton, or in the rumors of
ghosts residing in his home. His scholarly pursuits in
Greek history take precedence over the attentions of
young ladies seeking a husband, until Cassie's refreshing
presence makes him wonder if he's been spending too
much time with his nose in a book.

But for Cassie and Phillip to embrace their love, they're
going to need a little spiritual guidance...

0-451-20801-3